To Barbara,
Thank you for your
Loyal Support !
Arlyon-Thomas
3/30/2018

THREE SHEETS IN THE WIND

By Anita Dixon-Thomas

THREE SHEETS IN THE WIND

Copyright © 2017 by Anita Dixon-Thomas

Published by Tavares Entertainment, LLC.
Book cover design by Diego Larenas
Edited by Gary G. Tavares
Printed in the United States by Createspace

Gary G. Tavares
Tavares Entertainment, LLC.
3320 S. Cobb Dr. SE #21
Smyrna, GA 30080
678-437-4496

ISBN: 978-0-9833292-1-3

ACKNOWLEDGEMENTS

Although Three Sheets in The Wind is written as fiction, all of what follows could actually occur in a mental health facility. I would like to thank the people who helped me so much in making this novel an interesting, captivating and exciting read.

Laura Confer-Paylor, Educator and Long-Time Childhood Friend

Monica Nixon, PhD

Holly Lightkep, RN, Psychiatric Nurse

Amanda Wagner, LCSW, Social Worker

Diane Laing, LCSW, Social Worker

Esther Robinson, SFC, U.S. Army, Retired

Sisters, Crystal G. Dixon and Barbara L. Smith

"I have cried so much over these past few days, my eyeballs feel like they are on fire!"

-Jennifer Wiley, RN Emergency Room Nurse

CHAPTER ONE

Susan Cole sat alone in the dark with a loaded forty-four Magnum in her lap. She flinched when the cuckoo clock chirped twelve times in the next room. It was midnight, Monday, June fifth nineteen eighty-seven. Precisely three years since she and Doctor George Benny left Salter's Point. Tonight, he was late. He had been late many nights, causing her blood to boil with utter contempt. She knew why he was late. She hoped he would come to his senses sooner rather than later. But he hadn't. His blatant disrespect was worsening over time leaving her cold and feeling abandoned. She sat there with her finger on the trigger. Thinking, thinking, thinking. Reminiscing over the good times, distraught over the present.

When she and George Benny first arrived in France three years ago, the two of them settled in a little village outside of Paris. For the first two years of their life together they seemed happy and content. Every night, under the shimmering moonlight, they would make love outside on the terrace of their apartment flat. During the day, they would take short excursions along the countryside visiting vineyards, drinking wine enjoying the country's vast culture. On the surface, their life as fugitives appeared grand in comparison to their old life back in Salter's Point. It appeared, at least for a time, Susan's struggle with depression was in remission, no longer a menacing threat to her emotional wellbeing. However, in recent days, her depression had returned with a vengeance.

Her fragile state of mind constantly plagued her with intrusive, negative thoughts, cruelly reminding her of a checkered past. Forced to face her demons alone, she tried desperately to explain away the rapid deterioration of her once happy monogamous relationship with Doctor George Benny. For the past six months, he had been distant. Never around and she missed him. When she found out about his affair with a young French nurse half his age in a nearby village, she was devastated. His betrayal sending her over the edge. Pushing her down a deep dark road of impending doom. To cope, she purchased Xanax from a street dealer, hoping to numb her emotional pain.

After several days of taking the drug, she felt increasingly worse, unable to sleep, her suicidal thoughts stripping her peace of mind. As she sat in the dark, gazing out the window contemplating her own suicide, the bright gold moon caught her eye. The moon's shimmering glow lit up her entire living room, and she admired its beauty and excellent round size. Then it slowly moved west across the midnight sky, casting gray shadows on the wall behind her. Leaving her in complete darkness again, the black night a match to her dark, intense mood. She scooted further down on the sofa and contemplated shooting herself. Tears flooded her eyes and then streamed down her cheeks. She angrily wiped water off her face while rage burned deep inside her heart. Soon her thoughts switched from shooting herself to shooting him instead. After all, if she couldn't have him, why should anyone else. Suddenly footsteps approached the door of her apartment and stopped. The clicking of the lock startled her, and she swallowed hard.

7

Then the door swung open, and George appeared in the doorway.

"Why is it so dark in here?" He grumbled looking around and then slamming the door. "Why aren't the lights on?" There was a lump in her throat. It was difficult to speak. She gripped the gun so tight, her hand perspired. Her burning eyes followed his shadowy silhouette as he groped his way through the dark searching for the light switch. He found it and flicked it back and forth, but still there was no light.

"Damn it," he grumbled. He backed away from the wall and faced the dark living room again. He spotted the dark human figure parked on the sofa. His eyes, looking like slits in his glasses, squinted to see who it was.

"Susan," he called out. "Is that you?" Silent as snow, she sat there like a statue. Watching the outline of his tall, dark silhouette advancing her way. He recognized her and then he became angry.

"Damn it, Susan! Why are you sitting in the dark like a dimwit?!" He scolded her. His words stung, and her blood boiled. She pointed the gun at him and fingered the trigger. Every nerve ending in her body tingled, and a wave of adrenalin rushed up to her spine.

"Susan, answer me!" He demanded stepping toward her. "Do you hear me, woman? Answer me!" He lunged at her, and she squeezed the trigger. The force from the blast jerked her back. The bullet ripped right through him, and for a second, he froze in place. Then he stumbled back hitting the door, leaning against it. He tried to support his own bodyweight, but his strength soon gave out.

He slid to the floor in a crumpled heap, and red liquid poured from the gaping hole in his chest.

His gasps of pain were music to her ears and the corners of her mouth crinkled up. He cried out to her.

"Why are you doing this to me?! Why?!"

His pleas didn't faze her, and in a trance-like state, she slid off the sofa. She marched like a robot to the table as he continued to cry out in pain. She turned on the lamp, her movements methodical like a Stepford wife. She turned and gave him a blank, cold look. Sweat dripped off his face, and his eyes glistened with terror. She walked over to him and straddled her legs over his chest. She hovered in his face, with eyes cold and vacant, snarling at him. He stared down the barrel of her gun, and his blue eyes pleaded for mercy.

"You don't have to do this! Please don't do this!" He said. Tears stung her eyes. She pressed the forty-four Magnum to his forehead and squeezed the trigger. The bullet shattered his skull and warm red liquid spattered on her hands and legs. She stood there and stared at her bloodstained hands. Then she backed away from his bloodied body. A gust of guilt came over her, and silent tears ran down her face. She whispered.

"You betrayed me. I'm very, very sorry!" With the gun still gripped tightly in her hand, she stumbled to the sofa and flopped down. She engaged the safety and laid the gun in her lap. Her emotional pain was daunting, and she wrestled with ending her life again. Then she heard a light tap on the door. Her head jerked up. She stared at the door and she hesitated, afraid to answer. She trembled violently when the tapping became louder and louder, then she leaped to her feet and started for the door.

She wiped her wet face with the sleeve of her white blouse and her bloodstained hands she wiped on her black skirt. She stepped over George Benny's blood-soaked body, and she groaned with utter disgust.

"I guess I need to move this two-timing bastard," she mumbled to herself. She grabbed his feet and dragged him across the room leaving a trail of dark, sticky red blood on the carpet. Beads of sweat popped out on her forehead, and her shoulders sagged from the weight of his six-foot frame. She struggled to breathe, gasping with every step. The soft humming of her wheezing soon tired her out. She made it to the sofa and dropped his feet to the floor. Then she sat down exhausted, inhaling in deep breaths. She panicked when the tapping grew louder and louder. Her heart raced, and her brow was hot with sweat.

"Just a minute," she hollered barely getting out the words. She ran into the bedroom and snatched a comforter off her bed. She ran back to the living room and tossed the comforter over his body. The tapping grew louder and louder irritating her.

"Damn it, I'm coming," she cursed. She ran to the door and looked out through the peek hole. Martha Kendall, her neighbor who lived two doors down, was peering back at her through a magnifying eyeglass. She cracked the door just enough to see outside. She gave the old lady a measly smile and whispered.

"Hi Martha, what's up?!" Martha Kendall, a humped back woman in her late eighties had thick silver-gray hair, twisted in a bun. She leaned on her cane squinting through black bifocals.

"Are you alright dear?" She asked with her voice cracking.

"Yes, why?" said Susan.

10

"I heard a loud noise coming from your apartment," Martha said. "It sounded like a firecracker."

"Oh, I'm afraid I dropped one of my glass vases on the floor," Susan lied. "I have created such a mess for myself," she said.

"Oh," said Martha as she craned her neck trying to see around Susan, whose body was wedged in the doorway.

"Be careful honey," she said. "Cleaning up glass is no joke."

"You are right," said Susan. "I will be extra careful. I promise," she smiled. Susan then closed the door leaving Martha in the hallway. She lingered there, straining to hear, hoping the old lady would accept her explanation and leave her alone. Killing the old woman was not an option. She winced at the thought of it. Two murders, she just couldn't fathom it. She could never live with herself.

"Martha, take your old butt back to your apartment," she whispered to herself. "Please go," she pleaded. A few minutes later, she finally heard Martha shuffling down the hall with her cane tapping loud on the floor. She sighed with relief. Her eyes fell on her lover's covered body, and the comforter soiled with dark red blood reeked with a faint sour stench.

Overcome with intense sadness, she wondered what she should do next. Moving his six-foot frame was hard, and she knew she would never be able to move him from the apartment without the risk of being seen. So, she left him there and headed to the bedroom. She climbed into the bed and thought about killing herself again, but decided not to. She then ran back into the living room and snatched the gun off the sofa. She removed the weapon's remaining bullets and then disposed it along with the bullets down the garbage chute.

She returned to her room, grabbed her suitcase out of the closet and tossed it on the bed. She packed fast, her movements frantic, snatching clothes out of drawers and tossing them in the suitcase. She ran around the room like a little mouse, grabbing up personal items and throwing them into a make-up bag. Once packed, she showered and quickly dressed.

While combing her short, curly, blonde hair, she contemplated her next move. She knew she must leave France, but where? Frazzled, she plopped down on the bed again racking her brain for an exit plan. Her mind raced overtime as she thought, thought, thought of where she might go. Realizing time was slipping away, she decided on a plan. She reached for the telephone and dialed a number. A voice was heard on the other end of the line, and she cleared her throat.

"I...I...I need a one-way ticket to Seattle," she stammered.

"How soon do you need it?" The representative asked.

"As soon as possible," Susan replied in a hurry.

Meanwhile, overseas at Salter's Point Regional Hospital, that very same day, Nurse Teresa Boston chased Billy Moonwalker across the hospital campus. Billy, a paranoid schizophrenic, tried to hang himself three weeks earlier with one of his shoelaces. He wrapped the lace around his neck and then tied it to a doorknob in his room. Luckily one of the nurses passing by saw what he was doing and stopped him. When Doctor Ethan Poppy was notified about Billy's attempt, she swiftly ordered suicide precautions, finally releasing him seventy-two hours later when he promised not to hurt himself again.

It appeared he was doing much better after the doctor prescribed him a new medication to treat his stomach ulcer. He was more outgoing, talkative and gregarious with his peers. Doctor Poppy, pleased with his progress, had planned to discharge him home by the end of the week. However, when Billy woke up Monday morning on June nineteen eighty-seven, he didn't feel quite right. His stomach hurt, and soon thoughts of suicide swept across his psychic again.

The last thing he ate was a cupcake decorated with pink icing, a treat passed out in skills group from the previous night before. He managed to shower and dress despite the gnawing pain intensifying in his stomach. He snuck out of his room and then parked himself five feet from the unit exit. For a while, he watched the nurses go in and out of patients' rooms passing out medications. Then he zeroed in on Teresa. His light brown eyes followed her down the hall as she headed to the exit. He scooted out of his seat and followed her. Staying several steps behind to avoid being detected. When she exited the unit, she unknowingly, left the door ajar. Recognizing a window of opportunity, he eased out. He sprinted past her, nearly knocking her down.

"Billy, bring your ass back here right now!" She screamed. He ignored her and kept running. Then he bolted out the door. Fear clouded Teresa's face, and she yelled,

"Someone get security!" She took off running after him. His long brown, woolly hair blew wild in the wind, and he sprinted through the parking lot like a speeding bullet. Running through the rose garden and then across the soccer field. The hospital gate, a few yards ahead, beckoned his escape.

He was there in a matter of minutes, and he shook the gate with such intensity, he jarred it opened.

"Shit!" He screamed when Teresa caught up with him and wrestled him to the ground, stopping him cold.

"Get off me, you witch!"

"You are not going anywhere," Teresa shouted.

The two of them rolled in the grass like little bear cubs until Billy overpowered her and managed to break free. He jumped up and aimed for the gate again. With his face beet-red, he shouted.

"Leave me alone!"

He rattled the gate free and ran out into the street. Drivers honked and swerved around him as he stayed in one place, staring straight ahead in a deep, deep trance.

"Billy, get out of the street!" Teresa screamed running up and down the sidewalk. "You are going to get yourself killed!" Her screaming broke his trance, and he ran to the other side of the street hopping on the sidewalk. He teetered on the edge, eyeing Teresa the whole time.

"Stay there and don't move!" She screamed. She tried to cross the street, but the cars whizzed by her so fast she was unable to do so. Suddenly, Billy changed his mind and ran into the street again. A car out of nowhere slammed into him, sending his body sailing through the air like a soccer ball. His body landed a few feet away down the road with a hard thump. Speeding vehicles ran over him, crushing his lifeless humanity into the dark pavement. Teresa dropped to her knees.

"Oh my god, oh my god, oh my god," she bawled in anguish, rocking back and forth with her head in her hands.

Traffic slowed to a grinding halt. Seconds later, patients, hospital personnel, and terrified drivers surrounded the gruesome scene. Sirens were heard screeching in the distance and the circle of devastated onlookers grew larger around Billy Moonwalker's broken body. His bloody, broken body was barely recognizable to the naked eye. Finally, the ambulance arrived, and the attendants tumbled out of the vehicle. They carefully picked up Billy Moonwalker and placed him on the gurney.

Within minutes he was whisked away, while hospital personnel looked on in horror. In their moment of grief, they had no idea a storm was brewing in their mist. Susan Cole's heinous crime and Billy Moonwalker's sudden death was the first of many calamities to plague Salter's Point Regional Hospital. A frightening tale has just begun.

CHAPTER TWO

The Next Day was Tuesday morning. Cathy Ray, nauseated after binging on a plate of pancakes and eggs, hightailed it to the bathroom. It was her first full meal in three days, and she was hungry, at least she thought. She made it to the commode and fell on her knees. She lifted the toilet seat up. She twisted her long strawberry blonde hair in a neat ball on top of her head and then shoved a finger down her throat. She gagged and her eyes watered. A concoction of slimy food particles projected straight from her mouth. Each retching episode lasted a full minute until every piece of food was expelled from her stomach.

Relieved, she flushed the commode and watched the contents whisked down the drain. She shook her hair, and it fell gently on her shoulders in a tangled strawberry mess. She struggled to her feet and steadied herself against the porcelain sink. She took a deep breath, gripping the rim of the sink, feeling nauseous again. After a while, the feeling subsided, and soon she felt a lot better. She reached for her toothbrush and started scrubbing her teeth. After she was finished, she wiggled out of her pajamas, and a reflection of her skinny five-foot-four-inch frame caught her eye in the full-length mirror. No more than eighty pounds spanking wet, she inspected herself from head to toe searching for any evidence of cellulite. She was obsessed with her weight. Eating like a bird most days and then binging the next. A routine of self-imposed retching, a constant habit in her everyday life.

Her eating disorder began at the age of eleven when her father, an engineer and the family's sole provider, left her mother and moved to Nevada with his lover. Her mother struggled financially for a while but then the daily grind of supporting Cathy and herself became too much. One day she went home and overdosed on Benadryl, killing herself. After her mother's death, Cathy went to Nevada to live with her father and his new wife. She despised her step-mother. She blamed the woman for her parent's divorce as well as her mother's suicide. When Cathy was twelve, she became angry at her stepmother one morning and mixed rat poison in her orange juice. Her step-mother later died in the hospital, and no one connected Cathy to her sudden demise.

A year later, her father fell ill and died from a massive stroke, leaving Cathy orphaned and alone. Struggling with abandonment issues, she spent the rest of her teenage years in foster care, excelling in school and graduating with honors. She left Nevada and moved to a little townhouse in Federal Way, thirty minutes from the City of Seattle. She enrolled at the University of Washington, majoring in social work, and six years later she graduated with a Master's degree in the field. After graduation, she landed a job at Salter's Point Regional Hospital, and it was there her professional career began. She jumped when the shrill buzzing of the alarm clock went off. It was seven o'clock, and she revolted in panic. She had only an hour and a half to get to work, and she couldn't afford to be late. With just one month left on her probation, she had already been written up four times for being late. She showered and dressed, then she inspected herself in the mirror again.

She brushed her long strawberry blonde hair for a total of five minutes, and after she was done, she was finally satisfied with her appearance. Then she threw her jacket on, grabbed her handbag and dashed out the door. The traffic on interstate five was light and steady, an unusual occurrence during the work week rush hour. She zoomed down the highway, seventy miles per hour in her blue Mustang. She glanced at her watch. It was almost eight o' clock. For the next thirty miles, she weaved in and out of traffic until she spotted a State Trooper up ahead. He was parked in a grassy grove off the freeway between two big evergreen trees. She pumped her brakes, and her heart thumped hard in her chest.

"Please Lord, I can't afford to get a ticket," she prayed out loud. She passed him, and he didn't look up, and she sighed with relief. "Whew, that was close!" She said.

Taking precaution, she drove the speed limit until she could no longer view the trooper in the rearview mirror. Then she stepped on the gas, taking off at seventy-five miles per hour. Forty-five minutes later, she was turning right onto the hospital grounds. Her anxiety was off the charts, and she was fifteen minutes late. The guard, decked out in Darth Vader garb, waved her through. Sweat broke out above her brow as she drove closer to East Campus Hospital. She scanned the area like an animal on alert, looking for Doctor Poppy, and hoping not to run into her. The doctor tattled on her the other day for being tardy; prompting Beth to issued her a written warning and since that time, Doctor Poppy has been in her crosshairs. As she made her way up the hill to East Campus Hospital, she noticed police cars parked alongside the road. Looking befuddled, she wondered out loud.

"What's going on here?" She speeded into the parking lot and parked. She grabbed her things and scrambled out of the car. She ran across the parking lot and into the hospital building. The lobby, crowded with doctors, nurses, social workers and techs took her by surprise. Police officers slithered in and out of the crowd as they stopped periodically to ask questions.

"What's going on here?" Cathy wondered again with her eyes big as saucers. She gave the lobby a once over and spotted Rachel Thomas, now married to Doctor James, and Betty Jo Brewer huddled in a corner near the reception desk. Betty Jo wasn't pretty in a traditional sense, but she was tall and attractive in her own right, a dark-skinned woman with expressive almond brown eyes and thick long braids to her waist. She was married to Doctor Mark Brewer; a handsome, slightly built man in his early forties with blue-green eyes and thick blonde hair combed back away from his face. They were new to Salter's Point Regional, transplants from California. As Cathy forced her way through the crowd, Betty Jo noticed her and gave Rachel an elbow nudge.

"Look who just came in," she said. "The little witch has just flown in on her broomstick, and she's late as usual," she joked.

"Oh, be nice," Rachel giggled as she waved for Cathy to come over their way.

"Hi ladies," said Cathy finally joining them. "Do you guys know what's going on here?" She asked.

"You are late!" Betty Jo said not cutting her any slack.

"I know. I am optimally delusional on how long it takes me to arrive at places on time," Cathy nonchalantly said.

"Whatever!" Said Betty Jo rolling her eyes. Cathy raised up on her toes to see over the crowd.

"What's going on here? Why is everyone in the lobby?" She asked.

"Billy Moonwalker committed suicide this morning," Rachel said with her face grim.

"Oh, my goodness," Cathy said with big eyes. She squeezed her mouth with one hand. "What happened?"

"He eloped from the unit and ran out into traffic," Rachel explained. "He was hit by a car and died," she added.

"How terrible," Cathy said shaking her head.

"Yeah, it is," Betty Jo said still checking out the crowd.

"Maybe his voices came back," Cathy reasoned as she tried to make sense of Billy's untimely death. "His voices were destructive. They would tell him to kill himself," she pointed out. Her eyes searched the lobby for Ethan Poppy.

"Does Doctor Poppy know? Billy was on her caseload."

"Yeah, she knows, and she is devastated," Betty Jo said. "She told us Billy was in skills group last evening and he had fun decorating cupcakes. He even ate one!"

"And you are surprised by that?" Cathy smarted off.

"Well yeah," Rachel piped in. "You were the one who told us he suffered from stomach ulcers," she said surprised by her attitude. "He hardly ate!" Cathy shied away for a moment, with her cheeks a rosy red. She hated when others called her out on her mistakes. Feeling embarrassed, she reluctantly takes the hit steering the conversation another way.

"Where is Doctor Poppy anyway?" She asked observing the crowd.

"In her office," Rachel said. "She refuses to answer the door."

Cathy rolled her eyes.

"That woman is so weird," she said.

"Yeah, she's a little special," Betty Jo chuckled under her breath. Rachel frowned, and the vein in her forehead protruded a little.

"Give the woman a break you two," she said. "She just lost a patient, and she feels terrible about it."

"The woman is an idiot," Cathy blurted out showing no mercy. "She has a mind like a paper doll, and she sleeps in a damn coffin for goodness sakes!"

"She does not!" Rachel retorted taking up for the doctor. Cathy's eyes narrowed.

"I wouldn't put it past her and besides the cupcake thing was her idiotic idea," she disclosed. "She thinks serving cupcakes in the group brings the patients closer together, how ridiculous is that?" She huffed.

"I don't see anything wrong with it myself," Rachel said giving her the stink eye. "The group activity encourages patients to socialize with one another," she reasoned.

"I agree," said Betty Jo siding with Rachel. "Sharing a dessert promotes camaraderie, intimacy and good communication," she added. Cathy threw her arms across her chest and rolled her eyes again.

"Okay I get it. I see it from your vantage point. But, I still think the idea is ridiculous!" She insisted.

"All righty," Betty Jo sighed. "You are entitled to your opinion!" She and Rachel exchanged wary glances. Then Betty Jo announced,

"I'm leaving and going to my office. I'll see you guys later."

"I think I'll join you," Rachel said taking her cue. She and Betty Jo take off, leaving Cathy Ray alone in the lobby.

"She's exhausting," Rachel said taking a deep breath.

"Toxic more like it," Betty Jo interjected.

"The more I get to know her, the less I like her," Rachel shared.

"Me too," Betty Jo said.

Later, mid-morning, Doctor Everett James sat in his office, brooding. He just finished reviewing Billy Moonwalker's chart trying to identify any missing clues leading to his tragic death. On the surface, it appeared Doctor Ethan Poppy provided adequate medical care, and nothing was amiss as far as he could tell. However, deep down in his gut, he felt something wasn't right. He respected Doctor Poppy, although, he found her a bit strange. Every time she emerged from her office or showed up for a meeting she was wearing a different color pair of high top tennis shoes or her hairstyle had changed.

Her violet colored eyes, short frizzy white hair, along with her albino, ghost-like complexion, took a while to get used too. She had a germ phobia, often donning long gloves before shaking a colleague's or patient's hand. Her most striking feature was her bright, perfect smile. Her smile was known to light up the darkest of rooms, and he chuckled at the thought of it, despite himself.

"That woman is quite a peculiar creature with specific habits," he mused. He leaned back in his chair and placed his feet up on the desk. His dark brown eyes wandered to his wife's picture.

He grinned like a Cheshire Cat when he thought about making love to her. His wife and little girl, Jamie Lee, were the love of his life. Three years ago, six months after their friend and colleague Jamie Lee's death, he and Rachel married in front of the justice of the peace in downtown Salter's Point. They moved into a modest, three-bedroom bungalow home in the town of Seaside, not far from the beach. Attracted to the house for its breathtaking view of Puget Sound. On a bright sunny day, one could see white glistening snow on the peaks of Mount Rainier. A barely visible McNeil Island could also be viewed floating one hundred miles away from the rocky coast of Puget Sound. The small town feel of Seaside, Washington boded quite well for the couple. Everything was close, including Salter's Point Regional, which was ten miles down the road. The daycare center Jamie Lee, their two-year-old daughter, attended was a few blocks from the hospital.

Still very much in love, Everett and Rachel were very content with the life they had made for themselves there, and marriage had done wonders for Doctor Everett James. He had changed his overall look. He no longer wore his usual garb of combat boots, beret hats, and jeans. Instead, he dressed in suits and kept his afro cut very low. Still favoring his dark sunglasses, however, often wearing them to meetings. After reviewing Billy Moonwalker's chart for the third time, Everett gave up.

"This chart needs fresh eyes," he concluded. While he gathered up his notes, Doctor Mark Brewer barged in. He stood in the doorway, propped up by his cane. He sprained his ankle two weeks earlier while stepping off a curb, intoxicated in front of Sully's Bar and Grill.

"What's shaking?" He said

"What happened to knocking first?" Everett scolded him looking irritated.

"Sorry man," he apologized. He hesitated for a second.

"Are you going somewhere?" He asked with a curious look on his face.

"Yeah, I am going to see our boss," said Everett. "I know you heard what happened to Ethan's patient Billy Moonwalker this morning?"

"Yep, I heard," Mark said. "Very tragic!"

"Yeah…. I have racked my brain all morning looking for clues in his record that might explain his bizarre behavior," Everett said looking somber. "I think another pair of eyes needs to review this chart before I blame it on his illness."

"What was his diagnosis?" Mark asked.

"Paranoid Schizophrenia," said Everett. "Initially he was experiencing voices telling him to kill himself, but it appears Ethan had the symptom under control with medication." He surmised.

"Okay, then what's your problem then?" Mark asked scratching his head.

"My gut tells me there could be something else with this case," Everett said looking concerned.

"Don't be too hard on yourself there, buddy," said Mark. "We can't save everybody."

Everett's face tensed up. He closed Billy's chart and started for the door.

"Dude do you hear me?" Mark asked looking cross and feeling ignored. Everett turned to face him.

"I need a second opinion man," he snapped back.

"Okay, if you insist," Mark said backing off. "It's your call."

Everett opened the door.

"After you," he said gesturing for Mark to exit before him. The doctor limped passed him and stepped out into the hall.

Everett followed him out and locked the door.

"See you later dude," he said gliding down the hall.

"Good luck man," Mark said. He turned and limped back to his office in the opposite direction.

CHAPTER THREE

Back on the admissions unit, Ethan Poppy was hunkered down in her office trying to stay below the fray. A dowdy and peculiar woman, she wore a long black smock, red high-top tennis shoes and her short white frizzy hair was swept up into a bun. Named after her father, who expected a boy the day she was born, Doctor Poppy joined the psychiatry staff a year ago. Newly divorced, her husband, also a physician, ran off with his gay lover causing the demise of their marriage. Looking for a change, she sold her home in Florida and moved clear across the country to distance herself from the life she had there. However, her adjustment to her new job had been rough, often engaging in verbal scrimmages with the nurses at least three to four times a day.

Her bizarre reputation was comedic fodder around the hospital. Rumor had it she slept in a coffin, and her affinity for high-top tennis shoes and unusual pets was often the main topic in most gossip circles. She owned fifty pairs of tennis shoes she stashed underneath her desk, and she frequently changed her shoes two to three times a day. In a corner behind her desk were three scrawny black rats she kept as pets scurrying around in a cage. When the nurses discovered she had rats in her office, they reported her to the health department. However, the health inspector allowed her to keep the rodents after he found the animals were domesticated. Since then, the nurses refused to visit her office, forcing her to come to the nursing station to sign off on orders instead.

She reached down underneath her desk and grabbed a small bag of carrots. She scooted her chair over to the cage and dropped three carrots inside. The rodents fought over the carrots while she looked on in amusement. Suddenly her office door flew opened and slammed into the wall.

"My word!" She screamed almost falling over in her chair. "You scared me!" Robert Harris' six-foot-four-inch frame took up the entire doorway. He sashayed into her office wearing red, spiked high heel shoes and a tight-knit black dress. His heavily made up expressive green eyes sported a hint of dark eyeliner, and his thin lips were smeared with a bold ruby red lipstick. A few weeks ago, he tried to change his sex by snipping his genitals off. He was rushed to the emergency room and when stable, was transferred to Salter's Point Regional. When he puckered up his lips, his eyes sparkled.

"Well, well, well, I see you got the memo," he said with a raspy voice.

"What do you mean?!" She said with blazing eyes.

"Don't' you see doc? We're twins.... We got the same colors on today!" He chuckled, as she frowned.

"Next time, don't barge in here without asking permission to enter first," she chastised him.

"AW, don't get your panties in a wad," he joked. "I didn't mean to scare you!"

"Robert, what do you want?!" She asked looking pointedly at him.

"Can you pleasssse give me a pass for the library?" He whined. "I need to get an engineering book for my job." Her jaw dropped.

"You have a job?!"

"Yes, girl," he sweetly replied. "I am on medical leave."

"What do you do?" She asked raising an eyebrow.

"Girl, I thought you knew," he laughed. "I am an electrical engineer. Once I leave this crazy place, I'm taking my fine cute ass back to work!"

"We'll see about that, Mister Harris," the doctor said. "It depends on how well you adjust to your medication." Robert bucked his eyes and fluffed his hair up.

"I'm doing just fine girl, believe me!"

"We'll see," the doctor clarified again.

"Pleeease Girl, can I get a pass?" He whined again with his hands in a praying position.

"Alright," Ethan said with her brow wrinkling. "But just for the record, my name is not girl!"

"My, My, My, aren't we touchy this morning with your old lady hairdo," he teased puckering his lips again.

She ignored his salty insult and opened her desk drawer. She reached for a pad of blank passes and tore one off. She printed his name on the pass, signed it, then she gave it to him.

"Here you are," she said. "Remember, the pass is only good for two hours," she warned. "Keep track of your time." He blew her kiss.

"Will do," he said. "See you in a few! And change that awful old lady hairdo! It's so boring!" He then sashayed out the door leaving it wide open. Five minutes later, Everett darkened her doorway.

"Hey there Ethan," he said smiling. "How are you?"

"As well as to be expected," she sighed.

"What's wrong?" He said gliding in and shutting the door behind him. He propped himself up on the corner of her desk.

"It's Robert...... He's such a nuisance," she sighed again.

"Yeah, he can be," he said. "Well, if it's any consolation, I reviewed Billy Moonwalker's record, and I didn't find anything amiss," he told her. Her eyebrows went up.

"Really?" She said.

"Yep," he said. "But I thought I'd have Carl review it before we put the matter to rest, do you mind?"

"Oh, go ahead," she said nodding her head. "I don't mind." The rats fought each other on the cage floor, and the noise grabbed Everett's attention.

"It's true! You really do have rats in here," he exclaimed looking surprised.

"Yes, I do," she said cracking a slight smile.

"Rats for pets, are you serious?!" He asked moving a little closer to get a good look at the scrawny creatures. Her violet eyes crinkled up at the corners.

"Do they bother you?"

"Why can't you get a pet dog or cat like normal people?" He inquired. "A rat for a pet, I have to say is quite weird," he added not mincing words. Ethan grinned wide.

"Maybe to you, it's weird, but I find rats to be interesting animals." He observed the rats for a long moment, and then he said,

"Do you want to join me to see Carl?"

"Sure," she said.

"Well let's go," he said. He turned and went out, and she joined him, locking the door behind her.

As they headed to Doctor Beebe's office, Everett checked her out from the corner of his eye. He became tickled and laughed out loud.

"What's so funny?" She said giving him the stink eye.

"I just can't get over the fact, you have rats for pets," he said shaking his head again. She let out a small giggle.

"Oh, you'll get used to it," she teased.

"Don't count on it," he teased back.

Later in the afternoon, Rachel and Betty Jo were in the nursing station feverishly documenting progress notes in patients' charts. Soon Cathy Ray came in, and they moved over, making room for her to sit with them. They sat in silence, everyone writing up a storm with no one saying a word. After thirty minutes went by, Rachel broke the silence.

"Cathy, I need to tell you something," she softly said. "Doctor Poppy told me to remind you not to forget to document less restrictive plans on your assigned patients," she told her. Cathy bristled up.

"I thought I did that!"

"According to her, you forgot," Rachel said. "Anyway, it didn't get done."

"So, she's blaming me," Cathy charged with her fuse getting short.

"Well, she did mention it to Beth," Rachel revealed, her voice calm and steady. Cathy threw her arms across her chest in a huff.

"I hate that woman!" She hissed. "She's always criticizing me! Tattling on me! I can never do anything right around her. She reminds me of my stepmother!"

"Well she's not your stepmother, and you need to slow your roll!" Betty Jo said, her tone abrasive.

"But she's a nuisance," Cathy fumed. "And I'm still on probation!"

"I'm sure everything will be fine," Rachel tried to reassure her. "Just remember to do your plans. It's part of the discharge process," she said. Cathy felt out of sorts and looked down at the floor.

"Whatever," she muttered under her breath. Rachel glared at her.

"Cathy, what's wrong with you today? Did someone take your damn lollipop?!" Betty Jo snickered out loud, and Cathy turned beet red. She bolted out of her seat.

"I don't have to take this! I'm leaving!" She sharply announced.

"Suit yourself," Rachel shot back making a funny face. Cathy snatched the chart she was working on and stomped out the nursing station. Rachel and Betty Jo looked at each other, their eyes wide with utter amazement.

"That little chick needs some serious Xanax," Betty Jo said.

"No, she needs an ass whupping," Rachel fumed. Betty Jo looks worried.

"Do you think Beth will keep her on after she finishes probation," she asked.

"Probably," Rachel sighed. "The hospital needs more social workers, so I think we are stuck with that little witch for a while!"

"Damn," said Betty Jo scrunching up her face. Rachel shrugged her shoulders.

"We just have to find a way to work with the crazy chick," she said.

"Girrrl, I don't know if I can do it," Betty Jo responded in a melodramatic way.

"You can," Rachel said. "We just have to check her every time she gets out of hand."

"I think she and Hiram should get together," Betty Jo joked. "They both like to stomp around like little toddlers when they get mad!" Rachel hollered with laughter.

"Girl, they'll end up killing each other!"

"Yeah, you are probably right," Betty Jo said giggling.

No sooner than she uttered her last word, a six-foot yellow bird wearing a blue navy hat with a bright orange beak pranced into the nursing station. Doctor Michael Louis, not far behind, walked in seconds later and the bird hollered, "tweet, tweet" in his face. He scowled, getting very irritated.

"Who left the idiot bag open?" He snarled. The bird threw up one hand in a dignified fashion.

"You're not very nice today my friend!"

"I'm not trying to be nice!" Michael said with contempt.

"Tweet, tweet," the bird chirped flapping his arms.

"Please go and be stupid away from me!" Michael grumbled. Rachel and Betty Jo giggled like two little bandits. Then Rachel said.

"Doctor Louis, that's mean!"

"Mean? My foot!" He snapped frowning up. "There are too many morons working in this hospital!" The bird mooned the doctor and then sat on top of the nursing counter. The bird crossed its legs and made a face.

"See, that's what I'm talking about," Michael said shaking his head. "An educated moron!"

"Hiram, stop it!" Rachel said laughing her head off.

"Missy, I'm just having fun," he grinned flapping his arms. He scooted off the counter and broke out into the "running man" dance.

"Are you serious?" Betty Jo said rolling her chair back giving him more room. "You are crazy as shit! Why have you dressed like that anyway?!" He stopped dancing and placed one hand on his hip.

"You don't know?!"

"If I knew, I wouldn't ask fool," Betty Jo smarted off.

"It's big bird's birthday, and Hiram is celebrating on his behalf," he declared speaking in the third person. Rachel fell out laughing again.

"Hiram, you are absolutely out of your damn tree!"

"A straight up fool is more like it!" Betty Jo deadpanned under her breath. Rachel tried to redirect him.

"Hiram, is there something you need?"

"Oh, Hiram forgot," he said taking off his mask. His hazel-brown eyes zeroed in on her, and his face suddenly turned serious.

"Who you got coming to court on Wednesday?" He inquired.

"I don't know yet," Rachel said. "The doctors are still deciding. I should know later this afternoon."

"Okay, Missy," he said.

He broke out dancing the "running man" again and then he took off and jumped over the gate. He stopped a moment to adjust his costume.

"I'll be back!" He hollered. Then he skipped down the hall disappearing through the exit. Rachel and Betty Jo fell out in hysterics. They laughed so hard, tears streamed down their faces.

"This place is so full of nuts; I can hardly stand it!" Betty Jo said barely getting out the words as she dabbed her face with a tissue.

"Girrrl, you got that right," Rachel said. "And Hiram is the biggest nut of them all!"

Everett and Ethan were in Doctor Beebe's office, discussing Billy Moonwalker and Carl, short on answers, looked glum.

"I don't know what to think," he said. "Sometimes the medicine doesn't work." "But he improved after I put him on Abilify," Ethan protested. "He was making plans, socializing more and eating again."

"It doesn't take long for Abilify to work," Everett added. "Patients generally get better after taking it for a week."

"Maybe he wasn't taking it," Carl pointed out. "Maybe he was spitting it out when the nurses weren't looking."

"That's possible," Everett said nodding his head in agreement. Ethan sighed.

"I feel bad about all of this," she said with tears in her eyes. She bowed her head and stared down at her lap.

"I know," Carl said, with his soft voice feeling sorry for her. "I know."

By the time six o'clock rolled around Tuesday evening, the nursing staff was all over East Campus searching for Robert Harris, who never returned from his trip to the library. Frantic and upset, Sally telephoned Doctor Poppy's residence several times, but there was no answer. She called his wife, and there was no answer there either.

So, she left a message on the answering machine and hung up. She then called the City Police, and for several hours, the officers conducted an extensive search. However, Robert Harris was nowhere to be found. Thirty miles down the road across town in the suburbs, Ethan was curled up in her coffin with the covers over her head brooding and feeling sorry for herself. With her mind consumed with Billy Moonwalker, she never heard the telephone ringing off the hook in the other room.

She had never lost a patient in her twenty-year medical career, and the shock of losing Billy had rattled her. "How did this happen?" she kept questioning herself. What did she miss? Unable to come to a reasonable explanation, she finally gave up and climbed out of her coffin. The telephone had stopped ringing by this time, and she shuffled over to the kitchen and made herself a hot cup of tea. While sipping on her tea, she obsessed about work.

She wondered how she would ever make it through the day once she arrived there in the morning. Little did she realize her troubles were just beginning and Robert Harris' disappearance would be the least of her worries.

CHAPTER FOUR

Wednesday, the next morning, Ethan was trying desperately to unlock the heavy steel door on the admissions unit, and the lock refused to budge. She grimaced and grunted, feeling frustrated as she jiggled the key in the lock. After a while, she finally gave up and banged on the door. Sally Roberts heard the noise and came to her aid. She made a face when she peered out the door window and saw it was Ethan.

"Doctor Poppy I have been looking for you," she said as she promptly unlocked the door. She shoved it opened, and Doctor Poppy waddled in.

"Thanks," she said barely smiling. "For some reason, my key is not working this morning." Sally lit into her.

"There's more to worry about than your key!" Ethan's violet eyes became watery.

"What do you mean?!"

"Didn't you hear?" Sally asked her eyes big like a peacock's. Ethan looks at her dumbly.

"Hear what?"

"Robert Harris is missing," Sally informed her. "He never returned to the hospital last night." Ethan's face dropped.

"What do you mean he never returned?!"

"The man is not here," Sally firmly said. "We searched for hours, and we never found him!"

"Did you call his wife?" Ethan asked trying to be helpful. "Maybe he went home!"

"I certainly did," Sally snapped outwardly irritated. "And I called you too, and there was no answer!"

"I'm so sorry," Ethan said, feeling guilty. "I was feeling so bad about Billy......" Sally cuts her off.

"There's no time for excuses! His wife is on the way to talk to you, so you better get your story straight!"

"Oh my," Ethan shrieked. "I must see Doctor Beebe right away," she said. She took off leaving Sally at the door. Sally shook her head.

"Poor woman," she said. "She has no idea what she's in for!"

Rachel and Betty Jo stood outside Cathy Ray's office and knocked on the door. The doorknob rattled for a brief minute, and then the door flew open.

"Oh!" Cathy said looking surprised. "What are you two up to?" She asked.

"Can we come in?" Rachel asked.

"Sure," Cathy said as she gestured for them to enter her office. The two women bounced in and pulled up a couple of chairs and sat down. Cathy parked herself behind her desk and swiveled three times around in her chair.

"I love this chair," she said with a naughty grin on her face. "What's up?! Why the visit?!"

"We want to know how you are doing," Betty Jo explained forcing a smile. Cathy's grin faded immediately.

"No, you don't," she said sounding annoyed. "Just tell me what's going on."

"You don't know?" Betty Jo said looking at her side-eyed.

"Know what?!" Cathy snapped tensing up.

"Well, your patient, Robert Harris is missing," Rachel informed her. "We thought you knew!" Cathy cringed.

"It's news to me," she said feeling ambushed. "So, you are telling me this because you think it's my fault, right?!"

"Girl, get over yourself," Betty Jo hissed glaring at her. "Stop thinking everything that happens is your fault!"

"I second that," Rachel quipped staring her down. The women fell silent for a moment. Then Rachel calmly said,

"Cathy do you want to know what happened?"

"I guess so," Cathy said with her face full of apology.

"Well....." Rachel began. "Doctor Poppy gave Robert a two-hour pass, and he never returned to the hospital," she explained. Cathy threw her hands up.

"I told you the woman thinks like a paper doll," she smarted off. "Why would she do that?! He can't be trusted. The man tried to cut his dick off a couple of weeks ago!"

"Maybe she thought he was getting better," Rachel said looking introspective. "I do see what you mean. Her decision making is looking a little suspect."

"Now she has gotten rid of two patients," Cathy exaggerated as she folded her arms across her chest. "I wonder who she's planning to get rid of next!" Betty Jo twisted her face up.

"Oh, stop it," she said. "You act like the woman is a monster!"

"Maybe she is, and we don't know it," Cathy speculated. "She is a dangerous person!"

"Now, now, let's not get ahead of ourselves," Rachel said. "The police will find Robert Harris, and he will be just fine."

"You better hope so for her sake," Cathy warned. "You better hope so."

When Ethan arrived at Doctor Beebe's office, an entourage was there waiting for her. Thomas Marshall, the police chief, Sally Roberts, Beth Jones and Doctor Beebe. Sick with dread and worry, she fought back the tears as she found a seat and sat down.

"Good Morning," she mumbled. "I guess you heard."

"Yes," Carl said with a gloomy face. "Tell us what happened."

"He was doing so well," she began. "I thought he was ready for ground privileges. He gave no indication he would be a flight risk."

"Did he say where he was going?" Thomas yawned, tired from being up all night on a case. Ethan shrugged her shoulders and carefully recapped her conversation with Robert.

"He told me he had to go to the library," she said giving Thomas direct eye contact. "He stated he needed an engineering book of some sort...... For his job." Beth busted out laughing.

"For his job?!" She smirked. "He lied to you, honey! He was fired months ago for missing too many days at work!"

"Oh, my goodness," Ethan groaned. She cradled her head in her hands, now embarrassed.

"Oh, my goodness is right," Beth said rolling her eyes. Thomas arched both eyebrows.

"Doctor, you weren't aware of this?"

"No," Ethan said blinking her eyes in a dignified manner. Thomas glanced urgently at Doctor Beebe.

Beads of sweat broke out on the doctor's forehead, and worry had settled deep in his features. He turned to face Sally.

"Do you know if Robert has any, um... favorite hangouts?" He stammered.

"No," Sally said shaking her head. "His wife might know. I understand she is on her way here and she is mighty upset!"

Ethan sank deeper in despair. Wishing she could just disappear. She swallowed hard as tears welled in her eyes.

"You better brace yourselves," Doctor Beebe warned, his face grave. "She's worse than a pistol going off on a fourth of July holiday when angry!" No sooner than the words escape his lips, screaming and cursing was heard in the hallway. The screaming grew louder and louder, and then the door swung opened and slammed against the wall. The room shook like an earthquake, and Ginger Harris stood in the doorway, frowning with her hands on her hips. Carl grabbed the phone and called security.

"Where in the hell is my husband?!" She shouted with her eyes fiery and hot.

"You, lady need to calm the hell down. You're at a fifteen, and I need you like at a five!" Thomas warned her with his hand on his weapon.

"The hell I will," she shouted, her face beet red. "Tell me where my husband is?!" She stood there glaring at him with her thick arms folded across her chest. Ginger Harris was something to behold. She was stocky with light brown eyes, and she wore a buzz haircut with orange lipstick painted on her lips.

Her orange checkered plaid shirt was tucked into her green overalls, and her spiked black high heel shoes were covered with dust. Her fiery gaze fell on Ethan Poppy.

"Are you Doctor Poppy?!" She demanded.

"Yes," she said, her voice barely audible.

"Speak up," Ginger hissed. "I can't hear you!"

"Yes, I'm Robert's doctor," Ethan repeated, her voice a little louder but weak. Ginger wagged her finger in the doctor's face.

"Where's my husband, woman?!"

"I don't know," Ethan said scooting back in her chair. She began to cry, and Ginger glared at the doctor.

"Crying isn't going to help you chick," she shouted. Suddenly two security guards stormed into the room.

"Need help?!" One guard asked as he sized up the hostile scene. Carl gestured for him to wait. The guards parked themselves against the wall with their eyes fixated on Ginger Harris.

"Aren't you supposed to be looking after him?" She yelled, turning around to check out the guards.

"Mrs. Harris, please sit down so we can explain what happened," Carl calmly urged her.

"Stop telling me to sit down," Ginger screamed now facing the medical chief. "I will not sit down until I get some answers!"

"Mrs. Harris, let me explain," Ethan interrupted, her voice soft.

"Alright," Ginger said calming down a little. "Get on with it!" Ethan cleared her throat.

"Humph...I gave your husband a pass to go to the library yesterday morning," she explained.

"Huh, huh," Ginger said with her eyes blazing and fixated on the doctor.

"He seemed alright. He promised to obey the rules and come back on time," she said. Ginger threw her hands on her hips.

"Let me get this straight! You mean to tell me you let my crazy husband off the unit and out of your sight?" She yelled in her face. "Have you forgotten this is the same man who tried to cut his dick off two weeks ago?! Doctor, my husband is ill! You should not allow him to leave this hospital!"

"I'm sorry...." Ethan said. She fell silent and lowered her head. Tears dropped in her lap. Ginger frowned and looked at Doctor Beebe.

"I have one question to ask you. Is she a doctor or a freaking crybaby?!"

"Mrs. Harris...." He said. Ginger waved him off in a dismissive manner.

"One thing I know for sure. If anything happens to my husband, I'm suing you, and this here cry baby!" Thomas, tired of Ginger's insults, stepped in.

"Okay that's enough," he said. "Go home and get some rest. I will call you with updates."

"NO!" She shouted. "First I'm going to whip this cry baby's butt before I go anywhere!"

When she lunged at the doctor, the security guards pounced on her and yanked her off the floor. They dragged her to the door screaming.

"If anything happens to my husband, I will sue you! Do you hear me Doctor Crybaby? I'm going to sue you!"

The guards carried her out, and Sally got up and shut the door. She shook her head and sighed.

"Boy, that woman is something else," she said. Ethan, unable to hold herself together, broke down sobbing. Sally rushed to her side and rubbed her back.

"I told you she's a pistol!" Carl said with his face filled with exhaustion. He glanced over at Thomas looking worried again.

"What's next?"

"We will keep looking for Mister Harris. I will keep you advised of any updates," Thomas said with a strain on his face. "In the meantime, try not to worry."

"That's easy for you to say," Ethan sniffled. "Don't worry, we will find him, dear," Sally said trying to be positive.

"Sally is right," Thomas butted in. "We will find him, I promise!"

CHAPTER FIVE

Closed off in her office, Cathy stacked cupcakes on a large platter and covered them with saran wrap. Doctor Poppy's skills group was at six thirty, and she wanted to make sure everything was ready to go. Although it was Doctor Poppy's idea to serve cupcakes after the group, Cathy volunteered to supply them after she found out the doctor had rats in her office. She despised Doctor Poppy. The woman reminded her of too much of her stepmother. Always criticizing her and never satisfied with anything she did. She resented Ethan Poppy for going to Beth and complaining about her less than stellar work.

Later receiving a written reprimand of disciplinary action, just before her ninety-day probation was up. Determined to get revenge, she took every opportunity to discredit the doctor including blaming her for Robert Harris' disappearance, as well as the untimely death of Billy Moonwalker. She opened her office door and with the platter in one hand and two cans of icing in another, she walked out guiding the door shut with her foot. She headed to the nursing station and ran into Betty Jo.

"What you got there, girlie?" Betty Jo asked eyeing the cupcakes and grinning like nobody's business.

"These little goodies are for the group," Cathy replied.

"Need some help?"

"Yeah do you mind?" Cathy hands Betty Jo the cupcakes. They continue down the hall.

"Girl, are these chocolate?" Betty Jo asked getting excited.

"Yep," Cathy said.

"Girl, I love anything chocolate," Betty Jo giggled. "Can I get one of these here babies?" Cathy cracked up laughing.

"These little babies are for the group. I don't have any extras!"

"Next time make enough for me," Betty Jo said with a grin pasted on her face. Cathy had a wicked gleam in her eye.

"I'll try to remember that," she said.

"Where do you want these?" Betty Jo asked as they walked into the nursing station.

"In the refrigerator," Cathy said.

"You got it," Betty Jo said. They go in the med room and put the cupcakes and icing in the refrigerator.

"Thanks for your help," Cathy said.

"You're welcome," said Betty Jo as she bounced out of the nursing station.

"Remember I want a cupcake next time," she reminded her. Cathy let out a wicked giggle.

"I'll certainly keep that in mind."

It was twelve noon, by the time Susan Cole's plane arrived at SeaTac Airport. Wearing a black fedora hat with dark sunglasses, Susan exited the plane and headed to baggage claim. She strutted with purpose, looking straight ahead as she navigated through the thick, bruising crowd. She soon found the train and stepped on board, and within five minutes she was in baggage claim at the carousel. She waited on her suitcase, and minutes later, it came tumbling out onto the rotor belt. She grabbed her suitcase and dragged it over the railing then she made her way outside. It was chilly and damp.

A thick, dense fog hovered over the airport, and she was surprised by the crisp cold air. She shivered as she buttoned her sweater and rubbed her hands together.

"Brrrrr, its chilly for June," she thought to herself. She flagged down a cab. The cab driver pulled up to the curb and hopped out grabbing her suitcase. He opened the trunk and tossed it inside, and he slammed the trunk shut.

"Thanks," Susan said.

"No problem," he said in a rough voice.

He ran to the right side of the cab and yanked the door open. Susan climbed into the back seat and once seated, he slammed the door hard, startling her.

"My word," she shrieked. "You are so heavy handed!"

The cab driver ignored her comment and slid behind the steering wheel. He looked in the rearview mirror and checked Susan out. Mesmerized by her dark sunglasses and black fedora hat, he wondered who she was. He grinned wide, revealing two rows of gold straight teeth and Susan was secretly tickled. She smiled.

"Where to mysterious one?!" He seductively barked.

"Do you know where Salter's Point is?" She asked.

"Yep," he said.

"Take me to Salter's Point Hotel," she said.

He stepped on the gas and sped away from the curb. He weaved in and out of traffic on the airport byway until he reached the exit going south on interstate five. He barreled through the exit and then zoomed down the highway.

"Are you here to stay?" He said glancing in the rearview mirror again as he tried to make conversation.

"I hope so," Susan said. "I used to live here," she shared.

"Oh," said the cab driver. "Then welcome home!"

"Thank you," she smiled.

Fifty minutes later, he pulled up in front of Salter's Point Hotel and parked. It was one o'clock in the afternoon, and the hotel was covered with a thick white fog, barely visible to the naked eye. When the cab driver got out of his cab, a big black four-legged creature brushed by him with rapid speed.

"Yikes! What was that?!" He yelled.

"Is something wrong?" Susan asked rolling down the window, craning her neck as she peered over her sunglasses.

"See that cat over there?" He shouted with his nerves on edge. "It scared the hell out me!"

The cat sat in the middle of the street staring at the cab driver. Its golden eyes were captivating and the cab driver was too frightened to move. Then suddenly the cat darted across the street disappearing into the thick, dense fog. Shaken and on edge, the cab driver mumbled something incomprehensible to himself as he went to his trunk and unlocked it. Susan stuck her head out the window.

"What did you say?" She asked.

"Nothing!" He said grabbing her suitcase and dropping it on the curb.

He slammed the trunk shut and stepped to the rear of the car. He trembled inside, fiddling with the door handle, then he finally yanked the door opened. Susan got out.

"Are you alright?" She asked, noticing his discomfort.

"Yeah, just a little spooked," he said with fright in his eyes.

Susan stood on the sidewalk checking out her surroundings. The cab driver soon joined her scoping out the area as well. Susan paid him and reached for her suitcase.

"I can take it inside for you," the cab driver offered.

"No thank you," she said smiling. "I can handle it from here."

She grabbed her suitcase and strutted into the hotel lobby. A young freckled-face woman with thick auburn red dreadlocks was manning the reservation desk. The woman slid off her stool as Susan approached sizing her up with narrow eyes.

"Can I help you?" The woman said in a soprano voice.

"You can," Susan replied peering over her sunglasses.

"I need a room with a king size bed," she said.

"Let's see what we got," said the woman.

She searched the reservation log and found a room on the fourth floor. She opened the drawer and took a key out.

"Ma'am, I have a room with a king size bed available on the fourth floor," she said. "The room number is four hundred and twelve."

"I'll take it," Susan blurted out not giving it any thought.

The woman shot her an alarming look. Caught off guard by her eagerness.

"The cost is one hundred dollars a night," she told her. "Check out time is eleven o'clock."

"That's fine," Susan said reaching into her handbag for her wallet.

She paid the hotel fee, and the representative gave her the key. Susan thanked her and headed to the elevator. Minutes later she was in her room.

She left her suitcase by the door and fell on the bed. "Boy, I'm tired," she yawned falling back on the bed. She rolled over and searched for the television remote. The remote was lying on the nightstand at the head of the bed. She scooted over and grabbed it and switched on the television. She surfed the channels for a few minutes and then settled on KIRO news.

The color drained from her face when she saw George Benny's face plastered on the television screen. She sat straight up like a tin soldier when the newscaster reported his death as a homicide. Her heart thumped hard in her chest when her picture flashed on the screen a few seconds later. Not only was she reported as missing, but a possible suspect in his murder. She panicked and grabbed a pillow, punching it with her fists. It wasn't long before she came to her senses, realizing for the first time since the murder, she would never escape her heinous crime. Feeling very much alone, she decided to face the music.

Her mind raced as she thought about her next step and then an idea crossed her mind. A very, very dark idea. She decided once and for all to put an end to her miserable life. She rolled off the bed and ran to her suitcase. She unzipped it and grabbed her medicine. Then she ran to the bathroom and filled a glass with water. She loosened the cap on the medicine bottle and shook out several tablets into her trembling hand. She took the medicine all at once chasing it down with water. She laid down on the bed and stared at the ceiling. Her thoughts replayed her gruesome crime, and a tear streamed down the side of her face. Soon her breathing became labored, and she felt herself fading away.

Her eyelids flickered for a second, and finally, her body relaxed. As she slipped into a deep, deep slumber, the town clock in the city square chimed two times. It was two o' clock in the afternoon in the city of Salter's Point and several hours would pass before Susan Cole was found.

CHAPTER SIX

Seven-Thirty, Wednesday evening, Ethan Poppy was finishing up her skills group while Cathy was busy serving cupcakes and grape Kool-Aid to thirty-some patients. Ethan, in an upbeat mood, was pleased with the turn-out despite such a horrible start to her day. After everyone signed in and received a cupcake, Ethan waddled over to the nursing station and sat down. She took notes while she quietly observed the patients mingling with one another. Soon Cathy joined her.

"Great turn-out," she said plopping down in a chair next to her.

"Yes, I think so," the doctor said breaking out into a bright toothy grin. Her bright smile took Cathy by surprise.

"You should smile more often. It brightens up your face," she said complimenting her.

"Thank you," Ethan said turning rosy pink. Cathy got down to business but treaded lightly.

"I heard about Robert Harris," she probed. "How are you doing with all of this?" Ethan's face turned very grave.

"I'm still bummed about it," she softly replied. "He's missing, and I'm responsible."

"Try not to worry so much," Cathy said trying to be supportive. "He's probably hanging out with friends somewhere."

"Cathy, do you realize how serious this is?!" She asked with her eyes intense. "If he does something harmful to himself, I could lose my medical license!"

"I doubt that," Cathy said. "You can't predict every patient's behavior. They fool you sometimes. It's the nature of the beast."

"You didn't see how angry his wife was," she insisted frowning up. "The woman threatened to sue me for malpractice!"

"Then you need to get yourself a good lawyer and quick," Cathy urged. "Otherwise you are screwed!" Ethan gave her a sour look.

"Let's just hope the police find him alive and well," she quipped. "I want this nightmare to be over!"

"I know you do," Cathy smirked with one eye on Celeste Brown.

Celeste Brown, a petite brunette staggered up to the nursing station. She held her stomach, grimacing in pain. Concerned, Cathy scooted out of her chair with a quickness.

"What's the matter, Celeste?!"

"I have a tummy ache," she whined.

"Can I get something for it?" Ethan, already out of her seat, was by her side in a jiffy.

"Let me help you," she said throwing an arm around her shoulder. She escorted Celeste to a dining room chair and helped her sit down.

"Tell me about your pain. Is it sharp or achy?"

"Achy," Celeste whined. "It's like I have gas trapped in my stomach!"

"Well I got something for that," Ethan assured her smiling. A nurse ran over to assist.

"Let the nurse take you to your room, and I will order something for that tummy ache," she promised.

"Okay," Celeste groaned, rubbing her abdomen with her face pasty white. The nurse threw one arm around her waist and helped Celeste out of the chair. Celeste held on to the nurse for dear life as the two women shuffled down the hall. Cathy's smile was wicked.

"Poor child," she sighed. "I guess she ate way too many cupcakes."

An hour later, Sammie, the charge nurse was up on a creaky ladder removing the glass from the clock on the wall. Tina held onto the ladder while he fiddled with the time.

"Change the time to nine-thirty," Tina suggested. "The patients will think it's time for bed."

"You got it," Sammie beamed following her directive. After he changed the time, and replaced the glass covering on the clock, he climbed down.

"Hurry up and pass out those meds," he told her. "When you're finished I'll order pizza and beer so that we can get our party on!"

"Cool," Tina said as she ran to the med room.

Patients, confused about the time, began preparing for bed. Tina began dashing in and out of rooms administering medications, and thirty minutes later she was done. She made a sweep through the hall again, this time shutting doors to every patient's room. Then she locked her cart in the med room and made a beeline to the nursing station.

"I'm done with medication rounds!" She yelled. "It's pizza time! Let's Party!" Sammie reached for the phone.

"Party, party, party!" He shouted with glee on his long face. He dialed Shakey's Pizza. When he heard a voice on the other end, he barked into the phone.

"I want thirty large pizzas, ten bottles of sprite, fifteen six packs of Rainier Beer, and four bottles of Saint Michelle Chardonnay wine delivered to East Campus Hospital pronto!" He demanded, his voice hurried. He paused and bucked his big brown droopy eyes.

"What?! You didn't hear me?!" He yelled into the phone.

He took a deep breath and ran his large fingers through his thick brown greasy hair. He repeated the order, this time he spoke very slow.

"Thirty large pizzas, ten bottles of sprite, fifteen six packs of Rainer Beer, and four bottles of Saint Michelle Chardonnay wine."

When the order was confirmed, he hung up. Tall and lanky, he managed to climb on top of the counter sitting upright. He reached for the mic and hollered into it, his voice loud and booming.

"I need one hundred and fifty dollars for the pizza boy! One hundred and fifty dollars for the pizza boy right here!"

Nurses dug deep into their pockets, handbags, bras, and shirts for dollar bills as they lined up to give the charge nurse their money. Two male nurses moved tables and chairs up against the wall in the dining room; then they dragged a pool table out of a nearby closet setting it up in the middle of the floor. Soon everyone gathered around the pool table, smoking cigarettes, placing bets, and taking turns shooting the ball. Soon grey smoke hovered in the air above them, and they whooped and hollered, jostling with one another. Thirty minutes into their partying, the unit doorbell rang.

"The pizza is here you guys," Sammie yelled.

Two male nurses raced down the hall to the exit and unlocked the heavy steel door. One nurse shoved the door open while the other nurse leaned into it to keep it from closing. The baby-faced pizza boy, grinning like a hyena, was dressed in white shorts and a Shakey's Pizza Tee-shirt. His cart was overflowing with pizza, pop, beer, and wine.

"Here's your order, sir," he said with a deep voice.

"Thanks dude," said the nurse handing him a wad of dollar bills as he snatched the cart away from the boy.

"Move back," he demanded. Just when the pizza boy stepped away, the other nurse lets go of the door, and it slammed in the boy's face. The door frame rattled like an earthquake as they raced down the hall dragging the cart behind them.

"Time to grub!" Both nurses yelled as they charged into the dining room. They emptied the cart, placing the pizza and drinks on a table. One nurse arranged paper plates and napkins on another table while another took care of the drinks. Within minutes, staff surrounded the table piling up their plates with their favorite pizza. They laughed, talked, and teased each other hogging the table as they fought over the beer, wine, and soda. One nurse turned on the boom box and Kool and the Gang's song "Celebration" boomed through the loudspeakers. Several nurses took to the floor and danced the hustle. While some began to breakdance, and do the robot. When the security guard heard the music while out conducting his evening rounds, he hesitated and raised an eyebrow.

"What the hell?" He mumbled. His name was John, and he was a big man with a pot belly and a bald head. His uniform was busting at the seams, and he wobbled when he walked.

He took his time walking to the heavy steel door, and his bottom jaw hung opened when he peered through the window. "What are they doing in there? Having a party?!"

He unlocked the heavy steel door and wobbled down the hall. As soon as he appeared in the dining room, he couldn't believe his eyes. Nurses were huddled in small groups guzzling down beer, playing pool or doing the fast hustle. Two techs were in a nearby corner making out. One nurse was out cold on the sofa, snoring like a freight train and another nurse was dancing on top of the nursing station counter smoking a joint. John swung his keys high into the air and shouted.

"WHAT ARE YOU FREAKING PEOPLE DOING?!" Everyone stopped in mid-action and turned to face John. Male nurses lined up in front of the pool table while Sammie ran to greet him.

"Look here man," he said trying to smooth things over. "We are just trying to have a little fun here," he said. "Cut us some slack!" John stretched his neck to see over Sammie's head.

"Man, is that pizza over there?" He asked eyeing the pizza boxes on the table.

"Yep," said Sammie moving aside. "Help yourself."

"I think I will," John grinned.

Their eyes followed him as he wobbled to the dining room table. They watched in silence, holding their breath as he rummaged through every pizza box searching for a slice of pizza. Finally, he found himself a slice, and he devoured it in seconds. He smacked and licked his thick, crusty lips and then he looked over at Sammie.

"Got any beer to wash this down?"

"Sure do," Sammie said as he pointed to the table with the liquor. John wobbled over and grabbed himself a beer. He cracked it opened and guzzled it down.

"Ahhhh, that's good and cold," he said. He crushed the can with one hand and tossed it on the table. Then he glanced around the room. Oodles of eyes stared back at him, and no one said a word.

"What are you people looking at?" He chided them. "Let's Party!" Everyone broke out in a roaring cheer, and John helped himself to another beer. Several nurses joined him while others hauled butt to the pool table to play another game of pool. John lit his pipe, and a rich tobacco aroma filled the air. They partied late into the night, placing bets, arguing, drinking, eating and dancing, only stopping once to conduct rounds and check on patients.

By the time Thursday morning rolled around, the unit was in complete shambles. Pizza boxes, wine bottles, beer and soda cans were scattered on tables, chairs and on the floor. Nurses were either slumped over in chairs sleeping off a hangover or charting quietly at the nursing station. A faint odor of stale cigarette smoke mixed with marijuana lingered in the air. When Sally arrived for morning report, the chaotic scene took her by surprise and she threw a fit.

"Damn it!" She cursed. She looked across the room. Stretched out on the sofa, with an empty beer can on his stomach, was Sammie. He was snoring like a grizzly bear. Sally threw her Louie Vuitton handbag on a nearby table and marched over to him. She snatched the pillow from underneath his head and slapped him on the head.

"What the fuck?" He shouted falling off the sofa and bumping his head on the floor. He groaned loudly as he rubbed the back of his head.

"Get your ass up!" She demanded, glaring at him. "What kind of a charge nurse are you?!" He rose to a sitting position and massaged his lower back.

"Don't curse me woman!" He said grimacing with pain. "We were just having a little fun!"

"This is not the place to have fun," she hissed. "This is a hospital dirt bag not a nightclub!" She scolded him. He laughed, mocking her.

"Honey, don't get your panties in such a knot!"

She glowered at him, and he responded by sticking his tongue out. Disgusted, she turned around and stomped to the front of the room. She clapped her hands until she got everyone's attention.

"Listen up," she shouted her voice very shrill.

"You people should be ashamed of yourselves behaving in such an unprofessional manner! I want this place cleaned up now!" One nurse waved her off dismissively.

"Aww, Sally," she groaned. "Don't be such a hard...." Sally immediately cuts into her. Her face was wolfish.

"I SAID NOW!" She yelled stomping one foot on the floor.

The nurse's eyes widened. Then she spun into action like a frightened mouse and began scurrying around the room picking up pizza boxes. Other nurses followed suit, lining up like little ants, confiscating dirty paper plates, napkins, wine bottles, empty beer cans and cigarette butts.

They tossed the items in nearby trashcans on their way to their lockers and Sally, still disgusted, snatched her handbag and headed to the exit.

"I need a cigarette!" She muttered under her breath. Once she reached the heavy steel door, she spun around and shouted.

"Report in the conference room in ten minutes, and be on time!" Then she unlocked the door and stomped out.

Fifteen miles down the road, in downtown Salter's Point, the town clock struck seven times signaling seven in the morning. A maid at Salter's Point Hotel shoved her cart down the hall on the fourth floor starting her rounds.

She passed by room number four hundred and twelve and stopped when she noticed the door slightly ajar. She knocked three times and there was no answer. She hesitated and then listened. She couldn't hear anything. Not even a sound. She knocked on the door again, but still no answer.

Then she pushed it opened and walked in. Her eyes got big, and she gasped.

"Oh my god!" Susan, spread-eagled on the bed, had a bluish tint to her bloated heart-shaped face and her blue eyes, half shut, appeared still and glassy. The maid's face was white as a sheet as she crept over to the bed. Her heart jumped into her throat when she touched Susan's wrist. Her skin, clammy and cold, sent chills up her spine. She dropped Susan's wrist and reached for the telephone. She gripped the phone so tight, her knuckles turned a pasty shade of white.

She dialed 9-1-1. Within seconds, a dispatcher came on the line.

"Ma'am, what's your emergency?"

"Get an ambulance to Salter's Point Hotel right now," the maid yelled shaken to the core. "I think this woman is dead! I can't wake her up!"

.

CHAPTER SEVEN

Three hours later, over at Lakewood General Hospital, Susan finally came out of her drug-induced stupor. With her eyes sunken and swollen, she tried to make out her new surroundings. Disoriented at first, she thrashed around on the bed, kicking her blanket and sheets on the floor. Then she sat up and scanned the room like a scared rabbit. When she realized where she was, her face twisted up like a wrinkled prune.

"Damn, Damn, Damn!" She cursed with venom in her voice. She snatched the IV out of her arm, and the alarm went off. A nurse rushed into the room and snatched the IV tubing away from her.

"Miss Cole, don't do that," she warned. "I need you to lie down and be calm," she said.

"I don't want to be here," Susan groaned falling back on the bed.

"That's obvious," the nurse answered looking concerned. She dashed to the cabinet and grabbed two blankets.

"What do you mean by that?" Susan pouted giving her the stink eye. The nurse looked her straight into her eyes as she covered her with blankets.

"The maid at the hotel you were staying in saved your life young lady," she tersely informed her.

"Whoopee for her," Susan smarted off. The nurse gave her an anxious look.

"Stay in the bed," she ordered. "I'm going to get the doctor."

"You do that," Susan huffed folding her arms across her breast. She stared at the ceiling. Mad as hell her suicide attempt failed. She now must come up with an alibi, and she must do it fast. Her story must be airtight and make sense, she reasoned. Going to jail was not an option. Not if she could help it. While she waited for the doctor, she replayed different scenarios in her head. Finally, she came up with a halfway decent one. Why not play the jilted lover? Taken advantage of and cruelly abandoned by the good cheating doctor, a scoundrel by nature. She would tell everyone he evicted her, put her out on the streets. As far as she was concerned, he was alive the last time she saw him. A murder suspect? No not her. How could she kill him? She hasn't seen him for two weeks, and besides, she loved him. A naughty grin crossed her face, and she was pleased with her hatched up alibi. Doctor Henry knocked on the door and entered the room all at once. He was a tall man with a full head of white hair, a well-groomed mustache, and his pale, green eyes twinkled when he spoke.

"Good Morning Miss Cole," he said smiling. "My name is Doctor Pete Henry!"

"Good Morning to you," she said sitting up. "I need to get out of here," she immediately demanded.

"I can't let you do that," he said. "Yesterday you tried to take your own life, so I placed a legal hold on you for your protection."

"You can't do that," she shrieked with burning, swollen eyes. "I can't stay here!"

"Oh, you are not going to stay here," he corrected her. "Once you are medically stable I am transferring you to Salter's Point Regional Hospital!"

"Oh no you are not!" She screamed with her face turning apple red. Again, she tugged on her IV tubing. Doctor Henry motioned for the nurse.

"Get security," he ordered. When the nurse yanked the door open, Thomas Marshall was there in the doorway, his fist in mid-air ready to knock.

"Hello," he said. "I was just about to knock."

"I was just about to leave," she said with a terse tone to her voice.

"Well, let me move out of the way!" He said moving to the side. The nurse darted out, and he went inside. Sweat beaded on Susan's upper lip once she laid eyes on the police chief. She wondered if he could hear her heart beating from where he stood. It was thundering so wildly and loud inside her. Immediately, he noticed her discomfort.

"Sorry to startle you Miss Cole," he said with his voice deep and commanding. "I just have a few questions for you." He hurried over to the head of the bed and stood over her. She drew her legs to her breasts and pulled the covers up to her chin. She shook so badly she tinkled on herself.

"Are you alright Miss Cole?" He asked.

"Huh, Huh," she answered barely getting the words out.

"Do you know why I'm here?" He asked with his voice calm. Susan shook her head.

"No sir," she said.

"Well little lady you are a suspect in a murder," he informed her.

"Huh?" Susan said scooting over to a drier spot in the bed.

"The French Police are accusing you of murder," he rephrased his statement. Her teeth chattered, and she trembled inside.

"Mmmmurder?" She stammered. "What are you talking about?!"

"They are accusing you of murdering George Benny," he explained again.

"This is a joke, isn't it?" She asked sinking down in the bed with her heart about to burst out of her chest.

"No ma'am, it's not," he said. He reached into his coat pocket and pulled out his pen and notebook. He scribbled a few notes, and she gazed up at him, with her face childlike. Then she asked a question.

"My George is dead?"

"Yes ma'am," Thomas said in a matter of fact tone.

"Noooooooooooooo!" She whined shaking her head violently as she forced out tears.

"Oh my god, what happened?!"

"Someone put a bullet in him and killed him in his home three days ago," Thomas bluntly said.

"Oh, my god," she cried out laying her head on her knees. Thomas leaned in closer.

"Miss Cole, when was the last time you saw George Benny?" He whispered. Susan sobbed louder pretending not to hear him.

"MISS COLE!" He said raising his voice four octaves. She flinched and looked up at him with blurry eyes.

"You don't have to yell at me," she wailed. His hazel eyes narrowed.

"Where were you three days ago?" He badgers her.

"In Paris," she whined. "I was staying with a friend," she volunteered. Susan shook her head violently again and wailed.

"Oh, my George, oh my George, my poor, poor George."

"Ma'am," Thomas interjected getting frustrated. "I understand you and George were lovers, is that right?!"

"Yessssss," Susan sobbed. "He's the love of my life!"

"So, you saw him how long ago?" He probed again trying to trip her up. The words tumbled out before she knew it.

"He broke up with me two weeks ago and threw me out! I didn't have anywhere to go, so I went to my friend's house," she said. Thomas handed her a box of tissue, and she snatched a tissue and blew her nose. Then she wept and wept with her head buried in her blanket. Thomas saw through her act and became extremely angry.

"Miss Cole, stop the nonsense and answer my questions!" He said. Barely looking at him, she answered him with self-pity in her voice.

"He didn't want me anymore! So, I got some money together and returned to the states."

"Sorry to hear that," Thomas said his mood softening. "So, when did you leave France?"

"Two days ago," Susan replied as she dabbed her eyes with the tissue.

"What's your friend's name?" He asked.

"Who?" She said. Thomas took a deep breath, with his eyes void of pity.

"I need your friend's name," he repeated.

"Cookie Taylor," Susan informed him. "She lives in Paris."

"Do you have an address and phone number for this Cookie Taylor?" He asked.

"No, I don't...I mean I don't remember," she stammered correcting herself.

She scooted down on the bed and cried like a baby. Doctor Henry, feeling empathy for her, intervened.

"Mister Marshall, no more questions today," he said walking to the door. "Miss Cole needs her rest."

"Alright," Thomas said as he heads to the door.

"Miss Cole, I'll be in touch."

"Okay," Susan sniffled as she pulled the blanket over her head. The doctor opened the door, and Thomas Marshall walked out. As he made his way through the hospital corridor heading to the elevators, he thought about Susan Cole. He knew she was lying, but for now, he couldn't prove it. However, he was confident he would nail her. It was just a matter of time.

Everett and Rachel were in bed making love. He on top of her moving in a slow rhythmic motion, and she underneath moaning loud until she finally reached an exhilarating climax. He soon followed. Quivering and moaning with sheer ecstasy. He kissed her neck and shoulders with warm, soft kisses and then lay limp on top of her. He breathes deep while she caressed his back with one hand and ran her fingers through his afro with the other. He rolled over and pulled her to him. They wrapped their arms and legs around each other like a couple of octopuses. They lay there quiet, their hearts beating in sync, as they kissed and caressed each other.

"What time is it?" Everett finally whispered breaking the romantic mood.

"I don't know," Rachel answered.

She turned over and squinted, looking at the clock on the nightstand. Her eyes grew large when she realized the time. She pulled away from him and sat straight up.

"Everett, it's almost eight! We are late for work!" He pulled her down in the bed and held her tight.

"We can be a little late, can't we?" He teased. He planted a wet warm kiss on her lips before she had a chance to respond. He then ran his tongue down her breasts. Circling it around her nipples. She giggled with excitement. She tickled him, upsetting the mood, and he laughed. She wiggled out of his firm embrace and hopped out of bed. Then she hightailed it to the bathroom.

"You don't play fair," he hollered after her.

"Neither do you," she yelled back, laughing mischievously. She brushed her teeth and took a quick shower. Then she wrapped herself in a terry cloth towel and pranced out of the bathroom. She was surprised to see Everett, still in the bed chilling.

"What are you doing?!"

"What's your hurry," he chuckled fluffing up his pillow. "We are already two hours late to work. No point of rushing around now." Rachel made a face and wagged her finger.

"All I know is you better get your ass out of that bed," she chided him.

"Baby girl, come on," he gestured. "Jamie Lee is at her grandmother's house. We are finally alone. This is our chance to call out sick and make love all day!"

"I can't do that," she reminded him. "I have court this morning."

"Huh, huh," he mused. Her towel fell to her waist and she put lotion on her upper body. He checked her out, and he felt himself getting aroused again.

"Baby girl," he said his voice deep and sultry. "I believe there might be a spider crawling in your hair." Rachel's eyes got big.

"What?! A spider?!"

"Yeah, there's a spider in your hair," he repeated with a gleam in his eye.

"Get it out, get it out," she screamed hopping in a circle with her towel sliding to the floor. She fluffed up her hair, trying to get the spider out. "Did I get it, Everett?!" She screamed. "Did I get it?!"

He raised off the bed and craned his neck pretending to inspect the situation and then with a straight face he said.

"Oh, I believe it's still there, baby girl, it's still there!" She ran over to him.

"Get it off me Everett! Please get it off me!" She pleaded. He grabbed her and pulled her in the bed. He rolled on top of her and held her down, his body hot. Realizing she had been fooled, she immediately protested.

"You, horny turkey! You tricked me!"

"Baby, I am the master of all tricksters," he said with a Cheshire Cat grin.

He kissed her hard on the lips and then his hand crept down her body, stopping to caress her breasts and play with her nipples.

Turned on by his kiss and touch. She surrendered. She wrapped her legs around his hips and kissed his bare chest. He lifted her hips ever so slightly and squeezed her buttocks. Then he thrust his strong erection into her. She moaned when she felt the hotness of him inside of her, and soon she climaxed from the rhythmic motion of his lovemaking. It wasn't long before he climaxed too and the two of them rocked in place until their intense orgasms passed. He relaxed, with the weight of his body on top of hers and she breathed deeply as she caressed the small area of his back.

"You take my breath away," she whispered in his ear.

"Mmmmm," he moaned as he kissed her eyelids and nose. His hot tongue teased her lips making her ache for more. Then the telephone rang.

"Damn!" Everett said.

"So much for making love all day," Rachel giggled.
The telephone rang off the hook annoying Everett. He rolled off her.

"Who in the hell could that be?" He grumbled. "Why do they keep calling?!"

"It might be important," Rachel said. "Just answer it!" He reached over her and grabbed the phone on the nightstand.

"Hello," he said. As he listened to the caller, a pained look came over his face.

"What's the matter?" Rachel asked raising up on one elbow. She looked him dead in his face, searching for clues and then two seconds later, he hung up the phone.

"Well," said Rachel bracing herself. "Tell me, what's happened?"

"Celeste Brown was found dead in her bed this morning," he told her biting his lower lip. "She happens to be on Ethan Poppy's caseload, and this is not good," he said.

CHAPTER EIGHT

By the time Everett and Rachel arrived to work, it was eleven o' clock in the morning, and law enforcement was everywhere.

"The Police are becoming regular visitors around here," Everett remarked.

"It looks that way," Rachel agreed looking flabbergasted.

He parked, and they both got out of the car. Everett adjusted his sunglasses as they walked into the hospital lobby. Mark and Betty Jo Brewer were already there. Mark limped over and dryly said,

"They just transported Celeste Brown to the city morgue."

"What happened?" Everett asked looking bleak.

"Nobody knows," said Mark.

"This is the second patient death within a week," Betty Jo said joining them. "Doctor Poppy must be devastated!" Rachel nodded her head in agreement.

"Let's not forget about Robert Harris. We still don't know what happened to him!" Speculation over the matter was too much for Everett to bear. Making him uncomfortable.

"Where is Ethan?" He asked looking around.

"She's not coming in," Mark said. "Carl gave her the day off."

"Does she know?" asked Everett.

"Yep," said Mark. "She's at her wit's end, but she knows."

"I feel so bad for her," Rachel said shaking her head.

"Me too," said Betty Jo as she scuffed the tip of her shoe across the floor.

Doctor Beebe rolled into the lobby and brought his wheelchair to a screeching halt. His face said it all. He was white as a sheet.

"What's wrong with you man?" Everett asked.

"I need to see you two in my office," he said. "Something else has come up!"

"More bad news?" Everett inquired taking a deep breath.

"It depends on how you look at it," Doctor Beebe said shrugging his shoulders. "See you in my office."

He flipped his wheelchair around and took off down the corridor. Everett and Mark exchanged puzzled looks.

"We might as well find out what this is all about," Mark sighed as he started across the lobby.

"Yep," Everett said following behind him.

He waved goodbye as Rachel hollered after him with anxiety on her face. "Keep me posted!" She said. The two women stood there and watched their husbands until they disappeared around the corner.

"Boy, I wonder what's that all about," Betty Jo said with big eyes.

"Don't know, but I intend to find out," Rachel said.

"Well, let me know."

"I will," Rachel promised.

On the way to her office, Rachel decided to stop by the mailroom. She grabbed her mail and flipped through her messages. Suddenly, she felt cold air on her neck, and she looked behind herself and it was Beth Jones.

The supervisor was decked out in red and white from head-to-toe. She wore a pair of white knee-high go-go boots and a red headband in her gray curly hair. Her smile was crooked, and her big green eyes looked fierce behind her white framed bifocals. Tickled, it took all of Rachel's emotional tenacity not to break out into wild laughter.

"Good Morning Beth," she said pursing her lips.

"Mrs. James, I see you decided to come to work this morning," she said ignoring Rachel's greeting.

"I called Joyce. I told her I was running late," Rachel protested. "She didn't tell you?"

"She did," Beth answered cocking her head to one side like a jaybird. Rachel frowned, irritated by Beth's behavior.

"Beth, why are you doing that?"

"You have a glow about you," Beth observed. She moved in closer, her grin naughty.

"Tell me, why you are really late for work?!" Rachel was speechless at first, but then she became incensed.

"I just overslept," she murmured, red in the face.

"Oh really?" Beth chuckled. "Well, the extra sleep did wonders for you!"

"That is not funny," Rachel said grimacing, not at all amused. Beth cackled.

"You have a nice rest of the day sleepy head and tell Doctor James hello for me," she teased as she marched out of the mailroom.

"Ugh, I can't stand that woman, "Rachel mumbled under her breath.

She waited a full five minutes and then stuck her head out the door looking for Beth. When she didn't see her, she bolted out the door and hurried to her office. On the way, she ran into Hiram. He was grinning from ear-to-ear with his gray, blonde hair teased all over his head. His bulldog shaped head moved up and down as he carefully checked her out.

"What the hell are you staring at?!"

"You," he sweetly replied.

"Hiram, what do you want?" She asked glaring at him. He made a wave-like motion with his hands and then said.

"You look...You look simply marvelous! The glow on your face is so becoming?! What have you been doing with yourself, Mrs. Everett James?!"

"Hiram, what the hell are you babbling about?!"

"You have this glow about you like you just been had," he deadpanned. She cringed, madder than a wet hen.

"Oh, go to hell Hiram," she said gritting her teeth, stepping briskly around him. "This conversation is over!" She cuts out leaving him in the hall.

"Don't be like that Missy," he hollered after her. "I was just trying to give you a compliment!"

Everett James, Carl Beebe, Mark Brewer and Michael Louis were huddled together in the conference room, having a private meeting. They discussed the recent tragic events and Michael Louis, being his usual grouchy self, slammed Ethan over the details of Celeste Brown's death.

"Does she have any idea how the woman died?" He asked lighting a cigarette.

"She's too distraught to talk about it," Doctor Beebe said, his face grave.

"Too distraught?" He growled with shameless sarcasm. "Distraught my ass! She better talk, if she knows what's good for her," he said. Doctor Beebe looked at him with utter disdain.

"I know that Louis!" He said. Michael puffed on his cigarette with his nose up in the air.

"Does Celeste have family?" Mark inquired.

"Don't know," said Doctor Beebe. "For now, her body is at the city morgue until someone claims it. In the meantime, gentlemen, we have another problem on our hands."

"What's that?" Everett sighed with irritation in his voice.

"Remember Susan Cole?" Doctor Beebe asked looking around the table. The men glanced at each other momentarily. Then Mark, looking like a deer caught in headlights, broached a question,

"I'm sorry, who is Susan Cole?"

"Don't tell me she's back!" Michael growled snuffing out his cigarette. Doctor Beebe nodded his head and said,

"She's at Lakewood General Hospital." Everett became unhinged.

"You are kidding, right?!"

"No, I am not," Doctor Beebe replied.

"Excuse me," Mark interjected still confused. "Who is Susan Cole?"

"It's a long story," Everett said cutting him off. He faced Doctor Beebe again determined to get answers.

"So why do we need to know she's at Lakewood General?" He demanded.

"Three days ago, she tried to commit suicide. Now she's back. I need one of you to volunteer to take her on as a patient," he said looking sheepish. Michael shot out of his seat like a jack in the box. Knocking his chair on the floor. He rattled off profanities with his face puffed up like a red balloon.

"Hell fucking no! She's nothing but a pain in the ass!" Mark became infuriated.

"Who is this woman?" His question fell on deaf ears, and Everett said,

"So, where is Benny?" Doctor Beebe let out a long sigh.

"Oh, that's the best part," he pointed out. "The police suspect she killed him."

"Well, I'll be damned!" Michael said bucking his eyes. He snatched his chair off the floor and sat down.

"Now how in the hell did she manage to do something like that?" He asked.

"They believe she shot him," Doctor Beebe said. The shock of his words rested on their faces, and they all fell silent. He welcomed it. A chance to recollect his thoughts.

"I know this is a lot to take in, but......."

"But what?!" Everett quipped with the creases in his forehead deepening.

"SOOO, who is willing to take her on?" He asked again. "She's due here tomorrow!" Doctor Louis and Doctor Beebe gave Doctor James a pitiful look.

"Oh, FUCK Naw!" He said, as he took off his sunglasses, pushed himself away from the table and stood up. His six-feet-four-inch frame towered over them, and his face was wolfish.

"Don't you dare put that woman off on me," he said.

"Everett, you are the likely candidate," Doctor Beebe tried to explain.

"How so?!" Everett said folding his arms across his chest, his dark eyes fierce.

"Louis can't do it! You know he has no bedside manner whatsoever," Doctor Beebe argued. Michael massaged the deep crevices in his chin and flipped Doctor Beebe the finger.

"And Brewer over here is just getting his feet wet," he said. Mark looked dejected.

"Oh, thanks! I am glad you have such confidence in me," he angrily pouted.

"Those reasons are sappy," Everett charged pushing back.

"The woman is cunning and manipulative," Doctor Beebe continued to press his case.

"She can't manipulate you! You won't allow her too!"

"You have a way of getting information out of patients," Michael piped in. "They trust you more."

"Yeah, she'll spill the beans with you," Doctor Beebe added.

"The police need help to get a confession out of her!" Everett's lips curled up, mad as a firecracker.

"I'm not with this Carl," he said.

"Can you just do it this time man," Doctor Beebe begged. Everett wrestled with his conscious.

His instinct told him not to give in. Rachel would kill him if he took Susan Cole on as a patient. He needed to talk to her first before deciding.

"Can I think about it?" He asked trying to buy more time.

"No, I'm afraid not," Doctor Beebe firmly said. "I need you to agree to take her on right now," he insisted. "She's due here tomorrow." Everett felt ambushed.

"So really, I have no choice," he said, with his face tight.

"Not this time," Doctor Beebe sternly said. Everett took a deep breath, looking visibly cross. "What time do we expect her?"

"Tomorrow at ten," said Doctor Beebe. Mark struck the table with his cane, and everyone turned to face him.

"Oh, now I got your attention," he haughtily said. "I have asked you gentlemen repeatedly, but you keep ignoring me! Who in the hell is Susan Cole?!"

The men busted out laughing relieving the tension between them.

"Sorry man," Everett apologized. "I'll explain the whole story to you on the way back to the unit."

"Good," said Mark, still riled up.

"Are we done here?" Everett asked.

"I think we are," said Doctor Beebe.

"Let's go Brewer," Everett said. "Susan Cole's story is quite interesting."

"Can't wait to hear it," said Mark.

Sally was relaxing in her office, puffing on a Marlboro cigarette, thinking about Celeste Brown's untimely death. Six months ago, she took up smoking out of necessity to cope with the stress on the job. The daily grind and bizarre craziness at Salter's Point Regional had taken its toll on her. As she puffed grey smoke into the atmosphere, she admired the sparkling emerald diamond ring on her right finger. A wedding anniversary gift from her husband for twenty-five years of marriage. She held it up to the light inspecting every intricate detail. Then a knock on the door interrupted her thoughts.

"Come in," she hollered. Rachel busted in and immediately began coughing, bothered by the cigarette odor.

"Girrrl, when did you start smoking?"

"I know it's a bad habit," Sally protested not answering her question.

"I'm putting it out right now!" She grabbed an ashtray and snuffed out the cigarette.

"Thanks," Rachel said still coughing up a storm. She pulled up a chair and plopped down. Her dark-brown eyes got big when she noticed the ring on Sally's finger.

"Girrrl, where did you get that beautiful piece of jewelry?!" She asked raising out of her seat to get a closer look.

"It's my twenty-fifth wedding anniversary present," Sally proudly boasted. "My husband gave it to me this morning."

"Oh, how nice," Rachel said taking her hand to admire the ring. "It's so beautiful!"

"Yes dear, it is," Sally said batting her long eyelashes.

"Any romantic plans this evening?" Rachel asked, winking at her.

"No dear. We have been married so long.... we are just a couple of old farts who prefer to have a quiet evening at home," she chuckled. Rachel laughed.

"You two are boring as hell," she said.

"Don't worry you and Everett will get there one day," Sally predicted.

"Never," Rachel said shaking her head. "I plan to keep my mojo going well into old age sister!"

Sally giggled. "More power to ya!"

"Speaking of Everett, I think I'll pay him a visit," she said.

"Don't you have enough work to do, my dear?" Sally teased raising an eyebrow.

"Listen to you," Rachel teased back. "I have plenty. Just need to talk to my sweetie."

"Well you do that," Sally giggled. She pulled out another cigarette and reached for her lighter.

"Time for me to go," Rachel said looking disgusted. "You really do need to stop smoking," she said. Sally lit her cigarette, ignoring her.

"Adios dear," she said.

CHAPTER NINE

Mid-morning turned into early afternoon. After trying all morning to catch up with her husband, Rachel finally gave up. During lunch, she mentioned to Betty Jo and Cathy about conducting a support group for the patients so that they could express their grief over the loss of their comrades. Cathy, being her usual cantankerous self, wasn't feeling it, but Betty Jo was all for it.

"That's a wonderful idea!" She said with her face all lit up. An hour later, all three social workers were in the admissions unit, arranging chairs in a circle in the dining room. Rachel looked over at Cathy and gave her a warm smile.

"Need some help?" She offered, feeling pleased Cathy finally agreed to come on board.

"Nope," Cathy said in a cold tone.

Rachel didn't bite choosing to focus on the task at hand. Her eyes swept the room, and she noticed four male patients pacing back and forth like synchronized robots.

"Do we know how many patients are coming?" She asked.

"About fifteen," Betty Jo said coming over to hand her the list.

"I'll start gathering them up," Rachel said. She approached each patient on the list and gently encouraged each one to attend the group. They all accepted, each one taking a seat as they waited for the group to start. Soon they were all settled in, and Cathy reviewed the ground rules. When she finished, they all talked at once.

"What happened?" One male patient asked with angst on his face.

"Why did she have to die?" Asked another, her eyes wet with tears.

"Remember, one question at a time," Cathy urged. Rachel butted in.

"So far, we have very little information," she explained. "Their deaths are under investigation."

"I had a nightmare about Celeste Brown last night," Rosemary Broome softly said. She wrung her hands so tight they turned an orangey red. "I can't shake the image of her bloated face out of my mind." Betty Jo felt terrible for her.

"I hate you found her like that," she said. "I know it hurts."

"It was horrible," Rosemary said, her voice breaking. "It was just horrible!" A terrifying silence gripped the room and then Cathy took over treading with extreme caution.

"I know everyone is feeling sad right now," she said with her voice quivering. "But we are doing everything possible to find out what happened to Celeste."

"And what about Billy and Robert?" Clyde Brown asked wrinkling up his nose.

"I know what happened to Billy, but Robert has vanished into thin air! Nobody can find him! I'm scared for him!"

"We are too," Cathy said. "The police are looking for him. He'll show up soon."

"I hope so," Clyde sniffled as he rubbed his pants leg. Rachel stood on her feet.

"Let's look out for each other," she suggested. "If you see someone acting strange and unusual, please report it to us as soon as possible."

"Yes, this way we can act quickly and prevent another tragedy," Betty Jo added. "If we all work together everyone will be safer." Rosemary bolted out of her seat with red and swollen eyes.

"Will there be funeral arrangements for Billy and Celeste?" Rachel swallowed hard.

"We haven't heard anything yet." She softly responded. "We will let you know as soon as we find out," she said. Rosemary collapsed in her seat and violently shook her head. She rocked back and forth, sobbing her heart out. Rachel rushed to her side and hugged her neck.

"I'm so sorry," she said.

"I miss Celeste! She was my friend," she wept.

"I know you do," Rachel said rubbing her back. "Try thinking good thoughts…. think about the good times you had with her."

"But I will never find another friend like her," she whined looking up at Rachel with blurry red eyes. "She was the only one who understood me."

"I know," Rachel said patting her back. "She was a good friend."

The weight of Rachel's words weighed so heavily on her, she broke down and wailed. Taking short, halting breaths as her chest heaved up and down. Rachel hugged her, blinking back tears. "It's going to be okay Rosemary, I promise. It's going to be okay."

Early Thursday evening, Rachel and Everett were at home having dinner with Jamie Lee who was making a mess of her collard greens. She giggled hysterically. Mashing the greens into a gooey green mush all over the table. The decision to name their daughter after their fallen colleague, Jamie Lee, was a no-brainer to them. A remembrance of the sincere friendship Rachel had with her so long ago.

"Jamie Lee," Rachel yelled. "Stop it right now!" Jamie Lee sucked her fingers and giggled.

"Don't yell at my baby like that," Everett scolded her.

"Then you clean up her mess," Rachel said with her temper flaring. She wiped Jamie Lee's mouth with a napkin while Everett cleaned the table off. The silence between them was deafening. After a while, Everett spoke first.

"Susan Cole is at Lakewood General," he said, his voice hoarse.

"What?!" Rachel squeaked, not sure she heard right.

"Susan Cole is at Lakewood General," he repeats.

"You are kidding, right?" She asked looking mortified.

"Nope," Everett flatly said. "She was admitted there after she tried to commit suicide three days ago."

Her blood curdled when she heard the news. Clinching her jaw so tight, the vein in her forehead appeared more pronounced. She braced herself, choosing her words carefully.

"Why are you telling me this?"

"I'm telling you this because she will be admitted to our hospital tomorrow morning at ten," he announced avoiding eye contact with her.

"And her doctor? Who is going to be her doctor?" She managed to get out.

"Me," he said still refusing to look at her. A minute, two minutes...... and then the explosion came.

"Damn it Everett!" She shouted. "Why in the hell would you take her on? You know my history with her!"

"I was swindled into it," he yelled back. "I didn't have much of a choice!"

"Oh please! Everyone has a damn choice!" Jamie Lee began to whimper.

"Rachel, let's not do this in front of the baby," he read her.

"Fine," she hissed. "Fine, fine, fine!"

She stomped out of the kitchen, leaving him there with Jamie Lee. He pulled his daughter out of the high chair and placed her in his lap. She laid on his chest, and the pounding of his heartbeat was soothing to her. She stopped whimpering.

"Mommy is going to be alright," he said hugging her tight. "She's just a little pissed off right now."

CHAPTER TEN

Rachel sat in the middle of the bed, with her arms folded, sulking over Susan Cole. How dare that woman return to Salter's Point after the chaos and baggage she left behind. And the thought of her on Everett's caseload burned her up. How could he consider such a thing? Taking her on as a patient when he knew the history between them. Swindled into it? Who was he kidding? She fumed to herself.

She knew him too well. He would never allow anyone to swindle him into anything and for that reason alone, she was furious he made such a dubious decision. After obsessing about it for over an hour, her head began to throb. She swallowed a couple of aspirin chasing it down with a glass of water and then she took a long hot shower. Feeling better and less angry, she climbed into bed and settled in on a James Patterson novel. An hour later, Everett came in and sat on the edge of the bed. He carefully checked her out, inhaling deeply.

"Jamie Lee is asleep," he informed her trying to make conversation.

"Good," she said not looking up.

"So, how long do you plan to stay mad?"

"Forever if I have too," she sharply said. She knew she was unreasonable, but she didn't care. He yawned.

"Well lady, that's your choice," he nonchalantly said. He rose to his feet and glided across the room into the bathroom.

Three seconds later, water blasted against the shower wall, and his deep voice belted out an Earth, Wind and Fire tune. Rachel boiled inside. She scooted out of bed and slipped on her sweater. She stomped out of the room, making her way down the hall. She stood in the living room looking out the sliding glass window. The soft moonlight lit up her patio. The beach, decorated with little white pebbles and marble-like seashells, glistened under the moonlight. Small sandpipers scurried around in circles on the hard-pressed sand while seagulls soared back and forth up above squawking with laughter.

She flipped the lock forward and pushed the door to the side. Then she stepped out into the cool night air and collapsed in a patio chair. A brisk breeze blew off the southern part of Puget Sound, and she basked in it, with the crisp air caressing her face. The distant laughter of the seagulls and the whooshing waves of the Sound was soothing to her. Suddenly, she felt a chill. An eerie chill. She straightens up, now on full alert. Her dark brown eyes narrowed as she squints to see. Spooked, she reared back. Her eyes rested on a flat rock that was ten feet away. A big black cat with yellow, gold eyes stares back at her. His body almost taking up the entire rock's surface.

"Peepers," she whispered sliding out of her chair. "Is that you?"

With her steps measured and slow, she crept toward the cat. The cat sat there like a big statue, and his eyes stayed fixated on her. Suddenly it darted into the thick marsh, startling her. Forcing her to stop dead in her tracks. She squinted trying to see where the big cat was heading.

The rustling and cracking of the thick marsh was her guide as the big cat traveled swiftly through the brush. The lack of light hampered her vision and then she lost her way. The cat disappeared into the black night leaving her feeling dumbfounded.

"Well I'll be damned," she cursed. Excited, she ran to the house. Once inside, she stumbled down the hall screaming like a banshee.

"Everett!" She screamed. "Everett!" He came out of the bedroom with a towel around his waist looking bewildered.

"What's your problem?!" He asked. "You are going to wake up Jamie Lee!"

"I...I...I saw Peepers outside on the beach," she stammered.

"What?!" Everett said.

"I saw Peepers," she excitedly repeats again.

"Peepers?" He cracked up laughing and shook his head. He left her in the hall and went back into the bedroom. She followed him.

"Have you lost your mind?!" He said. "Peepers hasn't been seen since Jamie died!" Rachel shook her head hard.

"He's back!" She shouted. "I saw Peepers out there!"

"Shush!" Everett cautioned bucking his eyes. "You are going to wake Jamie Lee up!"

"I am telling you I saw Peepers," Rachel said lowering her voice as she took off her sweater.

"Okay, if you say so," he said too tired to argue with her. He dropped his towel and threw back the comforter. He climbed into bed, pulling the comforter over his head.

"Good Night. See you in the morning." Rachel fumed with spite in her eyes.

"So, you're just going to ignore me?!"

"Stop acting crazy and get some sleep!" His words pissed her off. She immediately became quiet and switched off the light. She climbed into bed. The warmth of his body usually turned her on, but tonight, she was too angry. So, to punish him, she turned her back on him. Not only was she mad at him accepting Susan Cole as his patient, but now he was calling her crazy, and crazy she was not. Peepers was out there, and she knew it. She saw him with her very own eyes. As she drifted off to sleep, the last image she visualized in her head was Peepers' golden, yellow eyes. She knew he would be back, it was just a matter of time.

Friday Morning, precisely ten' o clock, a Police Van with flashing lights whirled into East Campus Hospital Parking lot and came to a screeching halt. Two straight-faced, husky looking police officers jumped out. One officer opened the back door, and a hand-cupped Susan Cole emerged with a scowl on her face. The officer escorted her into the hospital lobby while the other officer stayed close behind. They approached the reception desk, and Joyce, perched on a stool with her beehive hairdo looming high above her head, greeted them with a cheesy grin.

"Good Morning," she said. "Long time no see, Miss Cole," she smirked. Susan glowered at her but remained quiet. One of the officers took the initiative and spoke first.

"Good Morning," he said. "Where should we take this young lady?"

"To the admissions unit," Joyce said. "But, wait for Doctor Poppy," she said stopping him. "She will be here in a few minutes to escort you over there."

"Will do," the officer said. It wasn't long before Doctor Poppy appeared in the lobby. She was decked out in a long black dress, with green high-top tennis shoes. She donned black gloves and her frizzy hair was braided into a ponytail.

"Good Morning, I'm Doctor Ethan Poppy," she said introducing herself.

"Good Morning," said both officers. Her violet eyes rested on her newest tenant.

"You must be Susan Cole," she said smiling.

"I am," Susan said, her voice dry and barely audible.

"How are you?" Asked Doctor Poppy.

"Fine," Susan said looking off to the side. Doctor Poppy turned her attention to the officers.

"Discharge papers? You have them?"

"Yes," said one officer handing her a large manila envelope. She snatched the envelope and sprinted off.

"Follow me," she called out. The police officers followed the doctor through the lobby with Susan Cole in tow. As they passed through the lobby, staff stopped to stare at her. Susan bowed her head, and she turned three shades of red. Water popped out on her forehead, as she was sweating profusely. Soon, they were standing in front of the admissions unit. Doctor Poppy jammed her key in the lock, and the heavy steel door clicked opened. She shoved her body into the door and held it back.

"After you my dear," she said gesturing for Susan to enter first. The officer took Susan's cuffs off, and she stepped inside. Doctor Poppy smiled at the officers.

"I'll take it from here," she said releasing the door. It slammed in their faces with the door frame rattling off its hinges.

"Let's not tarry young lady. Your room is waiting," she said as she trotted down the hall.

Susan was mum. She stayed with the doctor down the long, narrow hall, and her eyes burned. The florescent lights in the ceiling were too bright, hurting her eyes. Soon they arrived at her room. It was straight across from the nursing station.

"Here we are," Doctor Poppy said opening the door. Susan hurried by her and sat down on the bed. She grabbed a pillow and pressed it against her stomach.

"Doctor James will be here shortly to see you," Doctor Poppy told her. "So, settle in and familiarize yourself with the surroundings." Susan nodded. Doctor Poppy hesitated and then shot her a stern look.

"Keep your door open," she commanded. "You are on suicide precautions."

"Okay," Susan finally spoke, hugging her pillow. The doctor walked out leaving the door slightly cracked. Susan fell backward on the bed and stared at the ceiling. Soon her thoughts returned to the night of the murder. Rehashing every single detail. Struggling with guilt. Rehearsing the reasons why she killed George Benny in the first place. Betrayal, the primary reason, a justification for her heinous crime. She flipped over on her stomach, and her mind drifted to the beach, and before she knew it, she was fast asleep.

Court was in session, and Everett was preparing to testify. Christy Bowles was his last case for the day. Christy, somber and sitting at the end of the table, fiddled with a white bandage on her left wrist. A string of auburn hair rested between her deep-set brown eyes, and she sat there quiet, not looking up, preoccupied with her thoughts. A few feet away was Hiram Gottschalks. He wore an orange pinstriped suit, and his unruly blondish-grey hair was tied back in a bushy ponytail. He held up a pocket mirror, admiring himself. The judge, amused by his antics, cracked up laughing. Everett rolled his eyes.

"Satisfied with your appearance Hiram?" The judge asked.

"I believe so sir," Hiram said grinning like a hyena as he twisted his ponytail around his thick fingers.

"Let me know when you are finished grooming yourself, so we can proceed," the judge said giving him some leeway.

"Certainly," Hiram said. He tidied up his ponytail and slid his mirror in his coat pocket. Then he clasped his hands together.

"Your Honor, I am ready. You can proceed," he said.

"Thank you," said the judge. He mildly zeroed in on Everett and asked,

"Doctor, are you ready to start your testimony?"

"Yes," Everett said giving Hiram a dirty look.

"Proceed," said the judge.

"This is Christy Bowles," Everett started off. "I am requesting fourteen days in the hospital. She is a danger to herself. Three days ago, she cut her wrist after a fight with her pimp. The wound was so deep, it required stitches." The judge observed Christy for a moment, disturbed by her withdrawn demeanor and the information he just heard.

She played with her bandage, never looking up. The judge jotted down notes and said.

"Tell me her diagnosis."

"I believe she suffers from Major Depression with Borderline Personality Disorder," Everett said. The judge observed Christy again.

"Miss Bowles, can you tell me why you wish to harm yourself?"

"I don't know," she softly said with her deep brown eyes glued on her bandage.

"Do you think she will be ready for discharge after the fourteen days?" The judge asked.

"I believe so," Everett said. Then he added, "However, I'm not making any promises. It depends on her progress." The judge turned to Hiram who was applying a fresh coat of red polish on his fingernails.

"Mister Gottschalks, can you guarantee me this young lady will not go out and prostitute herself after she's discharged?" Hiram inspected his fingernails and made a face.

"No more than I can guarantee you won't go out and prostitute yourself, your honor!"

Christy's face brightened for the first time in three days. She giggled out loud, and the judge turned three sheets of red. He glared at Hiram then his eyes bore into Christy.

"Miss Bowles, I believe you need hospitalization. I commit you for fourteen days. Court adjourned."

The judge got up and marched out of the courtroom in a huff. Everett and Hiram laughed out loud.

"That was a dumb-ass question," Everett said.

"Dumber than a box of rocks!" agreed Hiram. Everett gathered his notes and headed for the door.

"Christy, come with me," he said. "I'll walk you back to the unit."

"Thank you, Doctor James." She said giggling.

CHAPTER ELEVEN

Susan Cole's return to Salter's Point Regional spread like a bad case of measles and Rachel, seething with anger over it, could hardly contain herself. She and Sally were hunkered down in the nursing office sharing a Shakey's pizza, and Sally listened to Rachel vent with amused interest.

"I can't believe that woman came back here," she said frowning. "Why didn't she keep her butt in France?"

"She's probably running from the law," Sally concluded. "They say she's a suspect in George Benny's murder."

"I think she's guilty," Rachel declared folding her arms in a huff across her chest.

"Girl, do you really believe that?" Sally asked with wide eyes.

"Yes," Rachel said glaring at Sally. "Why not?"

"I think your anger is about something else," Sally carefully pointed out.

"What are you trying to say?" Sally kept her voice even and calm.

"Admit it dear, you are still mad about your sorry ex cheating with her years ago. You need to let it go!"

"Oooooh, you had to go there Sally, didn't you?!" Rachel hissed with burning eyes.

"I call it like I see it," Sally shot back, batting her eyes trying to make a point.

Rachel sank low in her seat. Sally was right. She was madder than a wet hen about it even though she was married and in love with Everett.

"Okay, I'll give you that much," she finally said. "But, I still believe she killed Doctor Benny," she insisted. Sally sucked in a breath and lit a Marlboro cigarette.

"Girl, I just don't see it," she said shaking her head. "The woman is mousey and borderline."

"Borderline, I agree," Rachel said rolling her eyes. "Mousey, I don't think so," she said. "She's playing folks. She's manipulative and she's got everybody fooled."

"Mmmm... Maybe," said Sally taking a drag off her cigarette and looking doubtful. "Maybe."

After calling her husband's office numerous times, and finally losing count, Betty Jo left her office and headed over there. She was worried about Mark. He had been working late and spending nights in his office, and this bothered her. She ran into Cathy along the way and she stopped to chat.

"Girl did you hear this news about Susan Cole?" Cathy said looking wide-eyed.

"Yeah quite a story," Betty Jo said.

"Do you think she killed the dude?" Betty Jo shrugged her shoulders.

"It's hard to say," she said.

"If I didn't know any better, I would say Susan Cole is a woman scorned," Cathy chuckled. Betty Jo nodded in agreement.

"You might be right."

"Where are you going?" Cathy asked changing the subject.

"To see my husband," she said easing by her.

"Well, see you later, "Cathy hollered after her. Betty Jo didn't answer. She was already down the hall.

Betty Jo found her husband, stretched out on the floor drunk, reeking of alcohol. He snored like a grizzly bear, and there were empty bottles of wine on the floor beside him. She stooped to her knees and slapped him in the face. He bolted straight up with his blue-green eyes, frantic and wild like a frightened animal.

"What the fuck did you do that for?!" He shouted with his speech slightly slurred. Betty Jo was furious.

"You promised to stop drinking," she scolded him.

"Babe, I'm not......," She cuts him off.

"Don't lie!" She shouted snatching an empty wine bottle off the floor. "What the hell is this?!" Gritting her teeth and pointing at the bottle. He groaned.

"Yesterday was so damn stressful, I needed a little nip, "he half-heartedly explained.

"How drunk did you get last night?" She asked. He struggled to his feet and pulled up his pants.

"Well, I still have my pants on, so not that drunk!" He laughed pissing her off.

"Mark, those aren't your pants!"

"They' re not?!"

"NO!" She yelled. "Whose pants are those anyway?!"

"I have no idea," he said with a sheepish grin. Betty Jo's expression hardens.

"Mark, have you been cheating on me?!" He shook his head.

"Noooooo…... I…I…"

"Never mind! I hate you!"

"Awww, babe don't talk like that," he groaned trying to placate her, but Betty Jo wasn't having it.

"Brewer you need to get yourself together and fast!" She threw the empty wine bottle at him, and he caught it, his reflexes on point despite his drunken state. She stomped out his office in a whirlwind, slamming the door behind her. He laid down on the floor and clutched the wine bottle close to his chest. His head spun, and he felt a headache coming on. He groaned just thinking about it and his wife, he didn't blame her for being angry. His drinking was out of control, and he knew it. The alcohol was his crutch, a stress reliever, so he reasoned. He kept a stash underneath his desk. A case of Merlot wine. However, he wasn't ready to quit. He needed his wine. So, he closed his eyes and selfishly said.

"She'll get over it. She always does."

Betty Jo banged on the door.

"Come in," Rachel hollered. She walked in and slammed the door behind her. She collapsed in a chair and pouted.

"Girrrrrl, what's wrong with you?" Rachel said noticing the pain in her face.

"Mark makes me sick," Betty Jo mouthed off. "I am so tired of his shit!"

"What happened?" Rachel said her voice calm looking concern.

"I found him drunk on the floor in his office, and he had somebody else's pants on," she groaned. "He didn't come home last night, and he never called!"

"Girl, did you just say he was wearing someone else's pants?!" Rachel asked with big eyes.

"Yep! I'm so embarrassed! I don't want to claim him as my husband anymore!" She frowned.

"Did he say whose pants he was wearing?"

"No!" Betty Jo shouted.

"I see why you're pissed," Rachel said trying not laugh. She hesitated for a minute and with a twinkle in her eye, she said,

"How long has he been getting drunk and wearing someone else's pants?" Betty Jo paused before answering. She looked disturbed. Rachel soon realized her attempt to be funny didn't register.

"Look, I'm ......" Betty Jo interrupted her.

"It's okay. I don't mind talking about it with you," she softly said. "I have been dealing with his drinking most of our marriage," she explained with her face sad. "He promised to quit and go to rehab, but he never follows through." Rachel decided to be honest and not hold back.

"You know what they say about alcoholics? They have to hit rock bottom before change happens," she flatly pointed out.

"Yeah, I know," Betty Jo said.

"So, what are you going to do?" Betty Jo was quiet for a moment, and then she said,

"Maybe I should do something drastic like kick him out of the house! That would take real balls on my part!"

"Girl, women have balls too. God made them so big, he put them on our chest," Rachel said with a gleam in her eye. Betty Jo cracked up laughing.

"Girl you are too crazy!"

"I know," Rachel smiled. Then her face turned doubtful. "Do you think kicking Mark out would help?"

"It's worth a try," Betty Jo said. "I have never done anything that drastic before."

"Do you think you can emotionally handle it?" Rachel asked pointing out the obvious. The creases in her forehead wrinkled up.

"As mad as I am right now, "I probably could kill him!" Betty Jo said. Rachel lets out a nervous laugh.

"You don't mean that," she said.

"No, I'm just talking." She stood on her feet and headed for the door.

"I got to go," she announced. "Progress notes are calling."

"Okay," Rachel said. "Remember, I am here if you need to talk."

"I know," Betty Jo said. "I know."

Mark finally dragged himself off the floor. He tossed the empty wine bottles into the trash and grabbed his cane. His blue-green eyes searched the room for his overnight bag, and it was there on the desk. He grabbed his bag and staggered out of his office. He limped down the hall to the on-call room and on the way, he ran into Michael Louis.

"Brewer you look like hell," Michael bluntly said with strands of hair sticking up from his toupee. "What the hell have you been up to?"

"Stayed late last night to catch up with my documentation," he lied. "Man, I guess I'm exhausted."

"Where are you headed?" Michael asked.

"To the on-call room to shower," he explained.

"That should do the trick," Michael said being his usual sarcastic self. "Well carry on!"

"Carry on yourself," Mark muttered under his breath as he limped by him. "And go to hell!"

Everett knocked on Susan Cole's door.

"Come in," she called out in a weak voice. He opened the door and stood in the doorway.

"I'm Doctor James," he said. "Meet me in the dining room in ten minutes."

"Sure," Susan said as she shyly gave him the once over from head-to-toe. He pulled the door too, leaving it slightly cracked. While at the nursing station reviewing Susan's chart, Ethan bounced in wearing her favorite candy pink high-top tennis shoes. Her hair was styled in two frizzy ponytails, and she appeared giddy, almost euphoric. She leaned over the counter and smiled.

"I have good news!" Everett looked up giving her his full attention.

"Good news? We definitely can use some good news around here!" He said.

"Robert Harris was seen coming out of a surgeon's office in Seattle yesterday," she excitedly said. "He's alive and well!"

"Well that's great," Everett said feeling pleased for her.

"Where is he now?"

"The police don't know yet, but they have strong leads. It's just a matter of time before they find him."

"Do we know why he was there in the first place?" He asked, his curiosity piqued.

"I think he was trying to find a surgeon to change his sex," she recalled. His eyebrows went up.

"I see," he said. He was introspective for a minute, and then he said, "Once Robert is brought back here, you need to put him on lockdown."

"I plan to," she said taking off. She sprinted down the hall disappearing around the corner. When he looked across the counter into the dining room, Susan Cole was sitting at a table. She was twirling a blonde curl around her finger, and she was very quiet. With chart in tow, he crossed the room at an easy pace.

"Settle in yet?" He asked pulling up a chair and then sitting down in front of her.

"I guess," she answered avoiding eye contact, staring at the table instead.

"Do you mind if I ask you a few questions?" He said crossing his legs.

"Go ahead," she said still looking away. He flipped opened her chart.

"What's going on? Tell me why you tried to kill yourself the other day," he probed.

"Why do you care?!" She flippantly responded still not giving him eye contact.

"I do care," he said. He leaned forward on the table. "So, what happened with Doctor Benny that made you feel you needed to take your own life?" He said rephrasing the question. She gave him eye contact. Her gaze questioning.

"You know him?" She innocently asked.

"I do," Doctor James flatly admitted.

"Did he tell you about us?"

"No, I have to say he didn't," Doctor James replied leaning back in his seat. "But, I have to say I was surprised when I learned about your romantic relationship with him." Susan bowed her head, and a tear ran down her cheek.

"So, you think our relationship was wrong?"

"I am not here to pass judgment," Doctor James carefully said. "I'm here to help you with your depression." She glanced at the ceiling, and her left leg shook violently.

"He cheated on me," she revealed, her speech halting. "I had to get even with him!"

"Get even with him?" Doctor James paraphrased raising an eyebrow. "Tell me what do you mean by getting even?"

"I had to leave him," she said correcting herself and sobbing.

"Be right back," he said. He found a box of tissue and returned to the table with it. She snatched a tissue out of the box and wiped her nose.

"How did you find out he was cheating on you?" He asked not missing a beat.

"By accident," she sniffled. "I was going to surprise him with a picnic lunch one afternoon, and I caught him kissing some nurse who lives in the village down the road," she said.

"Did he see you?"

"No," Susan said. "I just left."

"Then what did you do?" Her shoulders sagged.

"I just went home," she said.

"So, you did nothing?" He said as he gently tried to pry more information out of her.

"I didn't kill him if that's what you meant," she blurted out getting defensive.

"I didn't accuse you of killing him," his voice calm and measured.

"Well, the police think I did it," she immediately said speaking rapidly. He examined her face.

"Did you?"

"I had nothing to do with his murder!"

"Calm down Miss Cole," he said. He allowed some silence between them and then he started again.

"Tell me how you two came to break up."

"He kicked me out after I confronted him about his cheating," she fibbed. "So, I went to live with a friend. Once I got some money together, I bought an airline ticket and came back to the states."

"I see," he said jotting down notes. "When was the last time you saw or talked to him?" Susan paused.

"It all happened so fast. Maybe three weeks ago," she said.

"I see," Doctor James said. She cries again, and he felt sorry for her. He closed her chart.

"Let's stop here for now and continue this another time," he said.

"Okay," she sniffled. She snatched a tissue out of the Kleenex box again and wiped her nose. Doctor James stood up.

"Try to get some rest," he said.

"Okay," she whispered. She watched him glide across the dining room until he finally disappeared down the hall. Then she got up and hurried to her room.

CHAPTER TWELVE

Friday at Dusk. The town clock chimed eight times and the clouds circling Mount Rainier were disappearing into the gray, dull sky. Soon stars appeared just over the horizon as dusk faded into night and the hustle and bustle of Salter's Point Regional was rapidly winding down. Doctor Poppy had just finished group and Cathy was back in her office finishing up last minute charting, determined not to give the doctor anything to complain about. Nurses eased in and out of rooms passing out medications while patients concentrated on getting ready for bed. Ten miles down the road, finishing up a late dinner, Everett and Rachel were enthralled in a heated argument over Susan Cole. The small vein in Rachel's forehead was more pronounced than ever as she became increasingly riled up.

"The woman is guilty as hell," she said. "She killed that man, and you know it!" Everett stared straight and level into his wife's eyes.

"You don't know that for sure, and you should not jump to conclusions," he said, his voice tight. "The law says she's innocent until proven guilty."

"Have you lost your freaking mind?" Rachel shouted. "The police in France are looking for her," she reminded him. "Remember, she left town under suspicious circumstances!"

"You're right to a certain extent," he said giving in a little. "But I don't think she's capable of murder!"

Rachel stared him down with burning eyes.

"Why?!" she quipped. "She's manipulative and crazy as hell!"

"I just don't think she did it," he said refusing to back down. "Besides aren't you holding onto the past unnecessarily?"

"Don't you dare go there!" Rachel hissed bolting out of her chair. Everett leaped to his feet in a hurry.

"Hold up Babe! Calm down!" He warned her. Rachel immediately backed down. Realizing she wasn't a match for her husband's physical strength.

"Let's not bring up the past," she quietly said with narrow eyes.

"Fair enough," he said returning to his seat with his eyes pinned on her. There was silence. They sat there not looking at each other. Neither had the patience or energy to continue the fight.

"I don't want this to come between us," Everett calmly said breaking the silence. "But Susan is my patient, and you must find a way to accept it," he said sounding resolute. She squeezed her chest with pretended pain on her face.

"You have just stabbed me in the heart," she whined. He rolled his eyes.

"Oh, stop being dramatic! How do you even know what it feels like to be stabbed?!" He groaned. She didn't answer him. Instead, she got up and left him sitting in the kitchen. Everett rubbed his face hard. He hoped she would get over it, but now he wasn't sure. Every muscle in his body was tense. He hated when she was angry at him. As he brooded about it, he noticed a half-empty bottle of Rose wine on the counter. He reached for the bottle and uncorked it. He downed the rest of the wine, then he tossed the bottle in the trash.

He flicked off the light and went to his bedroom only to discover the door was locked. "Rachel," he yelled. "Open up this door." His words were met with a deafening silence, and he boiled inside. Too tired to fight with her, he gave up and went to the living room. He fell on the sofa and kicked off his loafers. He laid down and stared at the ceiling. He wondered how long he would be in the dog house. Disappointed the whole matter had gone this far; he flipped to his side and angrily stuffed a pillow underneath his head. The ticking of the clock on the wall above him soothed his mind. Exhausted, his eyelids soon became heavy, and before he knew it, he had dropped off to sleep.

Cathy almost fell out of her chair, when Ethan stuck her head in the door. She just finished gobbling down a second lemon cupcake, and she was surprised to see her. This time the doctor was sporting a pair of yellow tennis shoes, trimmed in purple and black, and she grinned when she realized she startled the social worker.

"Didn't mean to scare you," she said. Cathy, red as an apple, straightened herself in her chair.

"I, I, I was just about to go home, but I guess I got hungry," she stuttered.

"I see," Ethan said giving her a sheepish look. "Those cupcakes sure are good," she said. "The chocolate ones are my favorite," she added.

"Thanks," Cathy mumbled, still embarrassed. Ethan glanced at her watch.

"Well it's getting late my dear," she said. "Have a nice weekend."

"You too," Cathy said.

Ethan left Cathy alone in her office. She grabbed her handbag and made a beeline to the bathroom. She threw her bag on the counter and ran into a stall. Seconds later, the sound of retching filled the room, and every bit of cupcake she consumed earlier was in the commode. After a while, her stomach ached, and she had nothing left to give. With a sour taste brewing on her palate, she went to the sink and rinsed her mouth. She noticed herself in the mirror. She cringed at the deep, dark circles underneath her blue eyes. "Ugh, I look absolutely terrible! Just terrible," she groaned. She snatched paper towel from the paper dispenser and dabbed her lips. Then she picked up her handbag and strutted out the door.

Susan was wide awake and disoriented. She sat up in bed and looked around like a frightened rabbit, as if expecting to be attacked. Sweat dripped off her brow, and her heart thumped hard in her chest. Then she realized where she was and began to calm down. The nightmares of George Benny's murder were getting to her. Sleep deprivation and guilt was eating away at her. She glanced at the clock, it was eleven-thirty at night. She scooted out of bed and wiggled her feet into her slippers. Then she threw on her robe. Light shone from underneath the door, and she was glad someone was still up. She opened the door and stood in the archway with bloodshot eyes. Sammie, the charge nurse, was at the nursing station kicked back in a chair. His size thirteen feet were stacked on the counter. He guzzled down a can of Rainier Beer, and when he realized he was being watched, he became annoyed.

He nonchalantly tossed the empty beer can in the trash, and he growled.

"Sneaking up on me?"

"No, I'm not trying to," Susan said. "I can't sleep."

"Why is that?" He asked, his tone sarcastic.

"I guess I had a bad nightmare."

"That's no fun," he said as he slid his feet off the counter. His long arms reached for the chart in the rack.

"Can I get something for sleep?" She asked.

"I'm checking," he said flipping through her chart. A minute later, he answered her question. "Doctor James hasn't ordered you anything I am afraid. I'll have to page him." She frowned, disappointed she must wait.

"I appreciate anything you can do," she humbly said. "I really need to get a good night sleep."

"No problem," Sammie said. "I'll let you know what I find out."

"Thank you," Susan said. Then she went back into her room and closed the door.

Across town at Sully's Bar and Grill, Mark sat at the bar nursing a shot of vodka. He watched customers meander in and out, talking and laughing, buying drinks, having dinner or shooting pool. Their carefree attitude irritated him, especially since he found himself sitting alone. Edgy, distracted and feeling out of sorts, he was still reeling from Betty Jo kicking him out, surprising the hell out of him. "How could she do such a thing?" he asked himself. He was drinking when she met him. Why was it a problem now? He shrugged it off. Deciding this little arrangement won't last long.

He would humor her, and in due time she would miss him and beg him to return home. He chuckled at the thought of it, amused by it all. The bartender who had been checking him out behind the counter made his way over. He was a short bald man with arms covered with skull tattoos and his light brown eyes danced when he smiled.

"What's so funny?" He asked.

"My wife thinks she's doing something by kicking me out," Mark jokingly replied. The bartender arched an eyebrow.

"Why? What did you do?"

"Aw nothing," Mark said waving him off. "She thinks I drink too much." The bartender, used to these types of conversations, leaned on the counter. Genuinely concerned, as he looked Mark square in the eye.

"Well do you?" He asked.

"Do I what?"

"Drink too much," the bartender curtly replied.

"Not enough to need rehab," Mark retorted with a hint of anger in his voice. The bartender picked up on his sarcastic, irritable mood and rolled his light-brown eyes.

"Are you sure about that buddy?" He asked not giving an inch. Mark's face turned to stone.

"Mind your own damn business, and give me another shot!" He demanded.

"You brought the shit up," the bartender angrily responded. Mark glared at him with malice.

"Man, get me another shot!"

"Coming right up," the bartender shouted turning his back on the doctor. He poured Mark another shot of vodka placing it in front of him.

"Take it easy there, buddy," he warned. But Mark ignored him. He threw his head back and gulped down the liquor and then he slammed the glass on the counter.

"Pour me another one dude," he demanded with glassy eyes.

"Whoa," said the bartender throwing one hand up. "You need to slow your roll!" Mark waved him off, slurring his words.

"Man, just get me another one and stay out of my business!"

"Okay, one more and that's it," said the bartender. He poured him another shot and slid the drink over to him. Mark downed the shot and slammed the glass on the table again.

"I'm done," he said sliding off the stool, almost falling over.

"Should I call you a cab?" The bartender asked getting concerned.

"Nope," said Mark grabbing his cane. "I got it from here!" Looking worried, the bartender watched Mark limp with his cane to the door.

"Be careful out there," he yelled. Mark didn't look back. He opened the door and limped out.

The next day, Saturday morning, patients were waking up and stirring in their rooms. The breakfast cart sounding like thunder rumbled down the hall to the dining room. The dietary aide hollered at the top of his lungs.

"Hot trays in the house, Hot trays in the house! Time for Breakfast! Hot trays in the house!"

One nurse prepared medications to pass out during breakfast, while the rest of the nurses were hunkered down at the nursing station giving the report to Sally and the day shift staff. Soon patients emerged from their bedrooms fully dressed scurrying down the hall like little ants to the dining room in anticipation for breakfast.

They meandered up and down the aisle between tables in the dining room taking seats while the kitchen staff passed out trays. Chatter broke out around the room while two nurses passed out the morning medications. Suddenly a blood-curdling scream halted the morning routine. Everyone froze in place with terror on their faces, and then a frightening hush fell over the room. The screaming continued, and Sammie hopped to his feet in a hurry.

"What the hell is going on down there?!" He asked.

"I don't know," Sally said jumping out of her seat. She ran out of the nursing station and collided into Teresa. The nurse's face was white as snow, and her eyes were stricken with fear. She screamed at the top of her lungs and Sally grabbed her and shook her.

"Stop that screaming and calm down," she urged. "You are scaring the patients!" Teresa stopped screaming. She began hyperventilating and taking short breaths. Sally stared straight into her frightened eyes and calmly said,

"Tell me what's wrong!" Her voice trembled as she spat out the words,

"Lisa Cooper and Rosy Jackson are dead," Teresa whispered. "Lisa and Rosy are dead!"

CHAPTER THIRTEEN

Sally ushered Teresa into the nursing station, and her heart burned with fire.

"Girl, have a seat," she quietly said trying to remain calm. "I'll handle it from here." Teresa bowed her head and cried softly while Sammie, a complete loss for words, looked dazed and confused. Sally noticed the confusion on his face and offered him direction.

"Sammie, I need you to seal off that room right away," she barked.

"Sure thing," he said finally jumping to his feet and getting in gear. "Don't forget to call Doctor Beebe," he reminded her now fully engaged.

"Don't worry I won't," she said. "Keep everyone calm in the dining room while I notify the police and make some calls," she told a nurse with dark curly hair.

"I'm on it," said the nurse with her face wrecked with fear. She hurried to the dining room.

"Doctor Poppy needs to be called," one nurse hollered from the med room window. "Those patients are hers."

Sally hesitated. Her eyes grew wild with genuine fear. She gasped, choking on her own saliva as she rushed to the medication room.

"What did you just say?" She managed to blurt out.

"Lisa Cooper and Rosy Jackson are Doctor Poppy's patients," the nurse informed her again. "She needs to be notified." Sally couldn't believe her ears. Four dead patients and one missing in the same week. All four patients on Doctor Poppy's caseload.

"What's going on here?" She wondered out loud.

The nurse, puzzled by Sally's reaction, spoke earnestly.

"Is there a problem?"

"What?" Sally asked, her mind a million miles away.

"Is there a problem?" The nurse asked again. Sally snapped back to reality.

"No, no, no, no problem! I'll call her. Thanks for reminding me!"

"You're welcome," the nurse said raising an eyebrow. Sally hurried to the nursing station and began making calls.

His beeper buzzed for the fourth time. Everett, fighting for every ounce of sleep he could muster up, finally got up. He sat there on the sofa with his head hanging low and his fists firmly pressed into the cushion. He yawned and stretched out his legs. For the past two nights, he had been sleeping there, still not talking to Rachel. The phone rang. He looked up. "Damn," he cursed as he struggled to his feet. He stumbled to the phone. It stopped ringing by the time he answered it. "Dat Blasted it!" He cursed again. He dialed the hospital number and received a busy signal. Frustrated, he hung up.

A minute later, his beeper began vibrating wildly on the coffee table, and his body tensed up. The phone rang again, and he answered it on the first ring. "Good Morning," he said his voice deep and rough. As he listened to the caller, his forehead crinkled, and the back of his neck tighten up. Grim-faced, he absorbed the horrible news. "I'll be damned. I'll be right there," he told the caller. He hung up the phone and sprinted down the hall to his bedroom. The door was still locked and his blood boiled.

"Rachel," he whispered trying not to wake Jamie Lee who was asleep in the next room. "Open this damn door, so I can take a shower!" he demanded. When his request was met with a deafening silence, he slammed his fist into the door and groaned.

"Damn you!" His hand burned as he returned to the living room. He grabbed his jacket and slipped on his loafers. He checked for his car keys. The keys were safe in his jacket pocket. Then he walked out slamming the door so hard, the frame cracked.

He ran and jumped over puddles of water. Barely able to keep his two-inch high heel shoes on. His satchel swung high in a circular motion over his broad muscular back. His heels clicked hard against the pavement, and each step echoed in the hollow darkness. Just a few yards away, his destination, a large black door. He could make out the door's outline with the help of his flashlight. Behind the door was a room filled with horrible secrets. A room with a cruel past, a forgotten history of terror. He was aware of the history, but he kept going. Determined, no matter what, to get to the black door. He held the flashlight in an iron grip. Aiming it at the ground.

As he dodged decaying rats, birds and trash along the way. The concrete walls seemed to close in on him, and the air, cold and damp cut him through the bone. His knit dress clung to his muscular body and his breathing was hard and short. He wheezed, taking in the musty, stale air and his chest burned with each inhaled, ragged breath. Then he stumbled. Tripping over a rock. He dropped the flashlight. Crashing down on one knee. His right hand in a puddle of muddy water. His left hand grabbing his knee.

He yelled out in pain. His painful cries bounced off the concrete walls, and deep in the muddy residue, he searched for his flashlight. He found it, gripping it tightly. Then he forced himself up. The gooey, cool mud dripped from his hands; and the flashlight, drenched with mud was radiating brightly. It gave him needed light to navigate in the dark, and he wiped his hands on his dress. Then he reached into his side pocket and pulled out a handkerchief. He wiped the mud off his flashlight. A rat, the size of a small cat, scampered in his path and he hollered, dropping his handkerchief. The flashlight's bright light momentarily blinded the rat, and it hesitated. Its beady eyes glistened with fear, then it took off scurrying down the concrete path, veering off into a muddy ditch. The decaying stench of dead rodents reeked in the damp air, and he felt himself getting sick. A stinging sensation burned in his throat and the contents of his stomach threatened to eject out. Three times, he swallowed hard and gagged. Gripping his mouth trying to fight back the urge to throw up.

Finally, he won the battle, and the urge subsided. Relieved, he continued his way. This is not the first time Robert Harris had traveled this tunnel alone. It was a massive structure, secretly hidden underneath Salter's Point Regional. A long passageway leading to the room with the large black door. The room of long ago horrors, forgotten by society in recent years. He discovered the tunnel one day while on a pass to the library and adopted it as his own secret hideout. It was here he could smoke weed and fantasize about becoming a woman. A lofty goal, but one he was willing to die for. Finally, he reached the black door and busted in. He hobbled into the room and dropped his satchel on the floor.

The flickering lightbulb swung from the ceiling and was close to going out. He searched for a replacement using his flashlight. In a corner, across the room was a debilitated antique wood desk with six drawers. The desk was missing handles, and the drawers were severely splintered and worn. A wood chair missing an armrest sat in front of the desk, and he hobbled over, taking a seat in the chair. He searched every drawer. He found a dusky lightbulb in the very last one. Will it work? He pondered. We will see, he thought to himself. He kicked off his high heels and blew the dust off the bulb. He got up and dragged the chair underneath the flickering light. Grunting with pain, he painstakingly climbed on the seat while blood dripped from the gash on his knee. Once he unscrewed the light bulb, the room turned pitch black. He struggled to replace it in the dark, and after five long minutes, the light bulb was in and working. Breathing a sigh of relief, he climbed down.

He shut the black door and grabbed his satchel. He dragged the chair back to the desk and sat down. His stocking badly stained with wet sticky blood was ripped where he fell. He tore his satchel opened and pulled out alcohol wipes, two rolled up marijuana joints and a pair of scissors. He tossed the joints and alcohol wipes on the desk and held the scissors firmly in his fingers, and then he snipped the blood-stained stocking away from the wound on his knee. His knee throbbed. He ripped an alcohol pack opened and cleaned the blood off. The exposed cut stung every time the alcohol touched it, and he flinched, whimpering in pain. Once the bleeding subsided, he wrapped his knee in thick white gauze. Suddenly he sneezed. The dampness in the room had a scent of rabid mold.

He wiped his nose on his arm sleeve and wondered how his wife and children would take it if he changed his gender. After all, he loved them dearly, and he had no desire to disappoint them. However, he was tired of living life as a man. A lifestyle he believed he wasn't made for. He was born a man, but his feelings were more of a woman's. While he mulled over his thoughts, he gave the room a once-over. Other than the old antique wood desk and the chair he was sitting in, nothing else was there except for a few dusty books, an old surgical table, a rusty bathtub and worn leather shackles hanging from the ceiling. The tunnel had been there a hundred years. A passageway to this very room was referred to as the black dungeon back in the 1930's. Salter's Point Regional was known as the Asylum for the Insane and Idiotic.

A place of horrors. A place where the crazies go to be fixed. However, the crazies were often the innocent. Subjected to needless frontal lobotomies, electric shock, freezing ice water baths and being shackled to the ceiling with leather straps and suspended in mid-air. A form of punishment for being mentally ill and misunderstood by the larger society. It was a terrible time for many. Sometimes many died in the process. Living in a culture ignorant of mental illness and tortured by those hired to treat them. The history behind the tunnel didn't faze Robert Harris a bit. He liked it there. It gave him comfort, for this was his hiding place. He spent the better part of the previous week visiting surgeons trying to convince them to surgically change him into a woman, but to no avail. He was frustrated and tired of living a lie. A man in his thirties, feeling like a woman most of his entire life.

He even married, had two children, hoping his feminine feelings somehow would disappear, but they never did. Now faced with a decision, a task he was not sure he dared to carry out. He reached into his satchel again and pulled out a pair of garden metal clippers. He examined the clippers' sharp edges, holding the tool to the light and eyeing every detail.

Making sure the tool was dirt free. He ripped another alcohol pack open and wiped the clippers down. Then he wrapped the clippers in a clean white towel and laid them on top of the desk. He reached into his dress pocket for matches. He lit a joint and sucked on the tip for a long minute. Inhaling the sweet aroma, smacking his lips. The weed tasted like cherry pie to him, his favorite and he sucked on it for a long while. The smell heightened his senses, and the weed's effect slowed him down. Soon he no longer felt pain, and he finally relaxed. Then he sank down in his seat and contemplated his final move.

The loud banging on the door jerked him out of his sleep. He tumbled off the sofa bumping his head hard on the floor. Empty wine bottles rolled across the floor, and he rubbed his head, wincing in pain. He was wide awake and mad as a hornet.

"Doctor Brewer, open this damn door!" Sally yelled as she banged hard on the door again. "Do you hear me? Open this damn door!"

"Alright, alright!" He hollered, hoisting himself up with his cane. He felt dizzy as he limped to the door. He snatched it opened and glared at Sally with red bloodshot eyes. His handsome face looked haggard and squished up on one side, and his thick blonde mane was tussled all over his head.

"What's wrong with you?" He growled.

"You look terrible," Sally said looking like a peacock. "What have you been doing in here?"

"What do you want?!" He growled ignoring her question. Sally stepped back, shocked by his grumpy attitude.

"There are two dead patients on the unit, and we need you now," Sally said looking at him with a wary eye.

"Two dead patients?" He said sounding like a parrot with a blank look on his face. "You say two?!"

"That's right," Sally said. "They were found dead in their beds this morning!"

"Damn," he groaned. He turned his back on her and limped to the sofa. He sat down and forced his foot in one of his boots. "Did you call the police?" He asked.

"Yes," Sally said as she ventured into his office sticking her head past the door. She gave his office a once-over and noticed empty wine bottles on the floor.

"Have you been drinking in here?" She asked, her eyes big like a jaybird's.

"Mind your own business!" He snarled as he laced up his boots. Sally gave him the stink eye, deciding not to force the issue further. Instead, she stayed on message.

"Doctor Beebe wants a meeting," she told him.

"Yeah, okay," he said as he ran his fingers through his thick blonde hair. "Where is the meeting?"

"In his office in fifteen minutes," Sally said. He cuts his eyes.

"I'll be there," he said.

"Fine," Sally said. She put her nose in the air and left his office.

Mark telephoned Betty Jo, and she answered on the first ring.

"Hello, may I help you?" She said, her voice sharp.

"Hi honey," he cheerfully greeted her. But, before he could get another word out, she lit into him.

"Mark, what the hell do you want?!"

"I am coming home tonight. I am not sleeping in this office another night," he told her.

"No, you are not!"

"Why not?!" He yelled.

"Go to rehab, and then you can come home," she shouted back.

"Honey hear me out......" She hung up the phone. He lowered his head and took a deep breath.

"Betty Jo, Betty Jo, Betty Jo, why are you doing this to me?" He whispered with his face sad.

"Are you alright in there?" Michael asked suddenly appearing in the doorway.

"I'm fine," Mark mumbled not looking up.

"You coming to the meeting, aren't you?" He said.

"Yep, I'll be there." Michael rolled his eyes.

"Good," he said. He shook his head and headed down the hall.

CHAPTER FOURTEEN

By the time Everett walked into the hospital lobby, the place was run over with Salter's Point City Police. Hospital staff huddled together in small groups, whispering and gossiping among one another, while security guards manned the area keeping nosy patients at a distance. When the coroner and his attendants appeared in the lobby carrying the covered bodies of Lisa Cooper and Rosy Jackson, a hush fell over the room. One officer ahead of the entourage yelled out,

"Everybody clear the area! Go back to your units!" He demanded. Staff scattered in different directions and Everett, very determined, forced his way through the crowd. He bumped into Mark Brewer.

"Going to Beebe's office?" He inquired.

"Yep," Mark replied. He checked Everett out. His afro was knotted and lopsided, and his clothes were wrinkled. Surprised by his disheveled appearance because he always admired Everett's good taste in fashion.

"What's up with you this morning? Did you forget to comb your afro?" He joked. Everett twisted his face up. He wasn't in the mood for jokes. He wasted no time tearing into Mark.

"Dude, you got nerve! You look like somebody's stray cat out of a back alley!" He snarled.

"Ouch," Mark said. "That hurt!"

"I'm not in the mood for your nonsense this morning," Everett said with his brow furrowing.

"I see," Mark calmly said trying to keep his cool. "Well I want you to know I slept in my office last night," he volunteered, ignoring Everett's frosty mood. "Betty Jo has a wild hair up her butt! She kicked me out!"

"Why?" Everett asked looking solemn.

"Claims I drink too much," he bitterly said.

"Well, I hope you two work it out," Everett said being dismissive, not in the mood for listening to a long drawn out sappy story. Taking the hint, Mark decided to zero in on Everett instead.

"So, what's your story?" He asked. A crease appeared on Everett's brow, and he took a deep breath.

"Well, I didn't get kicked out, but I might as well have," he complained.

"Why, what's going on?"

"Rachel is not happy with Susan Cole being on my caseload," he said.

"Why?" Mark asked with his blue-green eyes widening.

"It's a long story," Everett said. "I don't have time to go into it. We got bigger fish to fry."

"I'd like to hear about it sometime," Mark said. Everett didn't respond. Mark recognized the conversation was going nowhere, so he decided to back off. They walked the rest of the way without conversation. When they reached Doctor Beebe's office, Everett knocked on the door.

"Open!" Doctor Beebe hollered. They went inside and found Michael, Ethan, Sally, and Hiram sitting around the conference table looking glum.

A stack of charts sat in the center of the table waiting to be torn apart.

"Join us," Doctor Beebe said looking red-faced and flustered. "We have a lot to discuss." Mark and Everett took seats across from each other. Everett, anxious to get things rolling, spoke first.

"Obviously, we have a problem here," he said. "Four dead patients and one missing. Doesn't look good for optics," he pointed out.

"I know," Doctor Beebe agreed. He turned to Ethan. "Can you shed light on why these patients suddenly die on your watch?" He asked. Ethan's violet eyes watered.

"I have no idea," she said. "I have reviewed their charts repeatedly, and I don't see anything I did wrong." Realizing he may have hurt her feelings, he softened his tone.

"I'm not accusing you of anything," he calmly said. "I'm trying to get to the bottom of this that's all," he further explained.

"At least not yet," Michael smirked not willing to let her off the hook that easily.

"Louis…..." Doctor Beebe warned giving him the evil eye.

"Okay, okay," Michael said rolling his eyes and waving him off. Everett wasn't willing to let her off the hook either.

"Something is not right here," he said frowning. "We are missing something!"

"I agree," Sally nodded. "I think we need to find out what's going on here and soon," she urged.

"That's why I called this meeting," Doctor Beebe said. "We are going to sit here and conduct a chart review of each patient…… It's possible we may have missed something." Mark rested his chin on his knuckles.

"And if we didn't miss anything, then what?"

"I think we should schedule lab tests on these patients," Everett suggested. "This way we can find out for sure how they died."

"Great idea," Ethan finally spoke up with her face brightening a little. "Why didn't I think of that?"

"Maybe because you are clueless!" Hiram smarted off blinking his eyes like a bird. Ethan glared at him.

"Doctor Poopy, why are you glaring at me like that?" He grinned teasing her.

"I'm hoping, by some miracle, you'll spontaneously combust!" She quipped. Loud snickers broke out around the table.

"Hiram, you get on people's nerves," Sally said batting her long eyelashes.

"Why? I'm so damn good-looking," he said giving her a cheesy grin. Everyone cracked up laughing including Ethan herself. Then she turned serious and broached a question.

"Is there anyone on staff who can conduct these tests and keep quiet until we decide on a conclusion?" She asked.

"No," Doctor Beebe said. "But, I have a contact in the community who can."

"Who'd that be?" Hiram asked as he untied his ponytail.

"Zurich Weaver," Doctor Beebe said. Ethan's violet eyes narrowed.

"Do you trust him to keep things confidential and out of the media?"

"Oh, I trust him," Doctor Beebe said. "He'll keep things confidential. He's sensitive to these kinds of situations."

Hiram tilted his head back, and his long gray, blondish hair fell gently on his shoulders. Then he spoke in the third person.

"Hiram can draw up a legal document and have him sign it to keep his mouth shut," he offered.

"Why that's a good idea," Ethan sighed with relief.

"Anything for you Doctor Poopy," he said winking at her.

"It's Poppy, you moron!" She turned away from him, and he leaned over tapping her on the shoulder. She cringed.

"What is it?!"

"Sorry, missy," he said trying to be apologetic. "Don't mean to offend you."

"Okay," she reluctantly replied refusing to give him eye contact. Sally suddenly spoke up.

"So, who's going to call the families to obtain these consents?" She inquired looking around the table.

"I will," Everett volunteered.

"I'll help," Michael offered. Doctor Beebe was pleased.

"Very good then," he said.

"I have a question," said Mark. "Any word on Robert Harris?"

"No," Ethan sadly said. "He was last seen coming out of a surgeon's office last Wednesday, but no one has seen him since." "The police have no leads on him," she further added.

"Too bad," Mark said. "Have you hired an attorney yet?"

"Not yet," she said looking down into her lap twiddling her thumbs.

"Why not?" Mark asked as he tried to maintain a calm and rational voice. Very surprised she had yet to hire legal counsel. Her eyes teared up, too embarrassed to answer. Noticing her discomfort, he backed off and turned to Hiram.

"Do you think Ethan has a legal leg to stand on?" He asked.

Hiram leaned back in his chair and placed his hands behind his head. He was reflective for a moment as he considered the doctor's question. Then he cleared his throat.

"Legally, she has Robert's voluntary consent going for her. The fact he voluntarily signed himself into the hospital shows insight and competence on his part to make his own decisions and he wasn't a danger to himself or anyone else when he left here," he pointed out.

"Didn't he try to cut off his genitals a month ago?" Mark recalled. "I would say that's a danger to oneself."

"But he got over that," Ethan piped in getting defensive. "He was close to discharge that's why he had ground privileges."

"Then why was he at a surgeon's office the other day?" Mark asked frowning up. Ethan became quiet for a minute and then said,

"I assumed he was trying to find a doctor to surgically change his gender." Mark snapped her up.

"No doctor in this country does that kind of surgery you are referring to!" He said.

"Which makes him a danger to himself if he doesn't get his wish," Michael added siding with Mark.

Ethan took the bruising from her colleagues hard. She struggled to keep her emotions in check even though she was on the verge of tears.

128

Deep down inside she knew they were right. However, in her mind, Robert had improved and because he had he was ready for discharge. Now realizing, for the first time she may be in serious legal trouble, she turned to Hiram.

"Do you know any good defense attorneys in the area?" Hiram giggled like a little kid.

"I got the guy for you," he said with a gleam in his eye.

"What's his name?!" Ethan asked getting excited.

"Sugar Foot Kent," he declared flipping his hair back. "The guy has sugar in his tank! No pun intended, but he is a damn good attorney!" Everett rolled his eyes in disgust.

"Sugar Foot Kent? Are you kidding me? With a name like that, who would take him seriously!"

"A lot of people," Hiram said bucking his eyes. Everett shook his head.

"Are you sure he can handle my case?" Ethan asked hoping the attorney was not feeding her nonsense.

"He can handle it," Hiram flatly said. "He'll get you out of this mess in no time!"

"I hope so," Ethan sighed heavily. Everett shook his head again and grabbed a chart.

"Let's get this party rolling," he said. "We have a lot to do!"

"Here, Here," Doctor Beebe said. They all settled in for the rest of the morning chatting and reviewing charts.

Something sinister was in the air, and Rachel and Betty Jo could feel it. Cathy, on the other hand, seemed off in her own little world. Quiet and introspective, a million miles away. They were huddled together in Rachel's office over a pot of hot Starbucks coffee, and a plate of chocolate cupcakes left over from Friday's group.

"Four patients have died without explanation," Rachel said with fear growing in her dark brown eyes. "There's something weird going on around here," she surmised.

"Scary more like it," Betty Jo said feeling uneasy.

"I wonder if they took something," Rachel pondered out loud.

"Like smoked some bad weed or something," she continued.

"Did they have ground privileges?" Betty Jo asked.

"I think they did," Rachel said.

"Then you might be right," Betty Jo said with relief in her voice. Cathy, still quiet and deep in thought, nibbled on a cupcake. Betty Jo reached over and gave her a nudge.

"Hey girl, snap out of it! It's impolite not to tell your co-workers what's incubating in that noggin of yours!"

"Oh, I'm sorry," Cathy said getting red in the face.

"What were you over there thinking about anyway?" Betty Jo asked.

"Well......I...... Oh nothing," she stammered. Rachel was annoyed.

"Are you even listening to us?"

"Listening to what?" Cathy inquired with big eyes.

"What do you think about four patients dropping dead so suddenly?" Rachel asked with a strain in her voice. Cathy shrugged her shoulders.

"I don't have a clue," she said. "But, that idiot Doctor Poppy probably does!"

"What the hell do you mean by that?!" Rachel said frowning up.

"I was just thinking, maybe she gave them the wrong medication or something," Cathy reasoned.

"I doubt that," Rachel said giving her the side-eye.

"You need to be careful Cathy," she warned. "You are not entitled to your own facts!" Cathy rolled her eyes.

"It was just a thought," she insisted.

"A thought you don't need to have," Betty Jo interjected looking irate.

"Sorry, I didn't mean to offend anyone," Cathy said backing down. A hush gripped the room for a moment, and then Rachel asked a question.

"Cathy, why do you hate Doctor Poppy so much?" Cathy was quick to answer and eager to vent.

"The woman reminds me of my stepmother! Always finding fault and criticizing me all the time!"

"It sounds like you harbor some deep resentment toward your stepmother," Betty Jo said taking note. Cathy nodded her head, seething with anger.

"I really don't want to talk about it!" She said.

"Whoa! Don't get huffy with us!" Rachel said. Cathy reined in her anger.

"I'm sorry," she quietly said. "Sometimes when I think about how she used to treat me, I am glad......." She stops short of finishing her sentence and then changed the subject.

"Let's get back to Doctor Poppy," she said. Betty Jo wasn't having it.

"Let's not! I want to hear what you were going to say."

"Oh nothing. Don't mind me," Cathy said waving her off. Betty Jo still was not ready to let it go.

"I want to hear about your stepmother," she insisted.

Cathy fidgeted in her seat, and her lower lip twitched. Rachel and Betty Jo stared her down until she answered. Feeling caged in, she reluctantly gave them a glimpse of her childhood.

"When I was twelve, my stepmother caught me kissing a boy, and she told my father. He put me on restriction for two weeks, and I couldn't go anywhere except to school!" She shared.

"She had too! You were twelve!" Rachel pointed out. Cathy twisted her face up.

"But, it was none of her business!"

"What kid has business at twelve years old?!" Betty Jo said bucking her eyes and siding with Rachel. Cathy stuck her tongue out at them.

"That's my story!" She said. "Anyway, I fixed her!"

"How?" Rachel asked with a questioning look. Cathy's face went dark.

"Let' just say, the little wifey never tattled on me again!" Rachel felt uneasy and decided to change the subject.

"Let's get back to Doctor Poppy," she suggested.

"Let's!" said Cathy welcoming the diversion. Betty Jo huffed and folded her arms across her chest.

"Do you know if these patients had ground privileges?" Rachel asked.

"Yep, they did," Cathy said. "Why do you ask?"

"I think maybe they got a hold of some bad weed or something," Rachel brought up again. Cathy laughed like a witch.

"Bless their miserable souls," she said. "May they all be high in the happy hunting ground!" Betty Jo and Rachel exchanged worried glances. Disturbed by Cathy's strange and unusual outburst.

"Are you alright? You sure are acting funny," Rachel observed. Cathy quickly regained her senses.

"Oh, I'm fine," she said. "Just trying to make sense of all the craziness."

"Don't you think we all are?" Betty Jo snapped back irritated by her lack of empathy. Rachel sensing tension between them again quickly changed the subject. She pointed at a table wedged in a corner.

"Well, it looks like we have devoured the chocolate cupcakes. What about those strawberry ones over there? Who are they for?"

"Oh, those cupcakes are for the group tomorrow evening," Cathy said. "Sally suggested I store them in the freezer on the admissions unit."

"Girl, you are some baker," Betty Jo said complimenting her. "I'm calling you the cupcake lady!" She teased.

"Oh shut-up girl," Cathy giggled nervously while inwardly boiling with rage. She hated Betty Jo for making fun of her. She gathered up her cupcakes and started for the door.

"Where are you going?" Betty Jo asked.

"To put these up." Then she opened the door and walked out.

Robert Harris, high as a kite, was slumped over in his chair with a pool of blood at his feet. His knit dress was hiked up around his waist, and dried dark blood was stuck to his hairy thighs. The metal clippers, neatly wrapped in a blood-soaked towel, rested on top of the desk. His eyelids were heavy as lead as he fought to stay awake. Soon he loses the battle and closes his eyes for a brief minute. Then, he felt something breathing on his face. His bloodshot green eyes blinked open, and a big black cat with gold yellow eyes stared back at him.

He panicked. His breathing ragged and his heart raced at one hundred beats a minute. He mustered up enough physical strength to slide his chair back. The cat's frightening gaze bared into him, and he was terrified. Then he quickly regained his bearings and scooted his chair back to the desk. He reached out to pet the cat, but it disappeared into thin air. He blinked again.

He rubbed his eyes, but the cat was nowhere to be found. He sighed deeply, thinking the cat was a hallucination, a figment of his imagination from smoking too much weed. He fell back in the chair, incredibly weak. His energy seemed to drain from his body, and his limbs felt like rubber. Soon his head drooped to a ninety-degree angle, and his breathing became shallow. He was fading fast, but he didn't seem to care. He took another deep breath and then he was silent.

CHAPTER FIFTEEN

Cathy marched into the nursing station, with her plate of strawberry cupcakes straight to the medicine room.

"Where are you going?" Sally said peering over her chart.

"Didn't you say I can store these cupcakes in the freezer for the group tomorrow?" She reminded her. Sally slapped her forehead.

"Oh, I forgot to tell you! Doctor Poppy canceled the group for tomorrow. She's taking a couple of days off," she said.

"Really?" Cathy said. "I guess the stress of patients dropping dead around her has wigged her out," she quipped showing no sympathy. Cathy's words hit Sally the wrong way.

"Those deaths have gotten to all of us," she grumbled. "You scare me!"

"Well, I am naturally terrifying," Cathy joked in a low, raspy voice. They glared at each other and then Cathy said,

"Look I didn't mean anything by it. I just meant she's stressed out."

"Mm, Mm," Sally said, not convinced. Cathy tried to make amends.

"Look, since the group is canceled, why don't I donate these cupcakes to the patients to eat for a snack," she offered. "No use keeping them in the freezer to develop freezer burn," she reasoned. Sally looked pleased.

"That's a good idea," she said. "Leave them on top of the counter. I'll make sure the nurses pass them out."

"Very well," Cathy said leaving the cupcakes with Sally. She left the nursing station and returned to her office.

A few hours later, Rachel had just finished charting, and she was contemplating giving her husband a visit. Although it was hard to accept, Susan Cole was on his caseload until she was well enough for discharge. No longer willing to allow Susan to come between them, she decided it was time for a truce. She locked her drawer and dashed out of her office. She got on the elevator and rode it to the second floor, and when the doors opened, she stepped into the hall. His office was right there, and she walked to the door and tapped on it. There was no answer, so she took off down the hall to the nursing office. When she arrived, she found the door slightly ajar, so she invited herself in. Cooper, the assistant head nurse, was reading the Seattle Times with his feet propped on the desk. In his right hand, he was twirling a can of Rainer Beer. His eyes met hers, and he dropped his newspaper. He leaped to his feet in a hurry, tossing the beer in a trash can behind him.

"What's up Mrs. James?" He asked, with his voice very tense.

"I didn't mean to startle you," she giggled.

"I was just taking a break," he said.

"It's okay," she said gesturing for him to sit down.

"I'm looking for Doctor James. Do you know where he is?"

"He's down the hall chanting with a group of patients," Cooper informed her taking his seat.

"Huh?" She said looking at him wide-eyed. "What do you mean?"

"Just go to the group room," he chuckled. "You'll see what I am talking about."

"Okay, thanks," Rachel said looking confused.

As she hurried to the group room, she heard soft humming at a distance. The humming sounded like a swarm of bees the closer she came to the room.

"What is that noise?" She asked herself, looking quite befuddled. She quickened her step. Anxious to find out what's causing the noise. Within seconds she was at the door peeking through the glass window, and her jaw dropped when she lay eyes on her husband. "What is he doing?" She asked herself.

Everett, a devout practicing Buddhist was leading a chanting session with Susan Cole and a group of twenty patients. Each patient was kneeling on their knees, bowing up and down like synchronized robots. Rachel groaned with disgust. The blood in her veins curdled, and rage hit her with swift vengeance. Does he realize how unethical this was? And why was this witch sitting next to him? She contemplated busting in and breaking up the little charade, but she decided against it. Mad as hell, she kicked the door and stomped to the elevator.

Two hours later, Everett checked his watch and realized it was four thirty in the afternoon. While he finished his charting, he stopped a moment and thought about his wife. He wondered how long she would remain angry. After all, it had been three days since she had spoken to him, and he was tired of sleeping on a lumpy sofa. Besides, his back ached. As he brooded about his marriage, he heard a faint knock on the door.

"Who's there?" He hollered, his voice deep and gruff. No answer. Seconds later there was another knock, but this time the knock was a little louder. He jumped to his feet and glided to the door snatching it opened. Rachel stood in the hallway with a sultry look on her face, then she asked,

"Please, can I come in?"

He didn't answer. Instead, he left her in the hall and returned to his desk. He watched her as she sauntered in and shut the door. She dropped her coach handbag on his desk and gave him direct eye contact. She had decided ahead of time not to mention his little group. Deciding instead, the little fiasco wasn't worth it.

"Look, I have behaved pretty badly over the last few days, and I want you to know I'm sorry," she apologized.

"Mm-hm," he said maintaining a stone face as he stared straight into her dark brown eyes. He wanted her to grovel a bit, not willing to cut her any slack just yet. She read him like a book and realized she would have to do some fast talking to melt his frosty mood.

"I will make it up to you," she quickly offers, smiling seductively.

"How you plan to do that?" He finally spoke as he rose from his seat. He glided around the desk and parked himself in front of her. She hugged his waist.

"Well, I don't know, dinner, maybe," she sweetly suggested as she gazed up into his dark, handsome face. He thought about her suggestion for a moment and then frowned.

"I'm afraid dinner will not be enough." He coolly said.

"Well, what do you want?" She asked feeling flustered.

"A little TLC, baby," he said as he swept her off her feet and carried her to the couch. She held onto him.

"Everett, what are you doing?! Put me down!" He laid her on the couch, honoring her request. He climbed on top of her and covered her face with kisses.

She giggled hysterically as she fidgeted underneath him. He tickled her neck with his warm lips as he unbuttoned her blouse. He kissed her breast. His free hand slid underneath her skirt and caressed her thighs. She immediately became aroused, pushing him away.

"You are a bad boy, Everett," she giggled. "We are not going to do this here!"

"And why not?!" He teased as he moved his hand between her thighs. She felt herself getting wet with anticipation as she tried to wiggle out of his hot embrace.

"This is not appropriate," she protested. "At least not here at work!" He decided she was right and he rolled off her. He sat on the edge of the couch and then he stood on his feet as he adjusted the growing bulge in his jeans.

"We will finish this later," he promised her.

"We'll see," she grinned. He glided to the closet, snatched his jacket off the hanger, and slipped it on.

"Since you agreed to treat me to dinner. Let's go to Sully's," he suggested.

"Sully's it is," said Rachel as she buttoned her blouse. She slid off the couch and walked over to the closet door. She gazed in the mirror. Smoothing out her skirt and then fixing her hair.

"Ready?" He asked as he opened the door.

"Yep," Rachel answered. She grabbed her handbag and sauntered out. He followed her locking the door behind him. As they headed to the exit, he reached over and kissed her on the forehead.

"I'm hungry," he said throwing an arm around her shoulder. She smiled up at him.

"Me too honey," she said. "Me too."

Doctor Beebe slammed the phone down. He just finished talking to his friend Zurich Weaver, and he agreed to perform the lab tests as soon as the consents were signed. He couldn't help wondering if Ethan Poppy had something to do with her patients' deaths. It certainly appeared that way. He thought it would be best to give her time off. Deciding to cover her caseload himself for a couple days so he could figure out his next move. Besides, he needed to find Robert Harris, and soon. When he discussed Robert's disappearance with Zurich Weaver, the doctor suggested he hire a private detective to track Robert down.

After much thought, he decided to take Zurich up on his suggestion. He reached for the phone and called Thomas Marshall. While waiting for Thomas to answer, a six-foot black cat appeared in the doorway. "Meow," the cat purred cocking his head to the side. Doctor Beebe hangs up. His call to Thomas Marshall must wait.

"Hiram!" He sighed in exasperation. "You really do need to be committed! You have lost your cotton-picking mind!"

"Meow," Hiram purred again with furry claw-like hands pressed against his hips.

"Hiram, what do you want?!" Doctor Beebe asked getting frustrated.

"Hiram would like to tell you Sugar Foot Kent agreed to be Doctor Poopy's attorney," he said.

"Doctor Poppy Not Poopy," Doctor Beebe angrily corrected him. "Now please get out here! I have calls to make!"

"Sure," Hiram said. He dropped down on all fours and crawled away from the doorway. Doctor Beebe laughed out loud.

He just couldn't help himself. He grabbed the phone and called Thomas Marshall. When he finally heard the police chief's voice on the other end of the line, he cleared his throat.

"Hello Thomas, I need some information."

Later in the Evening, Donald Curtis thrashed back and forth in his bed, clawing at his bedsheets as he was hot and sweaty. With his stomach in knots, he moaned and groaned, foaming at the mouth. He hollered for a nurse, then Teresa came running into his room. She took one look at him, and terror crept over her face. She grabbed his shoulders and shook him violently.

"Donald, what's wrong?" She screamed. "Oh my god, what's wrong?!" He tried to speak, but the foam building in his throat choked him. He gagged and gagged, and his light brown eyes rolled back in his head. Frantic, Teresa ran out into the hall.

"HELP!" She screamed. "Somebody help Me!" Sammie and two nurses heard her screaming and sprinted to her aid. By the time they reached Donald's room, he was gone.

CHAPTER SIXTEEN

Two days later, the staff at Salter's Point Regional were still reeling over Donald Curtis' sudden death, and Doctor Beebe was stressed out. Everywhere he went, the staff was questioning him, and he had no answers to give. The city police made several visits to the hospital, but after questioning almost everyone who was on the admissions unit that night, they came up with absolutely nothing.

The vanishing of Robert Harris haunted him. The last report he received was a week ago when someone spotted him in Seattle coming out of a surgeon's office. Since then, Robert hasn't been seen. His wife Ginger, on a constant tirade, kept calling and harassing him every single day.

Cussing him out every chance she gleamed, blaming him for her husband's mysterious disappearance. At times, he could avoid her. Refusing to take her calls, wearied of the unrelenting pressure, and wishing he could disappear. When the pressure became too great, he often relied on his handy crutch, mad dog whiskey. A substance to soothe his tattered nerves.

As for Ethan Poppy, she has been absent from work for over a week. No one has seen or heard from her, not even Doctor Beebe. As each day passed, her colleagues were beginning to view her as a potential suspect. Doctor Beebe, feeling both pressured and burden was on a mission to get answers; even if it meant he must hire a private investigator.

When he solicited Thomas Marshall's advice for the name of a private investigator, the police chief told him about a young lady named Holly B Presley. She worked at King County Investigators in downtown Seattle, and according to him, she had an impeccable reputation and a knack for solving complicated criminal cases. Upon hearing this, Doctor Beebe, anxious to meet her, immediately scheduled an appointment. Hoping for a good fit so he could move forward in solving the hospital's unexplained patient deaths. Little did he know he was in for an unusual surprise.

Back on the admissions unit, isolated in her room, staying below the radar, Susan Cole struggled with demons of her own. Always wrestling with her guilt, she tried to hold on to the little sanity she had left. Every night after falling asleep, she would relive the murder in candid color. The gun blasting and the bullet hitting George Benny in the chest. Haunted by his cries and questions of why. Haunted by images of his bloodstained crumpled up body, and waking her up in a panic. Dripping with cold sweat and trembling in fear.

For the rest of the night, she tossed and turned unable to fall back to sleep; the image of him a permanent imprint in her memory. The strain of it all was beginning to show on her face. The dark circles around her eyes made her look much older than her stated age of thirty. This pissed her off every time she gazed in the mirror, and made her feel depressed and disgusted. She finally forced herself out of bed and took a shower.

As she dressed, she heard knocking on the door. She hesitated and then called out.

"Who's there?" No answer. She heard another knock, and the doorknob rattled. Then the door cracked open. A young beady-eyed woman with two long black pigtails peeked around the door. Her light-blue eyes zeroed in on Susan, and she gave her a big broad smile. Stunned, Susan wrapped her robe around her slender body and asked.

"Can I help you?"

"I'm checking for bats," the young girl said now looking serious.

"Bats?" Susan asked looking confused. "Did you say bats?"

"Yes," the girl said as she stepped inside and scoped out the room. She looked down and pointed at her crotch.

"I think the bats in my vagina are coming from your room," she explained.

"Huh?" Susan said even more confused as she tried to maintain her composure. She walked over to the girl.

"I think you are mistaken," she said standing in front of her with her hands on her hips.

"Are you sure?" The girl asked with watery eyes. "It feels like I am turning into a vampire with these bats living in my vagina." Susan cracked up laughing. She couldn't help herself.

"Girl you are no vampire, and no bats are living in your vagina!"

"Are you sure?" The girl asked again with puppy dog eyes. Susan was quick to reassure her.

"I'm sure," she said. The girl unzipped her pants and felt around her private area. Then she let her pants fall to the floor. Susan gasped.

"Girl put your pants back on!"

"But life is so freeing without them," the girl replied with a grin.

"Pants on. Now!" Susan demanded. The girl pulled her pants up and Susan, feeling uncomfortable, tried to distract her.

"By the way what's your name?"

"Country Fried Taylor," the girl proudly replied zipping up her pants.

"Country Fried Taylor?" Susan chuckled. "Now that's an unusual name!"

"I'm from the south," Country Fried explained. "My momma named me!"

"She must have been high as a kite to come up with that shit," Susan muttered under her breath.

"What?" Country Fried asked flipping her right ear forward to hear better.

"Nothing," Susan said. She thought about asking Country Fried to leave, but she didn't have the heart to do so. Instead, she took a softer approach.

"Look, I need to finish getting dressed," she said. "Can we talk later?"

"Sure," Country Fried said. She turned to leave and then she hesitated in the doorway.

"Are you going to the dining room for breakfast?" She asked.

"Thinking about it," Susan answered.

"Can we talk then?" Susan cringed inside. She wasn't interested in forging a friendship, especially with someone who believed she had bats in her vagina.

"If I decide to have breakfast, I will find you," she fibbed.

"Great," Country Fried grinned. She left Susan's room and went down the hall.

Susan decided to skip breakfast. She didn't want to run into Country Fried. She spent the rest of her morning in the lounge, sitting by the window and flipping through an Essence magazine. She liked it there. It was quiet and serene. A place to meditate and mull over her thoughts. An hour later, Rachel appeared in the lounge searching for one of her patients. Her dark brown eyes landed on Susan and blood rushed in her face. With her heart thundering, wild in her chest, she struggled to keep her cool as she headed Susan's way.

"Good Morning Miss Cole," she said with her dark eyes narrowing. Susan looked up. She recognized Rachel right away and out of self-preservation, she decided to play dumb.

"Do I know you?" She asked looking wide-eyed.

"You don't know me?" Rachel asked looking very surprised.

"I'm afraid not," Susan answered trying to look confused and giving no hint she recognized her.

"You are kidding me, right?" Rachel said, not convinced she had amnesia. Susan shrugged her shoulders with a blank expression on her face.

"I'm sorry, but I don't know you," she said.

146

"Then let me give you a hint," Rachel smirked. "Does Ray Cooper ring a bell?" Susan slapped her hands over her mouth.

"Oh my god!" She exclaimed being overly dramatic. "I don't want any trouble," she said shaking her head. She remembered the beating Rachel gave her because of Ray Cooper. If she had known Ray was cheating on his girlfriend, she would have never gone to his apartment that night. She got up to leave, and Rachel stepped in front of her.

"Where are you going?"

"I don't want any trouble," she repeated with her voice shaky.

"Don't worry, I'm not going to hurt you," Rachel reassured her. "That was a long time ago. Have a seat. I want to talk to you." Red-faced and scared out of her wits, Susan tried to leave again.

"I don't want to," she said. "I…I don't have anything to say to you."

"Sit down!" Rachel demanded. Susan sank down in the chair, and her left arm twitched. She held it close to her stomach. Rachel pulled up a chair and sat down crossing her legs. Her dark brown eyes gave Susan the once over as she squirmed in her seat.

"Tell me, where did you meet Ray?" Rachel asked out of the blue.

"I met him in a club downtown in San Francisco," Susan softly said. "He was nice," she added looking terrified.

"Did he tell you he was engaged and living with someone?" Rachel asked with thunder in her eyes. Susan let out a long sigh.

"No, he didn't," she said. "He told me he had broken up with his girlfriend. I had no idea he was lying!" Rachel felt her temper flaring.

"Girl get real," she hissed. "Didn't you see my makeup and curling iron in the bathroom? I can't believe you didn't know he was lying!" Susan shook her head feeling pressured.

"I noticed those things," she admitted. "But he told me his sister was staying with him!"

"So, you believed him, just like that?!"

"Yes, and I am very, very sorry," Susan apologized feeling flustered. Rachel rolled her eyes.

"You are so naïve." Susan became quiet. The two women sat there not looking at each other. After ten minutes passed, Rachel was less angry.

"Susan, you and Ray really hurt me," she softly said. "I felt betrayed. I was so angry, and as you know, you took the brunt of my anger." Susan, moved by Rachel's words, gazed into her eyes. She felt tears coming on.

"I know how you feel. I too was betrayed," she whispered. Rachel sensed something. A vulnerability about Susan. She felt sorry for her. A deep sense of empathy for her.

"Are you talking about Ray or someone else?" She asked scooting her chair closer. Susan looked down in her lap with tears streaming down her face.

"Someone else," she admitted.

"Tell me about it," Rachel probed. "It seems we have something in common."

"This man I was living with cheated on me right under my nose," Susan revealed as she wiped snot on her sleeve.

"Oh," Rachel said, with her eyes round like dark marbles. She knew this was her chance to find out what happened to Doctor Benny and she didn't waste any time.

"How did you find out?"

"One of my neighbors told me," Susan sadly said. "I didn't know what to do at first. I was so upset." Rachel studied Susan's face. Her gut told her she killed Doctor Benny, but her face gave off another impression. A child-like innocence, making it hard for her to tell. She gently pushed for more information, hoping to gain clarity.

"So, what did you do about it?"

"I can't talk about it," Susan tearfully said.

"Oh, it couldn't be that bad," Rachel said trying to get her to talk some more. She got up and went across the room. She brought back a box of Kleenex and placed it on Susan's lap. Susan took a tissue and blew her nose.

"I did a bad thing," she finally said.

"Really? How bad was it?" Rachel asked trying to remain calm. Susan snatched another tissue out of the box and dabbed her eyes. She looked Rachel directly in the eye and said.

"I'm not ready to talk about it just yet. It's too painful."

"I understand," Rachel said backing off a little. "We all have done some pretty awful things we are not proud of," she said. "But you are going to have to talk about it if you want to heal emotionally," she added.

"I know," Susan mumbled nodding her head in agreement. "I'm just not ready right now."

"Okay, I understand," Rachel said deciding to let her off the hook for now. "When you are ready, I'm here for you. I really would like to help you get over this."

"Really?" Susan sniffled surprised by Rachel's change of heart.

"Really," Rachel said.

"Thank you," Susan said. "Do you mind if I go? I'm so exhausted!"

"Go ahead," Rachel said. "We'll talk later." After Susan left, Rachel recollected her thoughts. She wondered if Susan committed such an awful crime. Maybe Everett was right. Perhaps she was innocent after all.

CHAPTER SEVENTEEN

Betty Jo jumped in her seat when she heard the phone ring. Too busy to talk, she ignored it at first and continued with her charting. The phone stopped ringing momentarily, and then it rang again. Irritated, she finally answered it.

"This is Betty Jo Brewer. Can I help you?"

"Girl, it's me," Rachel said breathing hard. "I need to tell you something."

"What's up?" Betty Jo asked, suddenly interested.

"Guess who I just finished talking to," Rachel excitedly said. Betty Jo sighed.

"I give up! Who?"

"Susan Cole," said Rachel.

"Girl, really?" Betty Jo said getting excited. "What did she say?"

"I think she knows something about Doctor Benny's murder. She was going to tell me about it then she got scared and decided not to," Rachel said.

"Get outta here!" Betty Jo giggled, very impressed. "How did you do it?"

"I used my own personal experience as bait," Rachel said. Betty Jo dropped the phone and then picked it up again.

"Girl, I didn't know you killed somebody!"

"No Silly! I didn't kill anybody," Rachel laughed out loud. "I just told her how I felt when someone I once loved betrayed me."

"Good thinking," Betty Jo said feeling relieved. "So, what's next?"

"I'm going to meet with her and talk to her again," Rachel said.

"Hold up, I think she's my patient," Betty Jo said feeling a little possessive.

"Oh yeah, she is," Rachel recalled. She thought for a moment and then she threw out a theory.

"Maybe she didn't commit the murder. Maybe she had someone else do it instead." Betty Jo was amused by Rachel's wild imagination.

"Girl, you are a trip," she chuckled.

"It's just a thought," Rachel said.

"Just keep me posted," Betty Jo sighed.

"I will," said Rachel.

"Well, I got to run," Betty Jo said. "Talk to you later!" She hung up the phone before Rachel could say another word. She sat back for a minute and chuckled to herself.

"Leave it to Rachel. If anybody can get to the bottom of this whole murder thing with Susan Cole, she can."

The very next day, Thursday morning, Holly B Presley was cruising down interstate five in her Honda Civic on her way to Salter's Point Regional Hospital. She accepted Doctor Beebe's invitation to meet, drawn by the mysterious deaths occurring in his facility. It's been two years since she's visited the city of Salter's Point. Her father, ill with bipolar disorder at the time, was the reason for her previous visit. Her parents divorced when she was ten years old. Her father, too ill to cope with the responsibilities of marriage and fatherhood, left town altogether and later divorced her mother. While growing up, she would see her father off and on over the years. However, his visits were often short.

Blowing into town like a whirlwind and leaving just as quick. When her mother remarried, she changed Holly B's last name to Presley. The name was much more comfortable to pronounce for teachers and students at the school. Despite her father's illness, he managed to financially take care of her and pay for her college education when the time came. As she zoomed down the freeway, she admired the fluffy white clouds circling around Mount Rainier. The mountain's high peaks were capped with glistening snow, a beautiful backdrop against the clear, deep blue sky. She rolled down the window, breathing in the fresh, crisp air.

It wasn't long before she was driving through the hospital gate and navigating her way up the hill to East Campus Hospital. She parked in the visitor's parking lot, grabbed her notebook and then scrambled out of the car. Once inside the hospital, she made her way to the reception desk. The receptionist was not there, so she waited; finger combing her thick blonde hair, twirling a strand around her index finger.

Her bright hazel eyes peered through black-framed prescription glasses as she inspected her surroundings with intense scrutiny. Soon Rachel and Sally mosey in; laughing, talking, and telling each other jokes. They walked by Holly B, and she stopped them.

"Excuse me, ladies! Don't mean to interrupt, but can you please tell me where Doctor Beebe's office is located?"

"Is he expecting you?" Sally asked shooting Rachel a suspicious look.

"I have a meeting with him," Holly B said with a warm smile.

"Is it business or personal?" Rachel asked being nosy.

Holly B laughed. "I'm a private investigator," she explained showing her badge. "So, I guess it's business." Rachel checked out her badge.

"Holly B Presley," she exclaimed. "Very cool name, I must say."

"Why thank you," Holly B said bowing her head with approval. "Tell me your names?"

"Oh, how rude of us," Sally said with her face turning a shade of pink. "I'm Sally Roberts, and this here is Rachel James."

"Nice to meet you ladies," Holly B said extending her hand. Rachel and Sally each shook the detective's hand.

"What do you ladies do here?" Holly B probed.

"I am the head nurse of the admissions unit and Rachel here is one of our social workers."

"Well, I'm sure I will be talking to you ladies again soon," Holly B said.

"How long will you be here?" Rachel asked getting suspicious.

"Don't know," Holly B replied with her hazel eyes narrowing. Rachel and Sally exchanged worried glances again, but Holly B stayed on mission.

"Can you direct me to Doctor Beebe's office?" She asked again.

"Oh, yes," Sally said getting herself together. She pointed across the lobby. "It's down that hall, room twelve."

"Thank you so much," Holly B said. She started across the lobby and then she hesitated and turned around. She placed a finger on her bottom lip and said.

"By the way, does Hiram Gottschalks still work here?"

"Yes, why?" Rachel asked.

"I'm his daughter," she revealed walking backward across the lobby. "Tell him his daughter is here."

Rachel's and Sally's eyes popped out after hearing Holly B's revelation. Shocked, they watched in silence as she walked across the lobby until she disappeared around the corner. Then, Rachel spoke first, barely able to contain herself.

"Can you believe this? Hiram has a daughter! Now that's unbelievable!" Sally, at a loss for words, tried to speak, but no words came out. Rachel kept fussing.

"I just didn't see that coming. He never mentioned he had a daughter!"

"I guess we need to tell him she's here," Sally finally said. They raced to the elevator and got off on the ground floor. Within seconds, they were standing in front of Hiram's office. Rachel pounded on the door. "Come in," he growled.

Sally opened the door and went inside with Rachel right on her heels. Hiram was picking his nose with his feet up on the desk. His frizzy grey, blonde hair was teased all over his head, and he wore a black tee-shirt with the words, "I'm Batman" on it. His big hazel eyes looked them up and down, and he growled.

"What can I do for you ladies?" Rachel and Sally looked at each other and giggled. Hiram bristled up.

"What's so damn funny?"

"Do you know Holly B Presley?!" Rachel excitedly asked. Hiram shot out his seat so fast, his wired frame glasses fell off his face.

"My Holly B is here?! Where is she?!" He shouted, with his hazel eyes ecstatic.

"She is meeting with Doctor Beebe right now," Sally informed him.

"Move out of the way!" He yelled, pushing Sally against the desk as he rushed by her to the door. "I've got to see my daughter!" Rachel stooped to the floor and swooped up his glasses.

"Don't you need these?" He snatched the glasses out of her hand and adjusted them on his face.

"Thanks, Missy! You're a gem!" He ran out leaving Sally and Rachel in his office. They fell out laughing. "Mannnn, he's off his rocker!" Sally chuckled. "He's so damn excitable!"

"He's a genuine nut! I wonder how he was as a father," Rachel mused.

"Crazy as hell," Sally said. "I bet Holly B was never bored!"

"Girl, we got to tell Betty Jo and Cathy about this," Rachel said.

"After you," Sally said as she followed Rachel out the door.

Hiram pounded on Doctor Beebe's door so hard, the frame rattled on its hinges.

"Go away," Doctor Beebe yelled. "I'm in a meeting." Hiram wouldn't take no for an answer. He forced his way in. He stood in the doorway with his hands on his hips grinning like a Cheshire cat.

"There's my sweet cakes," he said with his face lit up with joy. "It's been a long time!" Holly B slid out of her seat and ran to her father. She hugged him and kissed him on the cheek.

"I'm so glad to see you, Dad!"

"Me too, darling," he said holding her tight. Doctor Beebe lurched forward in his wheelchair with his mouth hanging open.

"This woman is your daughter? You got to be kidding me?!"

"This is my sweet cakes," Hiram proclaimed puffing his chest out with satisfaction on his face.

"Damn," Doctor Beebe said. "I had no idea!" He sat back and observed them with a bewildered look on his face.

"Are you going to stay with me sweet cakes?" Hiram asked with a sparkle in his eyes.

"Well, it depends," Holly B hedged giving her father a wary look. "Do you still live in that old garage?"

He nodded his head in the affirmative. Giving her a sheepish grin. Holly B sighed deeply and spoke in a low voice.

"Dad, I rather stay at Salter's Point Inn."

"If you wish, my dear," he grinned, bowing down before her. Holly B giggled. She noticed his tee-shirt and became ecstatic.

"I love it," she said.

"You do?" Hiram said as he spun around in a circle.

"I sure do," she said smiling from ear-to-ear. "I have one similar."

She unbuttoned her sweater and revealed a pink tee-shirt with the words "I love Miss Piggy" on it. Hiram cracked up laughing.

"Sweet cakes, I love it," he said with approval. Doctor Beebe shook his head in amazement.

"Two lunatics in the same family," he muttered to himself. "Unbelievable!" Hiram hugged his daughter again.

"After you finish with Doctor Beebe, stop by and see me on the way out. My office is on the ground floor."

"Okay Dad," Holly B giggled. Hiram let go of her and headed for the door.

"See you later sweet cakes!" He ran out leaving the door wide opened. Holly B went over and shut the door.

"My dad is a trip," she said. Doctor Beebe still visibly shocked didn't even respond. He had no words to describe the scene he just witnessed. Ignoring the shocked expression on his face, Holly B got down to business.

"Shall we continue doctor?" She suggested with piercing hazel eyes.

"I suppose so," Doctor Beebe mumbled, nervously looking down at his notes, and wondering if he made the right decision by hiring Holly B in the first place.

"Where would you like to start?" He asked

"Let's talk about the patients who mysteriously died," she suggested. "How many were there?"

"Five," Doctor Beebe informed her. "Billy Moonwalker, Celeste Brown, Lisa Cooper, Rosy Jackson and Donald Curtis."

"And Robert Harris?"

"He's missing," Doctor Beebe said. "As far as we know he is still alive." Holly B looked off into the distance, her mind working overtime.

"You told me earlier, these patients were on Doctor Poppy's caseload, right?" She probed.

"That's right," said Doctor Beebe.

"Do you have any reason to believe she could harm them?"

"Doctor Ethan Poppy has been a physician for a very long time. She came to us with a good reputation," Doctor Beebe said getting defensive.

"Doctor, you did not answer my question," Holly B said. Doctor Beebe squirmed in his chair. Feeling uncomfortable.

"No, I don't think she's capable of harming any patient," he finally said.

"Then why haven't you heard from her?" Holly B asked batting her eyes through her black framed glasses.

"I don't know," he said locking eyes with her. "I really can't answer that."

"Mmmm, very interesting," Holly B said scribbling in her notebook. Then she closed her notebook and stood up.

"I think I have what I need for now. I will keep you posted," she said. She moved toward the door. Doctor Beebe followed in his wheelchair. She opened it and then turned to face him.

"I look forward to working with you doctor," she said smiling.

"Likewise," he fibbed.

CHAPTER EIGHTEEN

Meanwhile, back in the nursing office; Sally, Rachel, Betty Jo and Cathy were chatting up a storm about Holly B Presley. They were shocked to learn she was Hiram's daughter. Rachel stretched her arms over her head and yawned. She fell back on the sofa and propped her legs up.

"I'm so tired," she said.

"Well if you would get some sleep instead of staying up all night making love to Everett, maybe you wouldn't be so freaking tired," Betty Jo teased.

"Mind your damn business girl!" Rachel quipped making a face at Betty Jo. Betty Jo made a face back by sticking her tongue out.

"I still can't believe Hiram is a daddy," she chuckled. "It's hard to wrap my head around."

"Yeah, it's hard to fathom," Rachel agreed.

"What's she here for anyway?" Cathy asked, her brow furrowing.

"I think she's here to investigate Robert Harris' disappearance," Sally said. "She did say she's a detective."

"Just Robert's disappearance?" Cathy asked. "What about the patients who recently dropped dead lately? What about them?"

"She's probably here for that too," Sally said. Cathy was skeptical.

"She's Hiram's daughter for goodness sakes! Is she competent enough to conduct a halfway decent investigation?"

"Let's hope so," Rachel chuckled. "In the next few days, we will know more about her and how she works," she said feeling hopeful.

"Maybe, we get a glimpse of the two idiots together," Cathy coolly said with spite in her eyes. Betty Jo cuts her eyes at Cathy.

"I am so tired of you calling everyone an idiot! You're the damn idiot!" She said getting loud.

"I beg your pardon?" Cathy said turning red in the face. Sally was quick to intervene.

"Ladies, let's not do this. We must be respectful to one another," she reminded them.

"Tell that to her," Betty Jo pouted as she folded her arms across her chest. She glared at Cathy.

"I'm sorry. I didn't mean ......" Rachel butts in and chastises her.

"Cathy, I agree with Betty Jo. You need to be more professional. Your comments are rude sometimes!"

"Okay, okay I get it!" She said now very embarrassed. She gave them a weak smile, but she was seething inside. Fully aware of her shortcomings, hating them for exposing her. Determined to stay in good with them, at least until probation was over, she decided to take a humbler approach.

"I apologize if I offended anyone," she said. "I can be nasty at times."

"That's more like it," Betty Jo said, her tone sharp and still not convinced

"Betty Jo," Sally urged. "She's putting out a good effort."

"Right," Betty Jo said still glaring at Cathy. She just didn't trust the woman. Since the day she stepped foot in Salter's Point Regional, there was something about the woman that wasn't right to Betty Jo. Something evil seemed to lurk within. A darkness she couldn't figure out. Rachel read Betty Jo's face, and she too had some reservations about Cathy. However, she was determined to remain positive, deciding to steer the conversation in another direction.

"Let's hang out at Sully's after work on Friday," she suggested. "The Average White Band is playing there this weekend."

"I love AWB," Betty Jo said taking Rachel's suggestion. "I'm in!"

"Whose AWB?" Cathy asked. "I'm not familiar with the band." Rachel waved her off.

"You are too young to remember. It's an R&B band from the seventies, "she informed her.

"Oh," Cathy said. She glanced at Betty Jo.

"So, you don't mind if I join you?"

"No, not at all," Betty Jo replied being very coy.

"And you Sally, are you coming?" Rachel asked.

"I'll pass," she said. "You ladies carry on. You need to bond."

"Ugggggh," Betty Jo groaned. "Really Sally?" Sally laughed.

"Yes dear, really."

Morning turned to early evening. Doctor Beebe was still in his office wrapping up the day's details. His off-colored meeting with Holly B Presley and her father, Hiram was still fresh on his mind. He hoped Thomas Marshall was right. He was not in the mood to deal with another knucklehead.

With his nerves on edge, he decided he needed a drink. He reached into his desk drawer and brought out a bottle of mad dog whiskey. Then he poured himself a drink and he gulped it down. Then he poured another, and then another, and soon he was feeling good and tipsy. With glassy eyes, he gazed up at the clock on the wall trying to make out the time. If it weren't for the town clock rumbling like a small earthquake, he would never have known it was five o'clock in the evening. He thought about the investigation and pondered whether he should hold a hospital-wide meeting to update the staff. The recent questions swirling around the hospital about Robert's disappearance and the number of patient deaths had become quite burdensome to him. He decided after some thought, it was probably best to schedule a meeting. He reached for the phone and dialed Joyce's number.

"Joyce Banks here," she said sounding cheerful.

"I have decided to schedule a hospital-wide meeting for Monday morning," he said slurring his words. Joyce paused momentarily. She had been worried about him since she discovered an empty whiskey bottle in his trash can recently. Suspecting he may have been drinking, she proceeded with great caution.

"Sir are you alright?" She asked. "You sound kind of funny."

"I'm fine," he burped. "Put a memo in everyone's box. Mandatory Staff Meeting on Tuesday morning at ten-thirty," he demanded.

"Can I say what's it about?" Joyce heard silence on the phone. He hadn't thought that far ahead. What should he tell her?

"Sir, did you hear me?" She asked again.

"Uhhh, just say, update on the investigation," he burped again.

"Okay," Joyce said. There's silence again. Then she heard ragged breathing and asked,

"Sir, are you there?" Nothing. "Sir?" Seconds later, she heard snoring and then a dial tone. She rushed to his office and barged through the door. She found him conked out in his wheelchair fast asleep with the telephone dangling off the armrest.

It was mid-evening at Salter's Point Beach. The blue sky above Mount Rainier had faded from sunset orange to the dull-gray night. Seagulls soared over the rocky waterfront laughing to themselves, while bats fluttered in and out in unusual, hurried patterns, resembling black polka dots against the dusky gray sky. Everett and Rachel were at home enjoying dinner with their daughter Jamie Lee. Rachel was anxious as she squirmed in her seat like a little kid. She couldn't wait to tell Everett about her conversation with Susan Cole. He took note of her fidgety behavior and called her out.

"Woman, what's gotten into you?"

"What do you mean?" She replied pretending not to know why he asked the question in the first place.

"You are all over the place," he said. "You got something to say, so say it!" She hated when he could figure her out.

"Welll…." She hesitated.

"I'm waiting," he said getting irritated.

"I had a conversation with Susan Cole today," she began. He raised an eyebrow.

"Oh," he said. "How did it go?"

"I almost got her to confess," Rachel proudly said. "But she got scared and backed down."

"Now girl, how did you do that?" He asked.

"I apologized for whipping her behind first," Rachel said. "And then…..." Everett busted out laughing.

"Now that's funny!" He said.

"Yeah, I think she was surprised," Rachel said with a smirk.

"I bet," Everett roared. "So, you apologized, then what happened?"

"I simply told her I wasn't proud of my behavior toward her and we all do things we are not proud of. Then she bit," Rachel said.

"Bit what?" Everett asked trying to keep a straight face.

"You know what I mean… She took the bait," she said giving Everett the eye.

"I'm afraid I don't, but go ahead, finish your story," he said giving her a half smile. She rolled her eyes and continued.

"So, anyway, she got all teary and told me about this man who betrayed her."

"Huh, huh," Everett said.

"Then she didn't want to talk about it anymore," Rachel said.

"Do you plan on talking to her again?" Everett asked.

"Yes," Rachel said. "I want to get the truth out of her."

"That's not your job baby girl," he warned. "Besides, she is not assigned to you!"

"I know, I know," Rachel said. "But......."

"But nothing!" He said cutting her off. "Leave that job to the police," he scolded her. She fell silent and pouted, disappointed he didn't see it her way. She got up and began snatching dishes off the table. He sensed her irritation and tried to smooth things over.

"I agree with you," he said. "She may know something about how Doctor Benny died, but murder? Baby girl, that's a real stretch!"

"We'll see," Rachel said wiping off the table. "We'll see.

CHAPTER NINETEEN

Thursday night became Friday morning, and the dark sky was showing a hint of blue-gray. The sun began to peek over Mount Rainier, and the rest of nature soon woke up. Holly B was on her way to her father's garage, a place he called home. Cruising down Sandy Beach Boulevard on the coast of Puget Sound. He invited her there for a late breakfast, and she happily accepted. Sandy Beach Boulevard soon turned into Seaside Drive. Winding down the coast of Puget Sound with its attractive bungalow homes and small manicured lawns.

She turned into a side driveway and came upon her father's humble abode; a deteriorating concrete building desperately in need of a good coat of paint. She parked her Honda Civic a few feet away from the garage next to a red Toyota missing tires; then she stepped out of her car. Little chickens, each a different color, red, brown, yellow and black scurried up to her. The birds chirped and pecked at her sneakers as they ran around her feet. Their claw-like feet made tiny scratch prints in the sand and Holly B, irritated to no end, waved them away.

"Shoot! get out of here!" She yelled. "Shoot! Get away from me!" The birds chirped and flapped their wings. Picking up speed as they took off and flew across the yard to a chicken coup nearby. Disgusted, Holly B slammed the car door and headed to the garage, stepping over chicken poop along the way.

The white smelly stuff was splattered in large spots in various places on the pavement, and she held her nose in desperation until she reached her father's door. She rang the doorbell. The door swung opened and Hiram, dressed in a Batman costume and combat boots, grinned back at her with pure joy.

"Good morning Sweet Cakes," he growled with his arms stretched out.

"Hi dad," she said. She ducked his embrace and stepped inside. He frowned, feeling slighted. He slammed the door and grabbed her, hugging her tight.

"What's wrong, Sweet Cakes?" He asked.

"Dad, you need to get rid of those chickens," she grimaced, while rubbing her nose. "I couldn't even walk to your door without stepping over chicken shit! It's everywhere!"

"Now, now, Sweet Cakes. It's not that bad," he chuckled patting her on the back. She recoiled. Irritated he was downplaying her feelings.

"Those chickens are a nuisance Dad," she protested.

"Ohhh, Sweetie," he said. "Why you think that?" She pointed to her sneakers.

"See what those little critters did?!" She said. "Their little beaks pecked holes in my sneakers!"

"So not good," Hiram said shaking his head as he glanced at her sneakers. Feeling responsible for her little mishap, he came up with a grand idea.

"I'll buy you new ones!" He exclaimed. "Will that do?" He asked trying to appease her.

"I guess," she said sighing. "Why are these chickens here anyway?" She wondered out loud.

"Those little babies will be my dinner soon," he said. "I'll wring their little necks, skin their little butts and fry them up! Then I will invite you over for dinner," he smartly proclaimed.

"Eew, gross," Holly B grimaced suddenly getting a visual. "Thank you, but I'll pass."

"Suit yourself, Sweet Cakes," Hiram said.

"What's for breakfast?" She asked as they moved into the kitchen, where a pot belly stove sat in the center of the floor.

"Well let's see," he said. "Make yourself comfortable!" She grabbed a folding lawn chair by the wobbly wood picnic table and sat down. Hiram stripped down to his multi-color long johns which sent Holly B in hysterics. She giggled out loud. She couldn't help herself.

"Dad, you are a man of many peculiar outfits. You never cease to amaze me!" He laughed as he skipped over to the stove. He snatched an iron skillet out of the cabinet and slammed it on top of the stove. Feeling whimsical, he joked.

"Fried chicken and pancakes coming up!"

"OOOOOH no!!!" Holly B said, raising her voice and violently shaking her head. "I am not eating any chicken today! Especially after meeting your little fowl friends outside on the curb!" Hiram cracked up. Tickled by his daughter's reaction.

"Then will you settle for eggs, bacon, and pancakes?" He grinned

"That's better," she sighed taking a deep breath and rubbing her forehead.

Hiram began cooking breakfast, and Holly B checked out her father's home. The garage, abundant in space, was cluttered with odds and ends. Pots, pans, newspapers, books, and magazines were scattered everywhere. Stacked on chairs or on boxes or against the wall. Two large, bright fluorescent light bulbs hung from the ceiling on opposite ends of the garage. One over the pot belly stove and the other over the picnic table. Across the room, a full-sized bed draped with a queen-sized comforter was pushed back against the wall. Spider webs lurked in corners while dust balls floated in the air. She rubbed her nose to keep from sneezing. Soon the sweet aroma of bacon filled the air. Holly B found some napkins and began tearing them up in little tiny pieces. Stacking the pieces in a neat pile and then flicking the paper all over the table. She repeated the action several times until her father took note of her compulsive behavior and became concerned.

"Feeling uptight, Sweet Cakes?" He asked.

"I guess I have some nervous energy in me," she said getting up from the table. She went to the cabinet and took out some dishes.

"Should I set the table?" She asked.

"Yes," he said cracking eggs in a skillet. She sets the table in deep thought, mulling over her investigation. She wondered if her father knew anything about Robert's disappearance. If he did, would he tell her? She wondered. She decided to take a chance and ask him anyway, hoping he would shed some light on the situation.

"Dad, what do you know about Robert Harris' disappearance?" She blurted out.

Hiram raised an eyebrow. Then he turned his back on her. Caught off guard by her question. Not sure if he should discuss Robert's case with her. He stirred the eggs with vigor, buying time so he could come up with a reasonable answer.

"What is it you want to know?" He finally answered.

"Well," Holly B said. "Doctor Beebe told me Robert had a pass for the library the day he disappeared, is that correct?" He turned and faced her, his expression serious.

"I believe that's right," he said. He brings the skillet of eggs and bacon to the table. Using a spatula, he scoops the food onto the plates.

"Where is the library?" She asked as she dived into her eggs.

"The library is on the first floor of West Campus Hospital," he said pouring pancake batter into the skillet. "Robert was an electrical engineer, and he liked checking out engineering books," he added.

"How well did you know him?"

"Not well," Hiram said. "I represented him in court a couple times, but that's about it." He brought the skillet back to the table and dumped three perfectly round pancakes on Holly B's plate.

"This smells so good," she said smiling.

"Eat up," he grinned. "You need some meat on those bones!" He fried more pancakes and then piled four of the cakes on his plate. Then, he took a seat across from Holly B. She continued to bombard him with more questions, annoying him.

"Why was Robert hospitalized?" She asked.

"He was depressed," Hiram replied.

"Depressed about what?" Before he answered, he paused for a moment. Should he break confidentiality and tell her about Robert's desire to be a woman? Or should he allow her to find out from another source? He decided on the latter.

"He had some problems," he softly said. Holly B 's eyebrows went up.

"What do you mean?"

"Sweet Cakes, I suggest you talk to his doctor," he said refusing to elaborate. She sensed his irritation and backed down for a brief minute. Then she threw another question at him, determined to get answers.

"Doctor Poppy was his doctor, right?" She asked. He glared at her. Getting more and more annoyed.

"Yes," he curtly answered.

"Do you know where she lives?" She inquired ignoring his intense glare.

"She lives at Salter's Point Loft Apartments downtown," he informed her.

"I hear she hasn't been to work lately," Holly B said. "Do you think she skipped town?" Hiram took a deep breath.

"Sweet Cakes, I wish I could help you, but I can't," he said. "Why don't you go to her apartment and see for yourself?"

"I think I will," Holly B said as she poured more syrup on her pancakes.

"Good," Hiram grinned, finally getting his point across. "That's my girl!"

Forty-five minutes later, Holly B was at Salter's Point Loft Apartments in the downtown district, where the property was very dated. Built in the 1960's, the property took up three acres of prime land with its groves of evergreen trees neatly placed around the parking lot. She struggled with the front door to the main entrance. The door made of oak was heavy and thick.

She hurled her body against it twice hoping it would open and after the third try, the door finally flew open. The weight of it threw her inside, and she almost fell face forward on the floor. She regained her balance and straightened out her clothes. While she checked out her surroundings, a whiff of musk assaulted her nostrils, and she sneezed. Like the property outside, the furnishings inside appeared dusty, old and outdated. She sneezed again and rubbed her nose hard, while she scoped out the place, looking for the occupant directory. She found it hanging on the wall by the elevator, and the name Ethan Poppy boldly stuck out on the register. Right next to the doctor's name, was her apartment number, five fourteen.

She tapped the elevator button, and the door squeaked opened. Feeling a little uneasy, she entered the elevator despite her reservations. The elevator rattled and shook as it traveled up to the fifth floor. Holly B steadied herself with arms stretched out against the wall, holding on for dear life. The elevator stopped and jerked her to the other side throwing her off balance. By that time, the door squeaked opened, and she was frazzled from the jerky ride.

She dashed out, and her body ached as she headed down the dimly lit hall. While she searched for the doctor's apartment, she kept an eye out for the stairs. When she turned left around the corner, she passed an exit sign leading to the stairway. She sighed with relief.

"I'm taking the stairs on the way out. I can't take another elevator ride." Three more apartment doors down, she finally arrived at Ethan Poppy's apartment. She knocked on the door. Heavy footsteps approached from the other side and then stopped. A big violet eye stared back at her through the peek hole and then disappeared. Then a woman called out from behind the door.

"Who is it?" Holly B held up her badge.

"I'm Holly B Presley from the police department," she said. "I need to talk to a Doctor Ethan Poppy," she further clarified.

Ethan cracked the door looking suspicious. Her hair was so frizzy and wild, it looked like it had been fried in a light socket.

"What is it you want?" She asked.

"I'd like to ask you a few questions," Holly B firmly said. Ethan opened the door a little wider and beckoned her to come inside. Holly B accepted the invitation and entered the doctor's dark and gloomy apartment. Then a creepy, monstrous feeling came over her, and she shuddered with fright. On an end table near the door, there was a small lamp barely giving out light, and next to the table was a large black coffin. Holly B was scared to death when she laid eyes on the black casket. She stood there in a trance, unable to speak.

"Have a seat," Ethan said. Holly B took a seat on the cranberry, velvet sofa in front of the window with jet-black curtains.

"Thank you," she said finally getting the courage to speak. She continued to check out her dark surroundings. Thin shadows, resembling spooks in a horror flick, danced on the walls and on the ceiling. Paintings of cats, owls, and mice wearing hats and bright red lipstick adorned the dark walls. The doctor's apartment reminded her of a funeral parlor, and she trembled inwardly, but managed to maintain her composure.

"Interesting art," she murmured sitting on the edge of her seat.

"Thank you," Ethan mumbled, with her words barely audible. Dressed in black, silk pajamas and red high-top tennis shoes, her outfit offset her bright violet eyes and white hair. Ethan made herself comfortable in her rocking chair and waited for Holly B to speak. Her violet eyes blinked every few seconds, and her chair squealed when she rocked. Holly B, captivated by the doctor's piercing gaze, promptly began her questions.

"I guess you know why I am here," she said. Ethan didn't say a word. Instead, she folded her arms and nodded her head in agreement. Holly B flipped her notebook open. Then she heard a rustling noise in a nearby corner.

"What's that?" She asked craning her neck to see across the room.

"Oh, those are my pet rats, Mickey and Harry," Ethan replied. "They are fighting over their breakfast." Holly B's eyes widened when she heard the word rats. She bolted off the sofa dropping her notebook on the floor.

"Oh, my god, you have rats?!" Ethan broke out into a small grin.

"Calm down. They are not going to hurt you. Besides, they are in a cage," she pointed out.

"Where?" Holly B asked.

"By the coffin," said Ethan. When Holly B laid eyes on the little critters, she almost fainted. She sat down and began hyperventilating.

"Are you alright?" Ethan asked getting concerned.

"I'm okay," Holly B said breathing deeply. "But why do you have rats?"

"I find the animals interesting," Ethan said. "That's all."

"My word," said Holly B. "Rats for pets! I have never heard of such!" Ethan smiled at the detective and apologized.

"I'm sorry you feel so out of sorts about this."

"It's okay," Holly B said, realizing she must live with the rats for now. She picked her notebook up off the floor, and her eyes rested on the black coffin. She took another deep breath.

"What's the coffin for?" She asked, trying to appear unruffled, but inwardly she was a mess. Her heart was jumping inside her chest like a basketball.

"I sleep in it," Ethan told her with a voice low and croaky. "I find it to be very soothing and relaxing." Holly B was visibly shocked, but she managed to remain calm. Her heart was about to burst inside her chest, and the palms of her hands were hot and sweaty. She told a joke, trying to relax.

"At least you will be casket ready for glory land!" She said. Ethan didn't respond. It was clear she didn't like the joke. She stared Holly B down with cold, violet eyes, never blinking once.

Feeling the heebie-jeebies, Holly B fidgeted in her seat bracing herself. Finally, Ethan spoke, her voice low and firm.

"You say you have questions? Then let's get on with it!" Holly B almost choked on her own saliva, scared out of her wits. She swallowed hard as she grabbed her pen from her coat pocket. Determined not to stay any longer than she had too, she began the interview.

"Okay, Doctor Poppy," she said in a hurried voice. "Tell me about the day Robert Harris disappeared."

"What do you need to know specifically?" Ethan coyly asked, still staring at her with cold violet eyes.

"Can you tell me how he got off the unit that particular day?"

"Certainly," she eagerly said. "He had earned ground privileges and requested a pass to go to the library, so I gave it to him," she said.

"Then what happened?" Holly B asked. Ethan's mood softened and her eyes watered.

"He took the pass, and he left," she said. "I told him the pass was good for two hours, but he never returned."

"Have you talked to his wife about where he might be?" Ethan fought back the tears, reluctant to answer. She knew she must be straight with the detective, so she forged on despite how she felt.

"His wife has no idea where he is, and she is furious at me," the doctor said with her voice cracking. "She's suing me!"

"I'm sorry to hear that," Holly B said now feeling sorry for her. Ethan scooted out of her rocking chair and went into the kitchen. A minute later, she returned with a box of tissue.

She sat down in her rocking chair sniffling and sucking in snot. She dabbed her eyes.

"I understand the library is a place he often visited when given a pass, is that right?" Holly B probed.

"Yes," Ethan tearfully replied. "He loved reading engineering books. He was an electrical engineer."

Holly B scribbled in her notebook documenting every detail as she came up with another question. Then she asked.

"Can you tell me what he was wearing that day?"

"Yes," she said. "He was wearing a black knit dress and spiked, red high heel shoes." The shock on Holly B's face was evident.

"He's a cross-dresser?"

"Yes," Ethan said. "He wanted to be a woman."

"I see," Holly B whispered. There was silence. The only noise in the room was Holly B scribbling in her notebook and the rats chasing each other's tails in their cage. Ethan broke the quiet by asking a question.

"Is there anything else you need?"

"Yes," Holly B said. "I understand five patients on your caseload suddenly......"

"Died," Ethan said finishing her sentence.

"Yes. Can you explain why?"

"I don't know," Ethan sadly said. "I wish I knew."

"Your documentation indicated these patients suffered from schizophrenia and suicidal thinking. Is that correct?" She asked.

"True," Ethan said. "The voices often instructed them to harm themselves, but the medication I prescribed each patient seemed to curtail that," she said.

"Did these patients have ground privileges?"

"No, not all of them," Ethan recalled. "Billy Moonwalker did not have ground privileges."

"I see," said Holly B.

"Do you think they took something you weren't aware of," Holly B suggested.

"It's possible," Ethan said. "The lab results will be back in the next few days, and we will know for sure."

"Mm, mm," Holly B replied. She took a moment to breathe as she mulled over the gravity of their conversation. Still wanting more information, she addressed the doctor one more time.

"Why haven't you returned to work?"

"I can't take the scrutiny, the stares, the accusations," she quickly responded. "I didn't do this, and I don't think anyone believes me. I feel so alone!"

"Do you realize the more you stay away, the guiltier you look?" Holly B pointed out to her. "You should get yourself a lawyer and go back to work!"

"I have talked to a lawyer," Ethan said. "He gave me the exact same advice you did."

"Then you should listen to him," Holly B said. "Your life depends on it!" Ethan bowed her head and tears welled in her eyes.

"You are right," she said. "I'll go back tomorrow."

"You need to," Holly B said. "I think it's for the best!"

CHAPTER TWENTY

Doctor Beebe hung up the phone. He was relieved to hear from Doctor Poppy finally, and pleased she had decided to return to work. He decided to schedule a doctors' meeting. There was a lot to discuss. The lab results came back, and the findings revealed a dangerous substance he didn't expect. The substance was very worrisome. He was now thinking about temporarily banning ground privileges. He needed to converse with his colleagues and Holly B about it before making such a decision but first he must call Beth. He reached for the phone again and dialed her number. When she doesn't answer, he hangs up. Then he called Joyce. She picked up the call on the first ring and her voice sounded hurried and short.

"Joyce Banks, may I help you?"

"Doctor Beebe here," he said. "Need to schedule a meeting with the docs. Can you type a memo and put it in everyone's box?"

"Certainly," Joyce said. "Need date and time," she said.

Monday morning at nine-thirty," he said.

"Will do," she said. She hung up the phone before he could say another word and he leaned back in his chair and sighed.

Cathy's heart jumped a little, when Beth informed her she passed probation. Overjoyed by her accomplishment, she was finally a full-time state employee. Her joy soon turned to rage after Beth dropped an unexpected bomb in her lap. Fighting to keep her temper under wraps, she heard Beth out.

"I have received complaints you are frequently late to work," Beth said, with her green eyes piercing. "This is unacceptable behavior and I want it to stop if you plan to continue to work here."

"Beth, I was only late a couple of times and I told you about it," Cathy reminded her defending herself. "Who is telling you this stuff anyway?" She asked. Beth was short with her.

"It doesn't matter. Just be on time!" She flipped through her notes and the phone rang. She answered it barking into the receiver.

"Beth Jones here!" She listened for a moment and then a big cheesy grin appeared on her face.

"Well that's good news! Thanks for the heads up!" She slammed the phone on the receiver and reached for her pack of Pall Mall cigarettes. Soon the office was filled with thick grey smoke. Beth's big green eyes glared over her bifocals as she brought up another pressing issue.

"It's been brought to my attention, you don't always complete your less restrictive plans for court in a timely manner," she announced.

"I forgot one time, but…." Beth cuts her off.

"Doctor Poppy and Betty Jo have relayed to me this happens often. It's important these plans are completed before court. No exceptions!"

"Yes Ma'am," Cathy said feeling both embarrassed and ambushed. She couldn't stand Doctor Poppy and she could barely stand Betty Jo.

These last few days without Doctor Poppy being around had been blissful for her.

"Has anyone heard from her?" Cathy asked trying to lighten the mood.

"Heard from who?" Beth asked taking a drag off her cigarette and blowing a puff of grey smoke into the air.

"Doctor Poppy," Cathy said.

"Oh, yeah," Beth said. "That was Doctor Beebe on the phone earlier. She's coming back tomorrow morning." Cathy forced a fake smile, trying hard not show any disappointment in her face.

"Glad to hear she's alright," she lied.

"Yep, she's fine," Beth said. "Just make sure you have those plans completed on her patients."

"Yes ma'am," Cathy said as she boiled inside. She got up to leave and Beth stopped her.

"Welcome to Salter's Point Regional, my dear," she grinned from ear-to-ear. "You are one of us now!"

"Thank you," Cathy said giving her a half smile. She opened the door and walked out. Seething with resentment, she was beside herself. How dare they tattled on her like that? Who do they think they are? She was hoping Doctor Poppy would be out for good, but she realized it wasn't happening. The woman was coming back, and she hated it with a passion. As she walked to her office, she thought of ways to drive the doctor to quit. She thought hard about it and then something came to mind. She laughed out loud just thinking about it. Her laugh shrill and wicked. Then she declared, "Doctor Poppy, I got something for you! I'm going to drive you plumb shit crazy! Then you will quit for good!"

It's nightfall, Friday evening. The pale, yellow moon radiated bright against the dark distant sky and stars resembling Christmas lights soon popped out throughout the universe. The night air, cool and breezy was unusual for June weather.

Mark Brewer, bundled in a leather jacket and scarf, drove his Mercedes into Sully's parking lot. He parked in a slant taking up two parking spaces. High as a kite, he had consumed two glasses of wine prior to leaving his office and he could barely get out of the car. He stumbled out and locked his vehicle. With cane in tow, he hobbled inside of the restaurant. Once inside, he sees patrons huddled together at the bar, having drinks while they yelled at each other over the loud jazz music playing in the background. He hobbled over and climbed up on a stool. He waved down the bartender who came right over.

"What's your drink tonight sir?" He asked.

"Need a shot of whiskey," he shouted.

"Coming right up," the bartender said. As he waited for his whiskey Michael Louis came in and spotted him at the bar. He stormed over, his face determined and serious.

"Brewer, is that your Mercedes taking up two parking spaces in the parking lot?" He demanded.

"Yeah, why?" Mark asked raising his voice.

"Geezus, Brewer! I hope you don't fuck like you park, you never get it in straight," he deadpanned.

"Ha, ha, very funny," Mark sarcastically replied. "What brings you here this evening?"

"Meeting my wife and Beth for dinner," Michael said.

"Well, I didn't know you and Beth were friends," Mark said looking surprised.

"Yep, we are," he said. "Care to join us?"

"Nope, I'll stay right here drinking my sorrows away," Mark grinned being sarcastic. Michael laughed.

"Don't get too wasted, Brewer," he warned.

"I can take care of myself," Mark shot back.

"Right!" Michael said rolling his eyes.

"Michael!" He turned to look and his wife was yelling at him across the room. She gestured for him to come over. Beth, hovering nearby, puffed on a cigarette.

"Got to go! The ladies are here," he said. "See you around!"

"Yep," Mark said. Michael leaves and the bartender placed a shot of whiskey on the counter in front of Mark. He picked up the drink, threw his head back gulping it down. Then he slammed the shot glass down on the counter.

"Need another one!" He shouted.

"Coming right up!" The bartender yelled back. As the evening wore on, the restaurant got lively. The sweet aroma of cigar smoke filled the air and members of the Average White Band were on stage setting up for their evening performance. Rachel, Betty Jo and Cathy soon bounced in and took seats near the stage. They ordered drinks as they settled in for the show. Mark, feeling good and toasted after finishing off his fifth shot of whiskey spotted his wife in the crowd. He slid off the stool and made his way over to her stumbling a few times.

Rachel sees him and nudged Betty Jo. "Girl, your husband is here, and he is coming your way. He looks really wasted," she warned. Betty Jo's face turned ashen when she laid eyes on her husband.

She cringed when he arrived at their table and stumbled against it, knocking a glass of red wine in her lap. She bolted straight up, shaking the liquid off her hands.

"Shit Mark, what's wrong with you?! Are you crazy?!"

"Crazy for you," he replied, his speech slurred. He tried to grab her, but she moved out of the way.

"Get a hold of yourself," she said, with her face red-hot. "You are embarrassing me!"

"Embarrassing you?!" He shouted. He turned and faced the crowd as he swayed back and forth.

"My wife just told me I am embarrassing her!" He shouted at the top of his lungs. Rachel hopped up and grabbed a chair from a nearby table and placed it behind the doctor.

"Mark, have a seat," she said.

"No," he shouted kicking the chair on the floor. "I want my wife to tell me how I am embarrassing her!"

With a stricken look on her face, Betty Jo broke down crying. Rachel, mad as a hornet, gets in Mark's face.

"You should be ashamed of yourself!" She said. "How dare you ruin her evening!"

"Get out of my way woman," he yelled as he shoved her to the side. He makes his way to the bar and two security guards meet him in the aisle. They grabbed him and dragged him toward the exit.

"Get away from me you sons of bitches!" He yelled. The guards lifted him up and carried him out the door. Everyone cheered. They stood and clapped showing their appreciation.

With her dark brown eyes wet with tears, Betty Jo faced her colleagues looking distraught.

"I can't stay! I'm going home!"

"Don't let him ruin your evening," Cathy pleaded. "You were so looking forward to this."

"Betty Jo stay," Rachel urged. "Cathy is right!"

"I can't!" Betty Jo sobbed. She tucked her handbag under her arm and dashed out the door. Rachel fell back in her seat in disbelief. Cathy, speechless felt sorry for Betty Jo even though she wasn't fond of her. The two women sat together in silence, alone in their thoughts. The band started playing and Rachel tried hard to relax. She leaned over and tapped Cathy on the shoulder.

"Let's enjoy the show. After all we paid for these tickets."

"I hope Betty Jo is going to be alright," Cathy said looking worried.

"Girl, me too," Rachel said shaking her head. "Me too."

CHAPTER TWENTY-ONE

It was midnight when Rachel arrived home. Still rattled over Mark's drunken fiasco down at Sully's, she felt sorry for her best bud, Betty Jo. She wondered how Mark could embarrass her like that. His lack of respect puzzled her. How could he do this to her? She pondered. The two of them make such an attractive couple. "What a damn fool," she mumbled to herself as she tossed her coat and handbag in the closet. Then her thoughts turned to Jamie Lee.

She hurried to her room and looked in on her. Jamie Lee was snoozing away with her little chest rising up and down. Rachel smiled at her with admiration, then she tiptoed over to the bed and planted a kiss on Jamie Lee's cheek. She covered her with the blanket and tiptoed out of the room, shutting the door behind her. Across the hall, she heard Everett snoring in the master bedroom. She tiptoed inside trying not to wake him. He was naked, sprawled across the bed, sleeping like a lion. Her dark brown eyes savored his smooth muscular body as she walked by the bed on her way to the shower.

Minutes later, she was drying herself off and wrapping a towel around her curvy body. She tiptoed to the bed and sat down next to him. She caressed his neck. Her wet fingers moved down the curve of his back, his skin smooth and silky. He stirred, sleepily opening his dark brown eyes, and then he flipped on his side facing her.

"You're home," he said sounding groggy. He stretched and let out a growling yawn. "What took you so long?"

"You are not going to believe what happened," Rachel said as she leaned over to kiss him on the lips. He stretched again with his toes pointing upward at a forty-degree angle.

"I'm listening," he yawned.

"Move over," she teased as she slid into the bed next to him. He scooted over giving her room.

"Mark was drunk as hell," she told him.

"He's always drunk!" Everett said. "What else is new?"

"Noooo, he was really drunk and out of control this time," she insisted, her eyes widening. He became suspicious.

"Tell me what happened baby girl," he said raising up on one elbow.

"He made a huge ruckus in front of the whole restaurant, embarrassing Betty Jo to the point she had to leave. Security threw him out," she excitedly said.

"Get out of here," he said raising an eyebrow.

"Yep," Rachel said. "I tried to get him to calm down, and he shoved me to the side," she casually said. As soon as the words left her lips, she knew she had made a grave mistake. Everett rolled out of bed and stormed to the closet. His dark brown eyes wild with fury.

"I'm going to kill that fucker!" He said. "He has no business putting his hands on you!"

"Everett no, don't get worked up," Rachel said shaking her head violently. "He didn't hurt me!"

"I don't care," he said. "He's history! I'm going to whip his ass!" Rachel hopped out of bed and ran over to him. "Calm down honey," she said holding onto his waist trying to stop him. "He's probably in jail anyway. Come back to bed."

He hesitated for a minute. Thinking.

"Pleeease," she pleaded.

"Alright if you insist," he half-heartedly said backing down. "But Monday, it's him and me!"

"You're so sexy when you get riled up," she teased dropping her towel on the floor to entice him. She pulled him toward the bed, and he felt aroused. "Mmmm," he murmured getting turned on. She fell on the bed, and he hovered over her nudging her chin. His heavy hot breath tickled her face as he slipped his tongue between her soft lips. She pulled him close, and he caressed her buttocks while his hot tongue moved from her lips to her nipples. Swirling around each one causing the hair on her body to tingle with erotic sensation and she moaned. His tongue then moved from her breast to her navel, slowly dipping in and out causing her to moan even louder with her body raising off the bed.

"That tickles," she whispered with a small giggle. She tried to wiggle out of his grasp, but he held her tight.

"Woman, you are not going anywhere," he said pulling her closer. "You taste so good."

He parted her thighs and stroked the lips of her fiery, wet sweet spot. She cried out with pleasure, the sensation intense. Her body rigid, finally rose off the bed, and he stroked her until her body exploded. The orgasm rippled like rushing water through her body, and she groaned with pleasure. Before she could catch her breath, he moved swiftly inside of her. She hung on to him as he pushed hard into her, over and over, deeper and deeper. Every muscle in his body was rigid and tense until he finally climaxed and collapsed on top of her.

They laid still, breathing heavily. Wrapped in each other's arms. Their hearts beating in a synchronized rhythm.

"Too heavy?" He said, his voice sultry and deep.

"Nope," Rachel said. He kissed her on the forehead. Then he rolled off her onto his back. She flipped on her side and cuddled up next to him.

"Don't start any mess with Mark on Monday," she cautioned. "He didn't mean anything by it. It's not a big deal." Everett made a face, but he didn't say anything. He wasn't buying her explanation for one minute. Sensing his sour mood, she grabbed his face and looked him dead in his eyes.

"Everett, I mean it," she said. "Don't say a word to him!"

"I hear you," he reluctantly said pulling away, not wishing to spoil the mood. "I'm cool," he lied. "Don't worry."

"Are you sure?" She asked, not convinced.

"Yes," he firmly said with a straight face. "I'm cool." In her heart, she knew he was lying, and his mind was made up. Mark Brewer will be the very first item on his agenda Monday morning.

Early Monday Morning around eight o'clock, still upset over Mark embarrassing her at Sully's, Betty Jo raced down the hall to Rachel's office. She had a lot on her mind, and she needed to vent. When she arrived at Rachel's office, the door was already ajar. Rachel, enjoying a cup of Starbucks coffee was buried in a social work journal. Betty Jo, on the verge of tears, bounced in uninvited. She flopped down on the couch and crossed her legs.

"Girl, I've had it!" She tearfully announced.

"Girl, what happened?" Rachel asked dropping her journal on the desk as she set her coffee mug down.

"I think I am going to file for divorce," Betty Jo said. Rachel got up and shut the door.

"Damn! What happened now?"

"I am so tired of dealing with Mark and his drinking," she whined. "He stops for a while and then he starts up again!! I am so tired of it!"

"Well, I don't blame you," Rachel said trying to be supportive. "But don't you think you should try marriage counseling first before taking such a drastic step?" Betty Jo bolted off the couch startling Rachel, who jerked back almost falling out of the chair. Too upset, Betty Jo didn't notice.

"Do you know how many times we have been to marriage counseling?" she screamed. "It does not work!"

"Shush!" Rachel said as she repositioned herself in her chair. "People can hear you! Calm yourself down!"

"Sorry," Betty Jo said as she flopped down on the couch again. She pouted, and tears flooded her eyes. Rachel offered her a box of tissue, and she snatched one and dabbed her eyes. "Thank you," she said.

"You're welcome," said Rachel. Her mind wandered off for a moment, then she gingerly said,

"Look, you and Mark are separated, right?"

"Yeah," Betty Jo replied. "What's your point?"

"You still love the man, don't you?"

"Yeah, like the Tina Turner's song says, what's love got to do with it?" She said looking flustered. Rachel chuckled.

"Look, before you take a drastic step like divorce, go to counseling one more time. See if you can salvage your marriage," she suggested. Betty Jo rolled her eyes.

"If he would stop drinking, everything will be okay," she said.

"Then make it a condition," Rachel said.

"What do you mean?" Betty Jo asked. Rachel stopped to think of the right answer. Then she simply said,

"Tell him, for this marriage to work, he must go to rehab. Get the marriage counselor to back you on it!"

"But I'm so frustrated," she said flinging her arms across her chest.

"I know," Rachel said. "Give it a chance." Betty Jo said nothing for an awkward moment and then she quietly responded.

"I guess I can give it another try."

"Good," Rachel said. "Everything will work out. Just be patient," she said.

"I hope you are right," Betty Jo said looking down in her lap. "I sure hope you are right."

Michael, Everett, Ethan, and Mark were in the conference room precisely at nine-thirty, waiting to meet with Doctor Beebe. Ethan Poppy, sporting fluorescent pink high-top tennis shoes, with gloves to match up to her elbows, made herself comfortable at the far end of the table. Everett glared at Mark from across the table and said nothing. Sensing something was seriously wrong, Mark squirmed in his seat. Then he let out a weak little wail of terror.

"Aaaaawww….. Brother, what's wrong with you this morning? You look pissed off!"

"Don't brother me!" Everett quickly retorted looking wolfish.

"What's your problem bro?" Mark questioned him feeling on edge.

"I hear you were quite the spectacle at Sully's last Friday," Everett said with a strained voice.

"A spectacle? He was a drunk babbling idiot!" Michael piped in offering his unsolicited two cents. Mark slammed his fist on the table.

"I resent the name calling!" He said. Michael nonchalantly rolled his eyes while Ethan shot out of her seat. With fear in her eyes, she dashed to the door and then stopped. She turned and faced her colleagues. Deciding at the last minute to hang out for a while to see what happened. She held her breath.

"I resent the fact you put your hands on my wife," Everett said gritting his teeth.

"What the hell are you talking about?" Mark said getting riled up.

"Let me show you what I am talking about!" Everett lunged out of his seat ready to punch Mark out. Michael leaped to his feet and stopped him cold.

"Hold up there, buddy!" He firmly said shoving him back. "He's not worth going to jail for and losing your medical license!"

Everett reluctantly backed off and pushed Michael off him. "Are you SURE I can't punch him in the face? He deserves it!" Everett said with icy dark brown eyes.

"The sapsucker is not worth it," Michael said.

"What if I break his nose a little?" He said not giving up.

"NO!" Michael yelled. "Just forget about it!" Everett returned to his seat, and in a terrifying calm voice, he said.

"Brewer, I will kill you if you touch my wife again!"

His terrifying threat left everyone in the room speechless for a long awkward moment. Ethan quietly returned to her seat at the end of the table with her eyes pinned on both men. Then, Carl speeded into the room with Holly B and Hiram close behind. Hiram, sporting a Shirley Temple hairdo, took a seat next to Michael. At first, Doctor Beebe didn't notice the thick tension in the room. He grinned from ear-to-ear, his mood cheerful and pleasant.

"Sorry, I'm late," he apologized looking around the table. "Good Morning everyone!"

Everett grunted while the others mumbled out a greeting with strained faces. Sensing something was amiss, he decided to address the situation.

"What's wrong with you people this morning?" He asked raising his voice.

"Not a damn thing," Everett cursed, still fuming as he glared at Mark. "What's this meeting about anyway?"

No one said a word. The spat between Everett and Mark was not worth bringing up again, especially after Everett agreed to calm down. His temper was a force to be reckoned with, and no one in the room was going to stoke it again. So, they focused their attention on the medical chief waiting for an answer to Everett's question. He glared at Everett. He wasn't happy with his nasty remark, but he answered the question in an earnest roundabout way.

"This here is Holly B Presley," he said introducing the detective. "I hired her to investigate Robert's disappearance and the deaths occurring in our facility."

"Hi everyone," Holly B said with a big smile. "Don't mind me. I'm here to listen and take notes," she said taking a seat next to Ethan. The doctor got up and moved her chair on the opposite end of the table. Holly B frowned, feeling a little insulted. She wondered why the doctor was so skittish. After all, she was just at her apartment the other day. She shook her head.

"Strange bird," she thought to herself. Ethan looked her up and down as if meeting her for the first time.

"You look like someone I know," she finally said surprising Holly B.

"Doctor, what do you mean?! We met the other day," Holly B said looking confused.

"I know that!" She said looking indignant.

"Then what do you mean?" Holly B asked her again shrugging her shoulders.

Ethan eyed her suspiciously. "You look like someone who works here," she clarified.

"You might be referring to my Dad," Holly B smiled.

"And who might that be?" Ethan asked with her violet eyes blinking fast.

"Hiram Gottschalks," Holly B announced giving Hiram a nod. Ethan slapped her hand over her mouth and almost fell out of her chair. Everyone in the room cracked up laughing. "Oh, my goodness," she exclaimed.

"Hiram Gottschalks is your father?" Michael chuckled. "Honey, bless your little soul!"

"Why you say that?!" Holly B asked, her face rosy red getting defensive. Carl felt bad for her and immediately interceded.

"Don't take it personally," he explained. "Your father and his peculiar ways have kept us entertained for years." Hiram flipped a curl away from his face and cackled like a hyena. Realizing Doctor Beebe was right about her father, Holly B let out a small giggle. She offered some of her own thoughts on the matter.

"He can be a real trip sometimes," she mused gazing lovingly at her father. Hiram bucked his eyes and wrapped one of his thick long curls around a chubby index finger.

"It takes one to know one," he chuckled. Michael, intrigued by Hiram's hairdo, decided to ask him about it.

"So, who fixed your hair like that?! Your daughter?!" He snorted.

"Nope," Hiram said. "I went to Fancy Peacock last night!"

"What, is that a strip joint with some fancy hoes?" asked Michael. Everyone cracked up laughing including Hiram himself. He shook his head, and his grayish-blonde curls swished gently on his shoulders.

"Dude it's a hair salon! Get real!"

"Damn," Michael said. "A hair salon with hoes and cocks!" Everyone laughed out loud, and Doctor Beebe, barely able to keep it together had to clap his hands to get everyone's attention.

"Let's get down to business. I have a lot to discuss," he chuckled. Soon everyone calmed down and flipped open their notebooks. They gave Doctor Beebe their undivided attention.

"The lab results are back," he informed them.

"Oh, they are?" Ethan said, her violet eyes narrowing.

"Yes, and the results are quite disturbing," he said. "Shocking I must say."

"Stop the suspense and come out with it," Everett snapped getting inpatient. Carl shot him a dirty look, but he remained steadfast.

"The results came back on everyone except for Billy Moonwalker," he said. "The blood work on each patient revealed the presence of strychnine."

"Strychnine?!" Ethan said with big eyes. "How did strychnine get in their system?"

"Now, you tell us," Michael snarled giving her the stink eye.

"Are you accusing me of harming these patients?" She said looking hurt. "How dare you?!"

"Then tell us how strychnine got in their blood," he said calling her out again.

"Alright, alright," Carl said waving both hands. "You two calm down." Michael rolled his eyes. He kept the heat on her.

"Maybe you gave them some marijuana laced with the stuff," he said under his breath. Ethan was peeved. She glowered at him from across the table. Furious by the accusation. She snatched the lab results off the table and began reviewing the paperwork herself.

"I don't believe this!" She said.

"I don't know why. The lab results don't lie," Michael chided her. He lit a cigarette, and soon a trail of smoke crept into the atmosphere. Mark, quiet as a church mouse, had been reviewing records during Ethan's and Michael's little exchange. He scuffed the floor with the toe of one boot, and then he softly pointed out.

"Every patient, except for Billy Moonwalker, had ground privileges. They also used marijuana as a recreational drug. It's possible they got a hold of some bad weed while out on pass causing their untimely demise."

"Maybe," Carl said nodding his head in agreement.

"Maybe we should suspend ground privileges until we figure out what's going on," Mark suggested.

"I was going to suggest that," Carl said. "Does everyone agree?" He asked glancing around the table.

"Before you decide, I have a question," Hiram said.

"Shoot fancy peacock," Michael smirked with a crooked grin on his face. Snickers erupted around the table. Hiram ignored them.

"In addition to the strychnine, was there marijuana in their system too?" He inquired.

"Yes," Doctor Beebe said. "All five had marijuana in their system."

"Mmm, interesting," Holly B mumbled under her breath. A significant clue she jotted down and must explore.

"So is everyone on board to suspending ground privileges?" Doctor Beebe asked again. Everyone nodded in agreement.

"Then it's settled," he said. He turned and faced Holly B who was quiet and introspective the whole time.

"What do you think little lady?" He asked, his eyes level with hers.

"I'm inclined to agree with Doctor Brewer," she said. "If he's right, someone out there is killing people," she said thinking out loud.

"You mean a serial killer?" Ethan asked with genuine fear in her voice.

"Possibly," she said. Michael roared with laughter.

"You nitwits! The serial killer is right here at this damn table!" He said, pointing directly at Ethan.

"That's enough!" Carl said frowning up. "Ethan is no serial killer!"

"That remains to be seen," he insisted. He stood up and snuffed out his cigarette. Then he stormed to the door. "I got work to do people," he said. "Let me know when you decide to arrest the little wench!" He swung the door open and stormed out.

"Good riddance," Ethan said. "I'm so tired of his insults!"

"He can be difficult," Carl said shaking his head.

"I would never hurt my patients," she said with watery eyes. "Why would he think such a thing?"

"Ignore him," Everett said. "He's just being an ass!"

Mark suddenly gets up and started for the door.

"Holly B, Good Luck with the investigation!" He said. "You have a lot to figure out!"

"I know," she smiled. He waved as he hobbled out the door. Ethan still visibly upset pulled off one glove and bit her fingernails. A tear rolled down her cheek and Everett, feeling empathy for her, got up and went to her. He gently squeezed her shoulder. She patted his hand, taking his warm gesture as comfort.

"I'll be alright," she said. "It's just so much to take in."

"If you need anything let me know," he offered.

"Thank you," she said. "You are a real gentleman!"

CHAPTER TWENTY-TWO

Later in the afternoon, on her way to her office, Rachel took a shortcut through the patient dining room and Susan Cole was there. Slouched in a chair with her curly blonde hair loose on her head, she was quite disheveled in her faded red plaid shirt and wrinkled, worn blue jeans. She stared out the window with a blank look on her face. Her mind, a million miles away. Rachel stopped and observed her for a minute. Her cute round face was tired and haggard, and the creases in her forehead were more pronounced. Rachel wondered why she looked so stressed. Could it be her demons had finally caught up with her? She pondered. Curious, she dragged a dining room chair over to the table. Susan, at first, didn't see her coming. When she finally did, Rachel was already there, parked in a chair in front of her.

"Oh my god!" She screeched as she lunged out of her chair almost falling on the floor. She regained her balance and stood there bewildered liked a scared rabbit.

"I didn't see you coming!" She said.

"Relax," Rachel said gesturing for her to return to her seat. "I thought you might need some company. You look upset."

"I'm okay," Susan fibbed as she sat in her chair. "I just have a lot on my mind."

"It's pretty obvious," Rachel said crossing her legs. "Care to talk about it?"

"Maybe," Susan politely replied not sure what to make of Rachel's kind gesture and changed attitude toward her.

She sat at attention like a tin soldier with her hands clasped tight in her lap; expecting a verbal confrontation, but it never came. Rachel took note of her discomfort and tried to reassure her.

"Look, I'm not going to hurt you. I told you earlier I just want to help if I can," she said.

"Really?" Susan said.

"Yes really," Rachel replied in earnest. Susan twiddled her thumbs and Rachel scooted in closer.

"How are you feeling today anyway?" She asked.

"What do you mean?" Susan said, barely giving her eye contact.

"Well, you made a suicide attempt a few days ago. Do you still want to take your own life?" Susan frowned.

"No, I don't think so," she said sounding evasive.

"Do you still have thoughts?" Rachel said trying to pin her down.

"I suppose so," she sighed.

"They come and go." Rachel decided to go out on a limb.

"Do these thoughts have anything to do with Doctor George Benny?"

"What do you mean?" Susan asked again fidgeting in her seat. Beads of water appeared on her forehead, and she suddenly felt hot.

"The last time we talked, you told me he cheated on you," Rachel reminded her. "That's tough to deal with. Especially when you love someone." Rachel's words sank deep into her soul and tears stung her eyes.

"I suppose," she mumbled wiping her face.

"Is it safe to assume his cheating led to your decision to take your own life?"

"I guess so," Susan tearfully acknowledged. Rachel gave her time to regroup. She hung back a bit and then she gently said.

"I remember you mentioning a neighbor told you about his cheating, is that right?"

"The truth is, I confronted him, and he kicked me out," she quickly responded.

"That must have been hard," Rachel said.

"Yes, it was," Susan said scooting back in her seat finally relaxing. "I was devastated!"

"What happened after he kicked you out?"

"I went over to a friend's house," she fibbed.

"How long did you stay?"

"Just a few days," Susan replied. "I just needed time to get myself together," she said.

Rachel studied Susan's face. Looking for clues. Wondering if she was being truthful. Although her baby blue eyes looked sad, she knew they harbored an awful secret. A secret she wasn't ready to reveal. Rachel sighed long and hard and said,

"Did you know Doctor Benny had been murdered at that time?"

Again, Susan fidgeted in her seat, and she hesitated before answering. Feeling pressured, she knew she must come up with a convincing answer to satisfy Rachel so she would stop with the questions. Sweat accumulating under her arms trickled down her side. Soon her shirt became damp and sticky, and she felt hot and anxious.

She looked deep into Rachel's eyes and gave a measured response.

"No, I wasn't aware of his murder at the time. I found out about it after the police chief came to see me in the hospital," she recalled.

"Oh, I see," Rachel said. "You must have felt awful after you found out," she said trying to sound empathetic.

"I just didn't believe someone could shoot him in the chest like that," she sniffled shaking her head. Rachel raised an eyebrow. She didn't recall any news reports describing how Doctor Benny died. Her leg shook, and her heart raced realizing for the first time she may have finally gotten Susan to confess. However, she was still doubtful. Maybe the police chief did tell her how Doctor Benny died. Cautious, she steadied herself and asked another question.

"You think someone shot him?" Susan, teary-eyed, ignored her question initially. She just simply replied,

"He was such a sweet man." Rachel took note of her avoidance and kept the conversation going to buy more time.

"Did you love him?" Susan grimaced.

"What kind of question is that?!" She said with a burst of anger in her voice. "Of course, I loved him!" Rachel backed off for a minute.

"I'm sorry. I didn't mean to offend you," she apologized. "But I know his cheating was a blow to you," she continued. "You must have been pretty darn pissed to shoot him in the chest!"

Susan's face turned dark. She sat straight up with her back rigid like a steel rod. She glowered at Rachel, and her lips twitched when she finally spoke.

"What are you trying to do? Trick me?!"

"No, I'm not trying to trick you," Rachel calmly said. "But if a man cheated on me, I would be pissed enough to want to shoot him!"

Susan relaxed a little. Rachel's words rang true to her because she had seen her in action. After all, she and Ray almost lost their very lives because of Rachel. The bullet missed Ray by a hair and Rachel beat her to an inch of her life. Suddenly realizing they had something in common, Susan felt better about exposing her horrible secret. She was confident Rachel would keep her secret. She just needed a little push.

"I admit, I thought about shooting him a time or two," she honestly said. "He hurt me so bad I often wished he were dead!"

"But he is dead, isn't he?" Rachel said as she stared straight into her eyes. Then she went out on a limb.

"You are the one who shot him! Didn't you?" Susan balled up her fist and jammed it between her teeth. She gnawed on it and rocked back and forth with her eyes singed with tears.

"He betrayed me," she sobbed. "I couldn't stand it anymore! I had his gun in my lap, and before I knew it, he was dead on the floor! I...I am so sorry! So very, very sorry!" Inwardly shocked, Rachel fought to keep her emotions in check by maintaining a straight face. She suspected Susan all along even when everyone else including her husband didn't.

Now faced with the truth, she knew she must notify the police, but she was conflicted. She understood why Susan did it. The act of betrayal could send anyone over the edge. She collapsed in her chair, feeling mentally drained. Susan, realizing she just confessed to murder, kneeled on her knees in front of Rachel and clasped her hands together.

"Pleasssse, don't call the police," she pleaded. "Don't you think I suffered enough?" The vein in Rachel's forehead popped out as her anxiety took over.

"Susan, you murdered him," she whispered leaning in closer to her. "I have to call them. It's the law."

"They will rape me in jail, I just know it!" She sobbed being dramatic. "Please don't call them!"

"Susan, get up!" She hissed in a strained voice. "You are going to bring attention to yourself!" Susan shied away and returned to her seat. She tried again to convince Rachel, playing on her guilt.

"Look, you almost killed Ray yourself when he cheated on you," she reminded her getting desperate. "You know what it's like to be cheated on! You know what this feels like!"

Rachel was even more conflicted and disturbed. The woman was right. She was no stranger to the sting of betrayal. How could she notify the police on Susan when she, herself faced the same dilemma many moons ago? Was she losing her mind? It felt like she was. She tried to rationalize the situation but to no avail. She knew Doctor George Benny was a scoundrel, and a manipulative, narcissistic horny jerk. She knew ultimately, someone was going to kill him for his cheating ways, but she never banked on Susan doing it.

Maybe she could help Susan get off somehow. She just needed time to help her find a decent lawyer. A nervous wreck, she reluctantly accepted Susan's request for the time being.

"Let me think about it," she whispered. "I'm not making any promises. I'll hold off telling the police for now."

"Thank you, thank you, thank you," Susan said feeling relieved. Rachel stood up on her feet.

"We will talk later," she promised.

"Okay," Susan said.

Rachel left the dining room with a burden on her shoulders. A burden she didn't ask for but accepted. She identified with Susan. She couldn't help herself. They were kindred spirits, so to speak, she reasoned. Now obligated to keep a horrible secret, she sighed, feeling emotionally weighed down.

"What have I done?" She repeatedly asked herself. "What have I done?!"

When Rachel returned to her office, she found Sally waiting for her by the door.

"What's up?" She said.

"Have you heard the news?"

"Heard what news?" Rachel asked still reeling over Susan's confession.

"There's a big staff meeting tomorrow," Sally said looking ecstatic. "They are going to tell us why the patients died!"

"Really?" Rachel said with her eyes widening. "That sure was quick!"

"I'll say," Sally agreed. Rachel unlocked her door and went inside her office with Sally following behind her.

Before Sally could shut the door well, Betty Jo barged in and shoved the door in her face.

"Ouch, that hurt!" Sally yelled. "Are you trying to kill me?!"

"Sorry," Betty Jo apologized. "I didn't see you!" Sally rubbed her forehead, wincing in pain.

"Are you alright over there?" Rachel asked looking concerned.

"I'll live," Sally said stumbling to the sofa. She sat down with a dazed look on her face. Betty Jo immediately felt guilty. She sat next to her and apologized again with genuine concern.

"Sorry about that," she said.

"No problem," Sally said.

"So, what's up?" Rachel asked.

"I came by to tell you something," Betty Jo said with urgency in her voice.

"And what is that?" Rachel asked raising an eyebrow.

"It's about the meeting tomorrow? Isn't it?" Sally politely interrupted.

"Yeah," Betty Jo said. "I heard they have a crack in the case."

"Me too," Sally said. "I wonder what they found out."

"I can tell you," Cathy said suddenly appearing in the doorway.

"Then come in here and tell us," Rachel said waving her in. Cathy stepped inside and shuts the door. She flopped in a chair and crossed her legs.

"Okay, we are all ears," Rachel excitedly said taking a seat at her desk.

"Doctor Poppy has informed me, ground privileges are temporarily suspended until the investigation is completed," she said.

"Why?" Sally asked raising both eyebrows.

Cathy sucked in air, bucking her eyes, and then she pursed her lips letting it all out.

"Are you guys ready to hear this?"

"Cut the suspense and tell us," Rachel huffed getting inpatient.

"Okay, don't be so bitchy!" Cathy retorted. Rachel gave her the stink eye and dismissed her comment with a wave.

"Just get on with it," she said.

"Well ladies, the lab results came back with strychnine and weed in the patients' systems," she said in a low voice. Sally's face dropped.

"My goodness, how did strychnine get in their system?" She asked looking confused.

"Doctor Poppy believes a drug dealer is selling weed laced with the stuff," Cathy said.

"I can see it from her vantage point," Betty Jo said looking introspective.

"Me too," Rachel said.

"Well, I don't!" Cathy angrily said with an ugly look on her face.

"Why?" Sally asked wrinkling her brow.

"I believe Doctor Poppy gave those patients strychnine," Cathy charged. "She is so creepy, and she has weird habits!" Rachel looked troubled.

"Oh, come on," she said. "Get real! Nobody believes that nonsense!"

"I second that," Betty Jo agreed.

"Me too," Sally said, very annoyed.

"That's my opinion," Cathy insisted not letting up.

Betty Jo exploded. "Damn it, you just don't like the woman! You just say anything to ruin her reputation!"

"Calm down, it's just an opinion," Cathy said with her face turning three shades of red.

"A damn wrong one," Betty Jo shot back glaring at her. Cathy felt tears coming on.

"Sorry, I....I... didn't mean..." Rachel cuts her off.

"Don't say another word, you hear me?!" She said with her temper flaring. A hush came over the room. A deafening silence. Cathy, realizing she made an awful mistake finally spoke with great remorse.

"Look I am sorry! I have been unfair to Doctor Poppy, I must admit. I am ashamed of myself!"

"You should be," Sally angrily interjected. "She may be weird, but she's not the kind to hurt anyone intentionally."

"Why you hate her so much anyway?" Rachel asked looking genuinely concerned.

"She's always tattling on me," she tearfully shared.

"Well if you do your damn job, you won't have to worry about her tattling on you," Betty Jo clipped, showing her no mercy. Cathy kept her cool despite her overwhelming urge to punch Betty Jo in the face. Instead, she stood tall and declared.

"I think I better go." No one said a word or tried to stop her as she headed toward the door. She opened the door and then turned to face them.

"I'm really sorry for what it's worth," she said. Then she walked out slamming the door behind her.

"She's hateful," Rachel said.

"Wicked more like it," said Betty Jo. Sally wrinkled up her face.

"Uh-oh, there's that crease between your brow," Rachel observed. "It comes out when you are anxious about something," she said.

"My gut tells me something is not right with that woman," Sally said still looking at the door.

"What woman?" Betty Jo asked.

"Cathy silly," she said. "I can't put my finger on it, but there's something very evil about her!"

"I have that same feeling," Betty Jo agreed. Rachel tried to be level-headed.

"Let's not jump to conclusions," she said. "My mother always told me the truth will come out in the wash."

"Your mother is right!" Betty Jo said.

Ethan Poppy had gone home for the evening, and Cathy who managed to talk maintenance into giving her a key to the doctor's office, quietly unlocked the door. She tiptoed inside and carefully shut the door behind her. She stood there in complete darkness as she fumbled around in her shirt pockets for her flashlight. Across the room, she heard Ethan's pet rats running inside a Ferris wheel, and she switched on her flashlight shining it directly on the cage.

The rats froze in place, stunned by the light, and their beady eyes looked like shiny little black dots. She hurried over to the cage and reached in her shirt pocket. She pulled out a small bag of white powder and shook it. She opened the cage and reached inside, grabbing a large piece of lettuce.

One of the rats clamped down on the vegetable setting off a tug a war. Then the lettuce tore apart leaving a significant portion in Cathy's fingers. She snatched it from the cage and laid it on the table. She then pried the plastic bag opened and sprinkled white powder on the lettuce. She placed the lettuce inside the cage and clicked the door shut. Instantly, the rats tore into the lettuce. Each one taking a piece and then scrambling to separate corners inside the cage. They nibbled on the vegetable while Cathy looked on with wicked amusement.

"Die you little rascals!" She cackled to herself. "Tomorrow, your momma is going to lose her freaking mind!"

CHAPTER TWENTY-THREE

The next day, Tuesday morning, Ethan flew through the lobby in her orange high-top tennis shoes. She had a satchel in one hand and a bag of carrots and lettuce in the other. Every morning around six, she would faithfully feed her pet rats, never missing a meal. She forgot to take the little critters home with her the night before. She was too exhausted to return to her office once she discovered she had left them there.

She entered the unit through a side door and sprinted down the hall to her office. She dropped her bags and unlocked the door. She flicked on the light switch and went inside. Immediately she sensed something was wrong. Her office was eerily quiet and very still. Her violet eyes wandered across the room, and her face turned a ghostly white. Her beloved pet rats were lying on their backs, stiff as boards, with their feet balled up into little knots. Heartbroken, she dropped to her knees and cried like a baby.

An hour later, Cathy found Ethan Poppy in her office with her head buried in her arms, bawling like a small child. Now feeling emboldened, a wicked smile appeared on her face. She tried to muster up some half-hearted sympathy to deflect guilt away from herself.

"What's the matter with you?" She asked with a hint of evil sarcasm in her voice. Ethan raised her head with her eyes burning red.

"My furry friends are gone!" She sobbed pointing at the cage and shaking her head. She wailed loud irritating Cathy.

"Are you kidding me?!" She hissed. "You are pissing over some damn rats?! Get over yourself!" Rachel overheard Cathy ridiculing the doctor while passing by her office. She stopped and poked her head inside.

"What's going on in here?!" She asked looking wide-eyed. She took one look at Ethan Poppy and immediately she became concerned.

"Who died?"

"My rats," Ethan sobbed. "My poor little babies!"

Rachel and Cathy exchanged quick glances and Rachel, trying hard not to break out in wild laughter, walked inside and closed the door. She looked in on the dead rodents and in her most sincere voice she said,

"I am so sorry this happened. I know they were very dear to you."

"Stop being ridiculous," Cathy said rolling her eyes with a hint of a giggle in her throat. "Who cries over dead rats?!" Rachel inwardly agreed with her, but was put off by Cathy's lack of empathy.

"You are so mean sometimes! When pets die, people grieve over them," she said under her breath.

"Okay, here we go," Cathy said pushing for an argument. "Blaming me for such foolishness!"

"Oh, don't you play the victim with me!" Rachel said clenching her teeth. "I'm not going to stand for it!"

"Okay Miss Perfect, but you are not going to chastise me either!" She huffed. She pounded on the cage. "Getting upset over some dead ass rats is just plain ridiculous!"

"You are heartless! It's like you have no soul!" Rachel charged. "What's wrong with you?!"

"What's wrong with you?!" said Cathy bucking her eyes. Ethan couldn't take it anymore. She popped out of her chair like a jack in the box and yelled,

"Both of you shut up and get the hell out of my office! I need peace and quiet!" Rachel and Cathy looked at each other. Shocked by the doctor's outburst. Ethan continued her assault.

"That's right! I said it! Get the hell out!"

"Okay," Rachel quietly said feeling very insulted. She stormed to the door with Cathy right on her heels.

"If you need anything, let us know," she said. Ethan didn't answer. She folded her arms and turned her back on the two women. When they left the doctor's office, they stood in the hall giving each other dirty looks and then they stormed down the hall in opposite directions without saying a word.

Twenty minutes later, a deep, masculine voice rumbled over the loudspeaker announcing a staff meeting in the conference room. The loud sound woke Mark up out of a deep alcoholic slumber. He had been living in his office since Betty Jo kicked him out two weeks ago. July Fourth was just a few days away, and he was hoping to return home for the holiday.

He frowned just thinking about it. Wondering how he could convince her to allow him back home. He yawned like a lion and ran his fingers through his thick blonde mane. He felt stiff, stretching his arms and legs to relieve the discomfort. Then a deep voice rumbled over the loudspeaker again.

"Another meeting?!" He groaned. "What in the hell is it this time?!" He sat up and reached for his cane. He hurled himself up too fast, and the room flipped upside down making him dizzy. He fell back on the sofa, and his head spun. A throbbing pain pulsated deep in his temple, and he rubbed his forehead hard. He laid back down and groaned.

"The hell with this meeting! I'm staying here!"

Everyone piled into the conference room, talking loudly amongst themselves as they searched for seats to sit down. Most of the doctors were there except for Mark and Ethan, and no one inquired about them either. Two nurses fought over chairs near the conference table.

"Give it up brother. I was here first!" One male nurse said to another.

"I don't see your name written on this seat," said the nurse inspecting the chair with a cheap grin. An argument ensued as several nurses sitting around them looked on in amusement. Soon Beth came in and made her way over to Doctor Louis. She sat next to him, and with synchronized coordination, the two of them lit up a cigarette. Soon the room turned into a smothering gray haze; and the smoke was so intense, several nurses and social workers moved to the other side of the room. Clueless, Michael and Beth kept puffing away. Occasionally they would reach underneath their seat and grab their coffee mug. The mug was filled with Mad Dog whiskey in place of Starbucks coffee. They sipped on it off and on, and before long their whole demeanor changed.

Their faces turned red and bloated, and their eyes became bloodshot and glassy. Their drunken appearance didn't escape two nurses who were sitting two rows behind them.

"They are so freaking rude!" One nurse boldly said, with her voice loud, trying to get their attention.

"Look at their eyes. They look toasted!" Said the other nurse checking them out.

"I'm not surprised," the nurse candidly responded. "The two of them spend all of their free time smoking and drinking at Sully's after work almost every day!"

"Are they fukernuking?!" One nurse asked with big round eyes.

"Ewe!" The other nurse replied. "I hope not!"

"Well, she's always around him," she said.

"I think they are just drinking buddies. Besides he has a young wife," the nurse shared.

"What does that have to do with it?" The other nurse said.

"I just think he prefers his women young," she clarified. The nurses giggled out loud shaking their heads.

Soon Holly B came in and sat on a seat in front of the room. She noticed her father and winked at him. He was sitting on the floor with his legs crisscrossed in a nearby corner picking his nose. Rachel, Betty Jo, Cathy and Sally finally arrived, taking seats against the back wall. Rona Berry, a patient on the second floor, slipped in unnoticed. She was a small woman, almost dwarf-like, with sad blue eyes and red hair tied up in big pigtails. She sat on the floor, not far from Hiram.

Doctor Beebe whizzed in precisely at ten-thirty with Thomas Marshall by his side.

"What's he doing here?" One social worker asked another as the chief took a seat in front next to Holly B.

"Something is going on," another social worker observed. Doctor Beebe reached for the mike and adjusted it. The mike squealed, and the staff covered their ears. Then he blew on the mike and yelled.

"Testing, testing, testing!" Michael, irritated by the noise, shot straight out of his seat.

"Alrighttttttt, already! The damn thing is working! Let's get this show on the road!" He screamed slurring his words. Carl's expression was tense. He would like to ram his wheelchair right into Michael Louis, but he managed to stay put and keep his cool. He began the meeting, focusing on his agenda, as he took a deep breath.

"Good Morning," he dryly said.

"Good Morning!" Everyone responded in unison.

"I called this meeting to give you an update on the investigation surrounding our patients' deaths. But first, I want to introduce you to our investigator, Holly B Presley," he proudly announced extending his hand in her direction. Holly B stood up and faced the crowd. With her cheeks rosy pink, she was embarrassed by the attention. She half-heartedly waved and sat down.

"A shy one, isn't she?" Sally noticed.

"She sure is," Rachel agreed.

"Yesterday the lab results came back, and we discovered something irregular," Doctor Beebe said. "It appears the patients had strychnine and marijuana in their system." Loud whispers broke out around the room and Carl clapped his hands.

"Quiet please," he yelled. "Let me finish!" The whispers died down, and everyone gave him their full attention.

"We believe there may be a drug dealer out there, lacing marijuana with strychnine," he informed them. Everyone around the room groaned with disgust. A male social worker stood and asked.

"Doctor Beebe, do you know who it is?"

"Not yet," Carl replied. "However, in the meantime, we will protect our patients by suspending ground privileges."

"Shit!" Cathy blurted out unintentionally. Everyone turned to face her. Their eyes bored into her as they waited for another response. She slouched down in her seat, red in the face, wishing she could disappear.

"Sorry, it just slipped," she mumbled. "Don't mind me." Beth glowered at her from across the room, and Cathy shielded her eyes with one hand. Gradually everyone took their eyes off her and refocused their attention back to Doctor Beebe. He made a half-hearted attempt to lighten the mood.

"If you see any weirdos lurking around selling weed, please notify me as soon as possible," he joked. Everyone cracked up except for Cathy. She was too embarrassed to look up. Sally, blinking her eyes like a peacock, stood up and asked a question.

"Any word on Robert Harris?"

"He's still missing," Carl sadly revealed. "He hasn't been seen for three weeks."

"So, what are the police doing about it?" Thomas sprang to his feet in an instant with his hand gripped tight on his forty-five. He was an average-looking man with a pot belly and receding hairline. He took long strides to the podium.

His expressive hazel brown eyes peered over the crowd with intense scrutiny. Carl handed him the mike.

"Let me address this," he said.

"Be my guest," Carl said as he gestured for him to proceed.

"The investigation into Robert's disappearance is ongoing," he said. "We will keep looking for him until he is found," he promised.

"Any clues where he might be?" Sally asked showing concern.

"No, not yet," he said. "However, if you stumble upon any helpful information, please come by and see me."

Hush whispers rumbled across the room as Thomas handed Carl the mike. He returned to his seat looking straight ahead. Carl rubbed the head of the mike making a scratchy noise. The whispers died down, and he continued with the meeting.

"Does anyone have more questions?" He asked.

"I do," Betty Jo said raising her hand.

"Shoot," said Carl.

"Do you think Susan Cole killed Doctor Benny?" Everyone let out a loud sigh.

"Look I'm just posing the question," she quickly responded irritated by everyone's reaction. Thomas turned around in his seat and looked back at her.

"We are still investigating. There are no definitive answers yet," he vaguely replied. Betty Jo wasn't buying his evasive explanation.

"All of the news reports gleam her as a suspect. There must be some truth to it," she insisted.

"Again, we are still investigating. That's all I can say right now," Thomas said. Rachel poked Betty Jo on the small of her back.

"Girl, sit down and stop embarrassing yourself," she whispered. Betty Jo slowly took her seat.

"Don't you want to know if she's guilty or not?" She said.

"Let the police do their work," Rachel calmly said. "We will know in due time. She is innocent until proven guilty. Let's not jump to conclusions just yet." Betty Jo gave Rachel a wary look. Wondering why the sudden change of heart.

"You are the one who thought she may be guilty," she reminded her. "Have you changed your mind?"

"I just want the police to do their job," she replied avoiding the question.

"How admirable," Betty Jo smirked not buying Rachel's explanation. She decided to drop the subject despite her suspicions. Right before the meeting adjourned, Harvey, a social worker, who is a tall, muscular man with a shiny bald head and a thick dark mustache sprung to his feet. His expression was intense, and his dark brown eyes shined through large wire-frame glasses. When he spoke, he told it like it was.

"Sir, I have a question!" He said with authority.

"Go ahead, I'm listening," said Doctor Beebe.

"There's a sign hanging in the patient lounge directing patients to call the Mental Health Asses Team if feeling suicidal. Why on earth are we directing our suicidal patients to call a bunch of assholes for help?!" Everyone roared. Doctor Beebe's face turned four shades of red and steam came out of his ears.

220

"It's a typo Harvey! It's supposed to read Mental Health Assessment Team! I'll make sure it's corrected!" He said with a strain in his voice.

"Well good! I was beginning to think I needed to find another job. I certainly didn't want to be on a donkey's team!" Everyone fell out laughing. Rachel was doubled over in hysterics with tears streaming down her face. Doctor Beebe twisted his face up. He was furious at Harvey.

"You made your point! Thank you!" He said. Satisfied his question was answered, Harvey strolled out of the room waving as he exited. Doctor Beebe, feeling exhausted, finally adjourned the meeting. Everyone piled out of the conference room back to their work areas. On the way to her office, Rachel ran into little Rona Berry who deliberately stepped in her way.

"Need to tell you something," she said, with her voice urgent, and her words broken and disjointed. Rachel grabbed her hand and ushered her to the side.

"Rona, what is it?"

"Harris……high heel man," Rona said shaking one hand.

"You mean Robert Harris?" Rachel clarified. Rona nodded her head. Her face tormented.

"Yes," she replied.

"What about Robert?" Rachel asked leaning closer.

"Man, by tunnel," she said jumping up and down. "Man goes into tunnel!"

"You saw him?"

"Yes," Rona replied nodding her head up and down.

"How long ago?" Rachel asked looking tense.

"Know don't," she said shaking her head with watery eyes.

"Man, still there," she said wringing her hands. Rachel, recognizing her discomfort, held off asking any more questions. She hugged Rona who was trembling in her arms.

"Don't worry," she reassured her. "Everything is going to be okay." Rona looked up at Rachel with sad blue eyes.

"Cat in tunnel too," she told her. "Big cat, gold eyes!" Rachel's eyes grew big as saucers.

"Where is this tunnel?"

"Right here," Rona said pointing to the ground. "Right here!"

"The hospital?" Rachel asked with a crease in her forehead. Rona shook her head up and down. Rachel held Rona's chin and said.

"Listen, let's keep this between us. Can you promise me you will do that?" Rona nodded her head vigorously in agreement.

"Good," Rachel said. "Now run along!" Rona took off, skipping down the hall and Rachel with her mind all over the place quickened her step and hurried to Betty Jo's office.

"Peepers and Robert Harris in a tunnel? Right here on the grounds? I got to tell somebody about this," she said.

CHAPTER TWENTY-FOUR

Rachel heard soft mumbling behind the door in Betty Jo's office. She knocked three times, and no one answered. Frustrated, she opened the door and invited herself inside.

"Didn't you hear me knocking?" She asked looking crossed.

"My, my, aren't we impatient?" Betty Jo responded with a gleam in her eye.

"Well I knocked several times, and you just ignored me," Rachel quipped not at all amused.

"Poor baby," Betty Jo grinned. "Come in and rest yourself. It's not that serious my friend." Rachel was peeved.

"Not funny!" She sat down on the sofa next to Holly B. The detective sat straight like an arrow with her unruly blonde hair tangled in a mop. Rachel noticed her rigid posture.

"Tense?" She said.

"No, not really," Holly B replied scooting back on the sofa. "I guess I am always on edge," she answered dryly. She crossed her ankles and started cracking her knuckles.

"Well you're the person I need to see," Rachel said. "I have some interesting info to tell you!" Holly B raised an eyebrow.

"Oh, you do? What do you have?"

"Apparently, there is a tunnel on the hospital grounds," Rachel said. "A patient told me about it. She told me Robert Harris might be hiding there." Holly B flipped opened her notebook and jotted down notes.

"Where is this tunnel exactly?!"

"I really don't know," Rachel said. "But, it's on campus somewhere, and it should be investigated."

"I most definitely agree," Holly B nodded as her hazel eyes grew larger behind her prescription glasses.

"The patient, what's her name?"

"Rona Berry," Rachel said.

"Can she tell me where this tunnel is?" Holly B asked.

"I think so," she said. Rachel paused a moment. Then she made a point.

"I need to be there when you question Rona. She is fearful of people she doesn't know very well."

"Will do," Holly B said slamming her notebook shut. She hurried to the door and looked back at Rachel.

"Let's go talk to her," she said.

"Right," Rachel said. Holly B opened the door and ran out with Rachel right behind her. "See you later girl! I got bigger fish to fry!" Betty Jo sighed.

"Good Luck!" She hollered after them. "You are going to need it!"

Mark Brewer wandered by Betty Jo's office, on his way to the cafeteria. He lingered there a moment and ran his slender fingers through his thick blonde mane. He hesitated a minute and then he tapped timidly on the door.

"Come in," said a weak voice. He sighed deeply and then he opened the door. Betty Jo was mortified when she realized it was him. Twisting her face like a prune, she spoke with furor in her voice.

"What do you want?"

"I was just passing by. Thought you might want to join me for lunch," he said ignoring her terse tone with him. Betty Jo tore into him with daggers in her eyes.

"Really?!" She said. "After you embarrassed me the other night at Sully's?! I don't think so!" He stepped inside shutting the door.

"Look I am sorry about that," he apologized. "Please forgive me! It wasn't my intent to embarrass you...I was....

"DRUNK!" Betty Jo shouted in his face. "JUST ADMIT IT! PLAIN DRUNK!" With his eyes cast down to the floor, his shoulders caved in.

"I was drunk, and I am ashamed of that," he said.

"You should be!"

"I know! I'm really sorry," he apologized again. "What can I do to make this up to you?"

"Go to alcohol treatment," she immediately said. "That's how you can make it up to me!"

"Okay, but can I come home first?" He asked. "I'm tired of sleeping in my office." She loved watching him squirm but coming home, not so much.

"No, you can't," she said with little pity in her voice refusing to give in. "Stop being cheap and get yourself a hotel!" He immediately bristled up, and she braced herself for a brutal fight.

"Who do you think you are telling me I can't come back to my own house?!" He childishly argued. "I'm coming back, and you are not going to stop me!"

"Well, you won't be able to get in the house," she flippantly informed him not batting an eye. "I had the locks changed!"

Her cruel words sent him back on his heels, and for a few minutes, he stood there speechless. She knew she had hurt him. It was written all over his face. Feeling guilty, she softened her tone, but her voice struggled to engage. Trying to find the right words and fearing her effort may not be enough.

"Mark, I'm not trying to be mean," she said with a hoarse voice. "I just can't take your drinking anymore. I want you in alcohol treatment, and then you can come home." At first, she saw the recognition of remorse on his face and then his eyes turned icy cold. When he finally spoke, his voice was harsh and cold.

"You are right! I think this is over. Once I find me a place to live, we can file for divorce. The house is yours." Then he stormed out, leaving her alone with her thoughts. Shaken to the core. Tears flooded her eyes. The thought of her marriage ending like this never once occurred to her. She sank back in her chair, frozen and unable to move. Despair crept over her, and she sat there for hours and hours. Soon the evening came, and she finally left her office and went home.

Meanwhile, on the admissions unit, Susan hurried down the hall to Rachel's office. Fresh off a bruising nightmare and another interview with the police chief, Thomas Marshall, she had it. Completely stressed out, it felt like her insides were ripping apart. George Benny's murder continued to haunt her. Short-circuiting her brain, making her crazy, and tearing her apart. Within minutes she was in front of Rachel's office, and she pounded on the door. Her eyes swam with tears when she received no response. Again, she banged on the door, and still no answer.

Then she kicked it, cursing. "Damn it, Rachel! Where are you?!"

"Can I help you?" A voice came from behind her. She spun around, and Cathy was standing there looking quite amused.

"Is there a problem?" She asked.

"I... I...I was looking for Rachel," Susan stuttered feeling embarrassed. "I'm sorry, I didn't mean..."

"It's okay," Cathy said cutting her off. "You looked like you are having a panic attack," she said examining her face. "Do you want to talk?"

"No, no, no, I'm fine," Susan said looking dazed. Cathy knew she was lying. She could see it on her face.

"I am happy to sit with you and talk," she offered.

"No, I rather wait for Rachel," Susan insisted. "If you see her, please tell her to come by my room."

"Sure," Cathy said. Susan took off disappearing around the corner.

"Who spooked the hell out of her?" Cathy wondered as she continued down the hall.

"I'm coming," yelled Rachel, as she stumbled along the grassy lawn trying to keep up with Holly B. The detective, on a mission, was speed-walking across campus leaving poor Rachel in the dust. The sky, morphing into a nasty, gray color was threatening rain, and a splash of water dropped on Holly B's cheek. She broke out into a light jog and hollered.

"Hurry up! It's going to rain! I don't want to get wet!"

"Don't worry," Rachel said glancing up at the dark gray sky, huffing and puffing and out of breath. "We are almost there!"

"I'm glad Rona remembered where this place was," Holly B said hiking down a small hill.

"Me too," Rachel said as she finally caught up with her. Soon they reached the tunnel entrance. They strained their eyes to see down the tube-like structure, with the inside dark as night. With fear in her eyes, Rachel hesitated to go in.

"I hope you have a flashlight," she said with a slight tremor in her voice. Holly B cracked a smile.

"I sure do," she said pulling a flashlight from the back pocket of her jeans. She flicked it on and stepped forward, aiming it into the darkness. The light lit up the massive structure exposing foliage, graffiti on the concrete walls and garbage on the concrete floor. Twigs, rotten food, dead rodents and birds floated in puddles of water on the concrete paved floor. Holly B sighed and braced herself as she looked at Rachel. She stood there with her hands in her pockets, with eyes twinkling like shiny black marbles.

"Are you ready?" She asked. "You look scared!"

"I'm not scared!" Rachel said looking indignant. "Let's go. What are we waiting for?!"

"Then follow me!" Holly B took off with Rachel following behind her. Thunder clapped in a distance and pelts of water beat down on the tunnel. They ran through the tunnel like a couple of demons. Their steps echoed in the dark bouncing off the concrete walls. The walls vibrated every time the thunder clapped, and a stream of water rushed along the side of the tunnel in a nearby ditch. The stench of decaying rodents and fowl assaulted their nostrils, and Rachel gagged.

"I can't take the smell! It's so nauseating!" She yelled. Holly B didn't answer. She was too focused and intense. Jerking the flashlight back and forth, searching for clues. There was a footprint here, knee prints over there and then she noticed a dried, bloody handkerchief embedded in a crack on the pavement. She ran over and shined the light on it, studying it. The handkerchief, stained with dried blood, had the initials "RH" emblazoned on it.

"This handkerchief may be Robert's," she whispered. "From the look of things, he suffered a fall."

"Oh my, I hope he's alright," Rachel said looking worried as she stooped down to get a closer look. "Those are his initials alright," she said feeling uneasy. A flash of light caught Holly B's attention.

"What was that?"

"I don't know," Rachel said with her heart beating fast. Again, the light flickered, and this time it exposed an outline to a door a few yards ahead. Holly B aimed her flashlight on it.

"That's a door! I wonder what's behind there." Wasting no time, she took off running. Shining the light in front of her as she hopped over puddles of water.

"Wait for me!" Rachel hollered scared out of her wits. She raced after her and screamed when a big black cat with yellow eyes ran in her path-breaking her speed. She stopped and stared at the cat.

"Peepers!" She shouted. The cat stared back at her for a moment as if he recognized her. Then it darted off disappearing into the darkness.

Spooked, she took off, huffing and puffing, running through puddles of water with the liquid splashing on her pants. She collided with Holly B, and the two women fell on the wet, muddy pavement in front of the black door. Immediately they both struggled to their feet.

"Ewe!" Rachel screamed. "It stinks like a latrine!" The decaying odor of rotten flesh took their breath away, and they recoiled, backing up.

"There's something dead behind that door," Holly B grunted. She grabbed her flashlight and aimed it at the door. Mud dripped off their clothing as they stood there, shivering, staring at the black door. They were too scared to move.

"Are you going in there?" Rachel finally asked with her teeth chattering from anticipation.

"I have to," Holly B whispered. She reached inside her jacket and brought out her pistol.

"Stay here," she said.

"No problem." Rachel was glad she didn't have to go with her. She stepped to the side giving the detective room. Holly B raised her foot and kicked the door open. A rotten stench slapped them both in the face, and they jumped back.

"Geeze, that's awful!" Holly B said.

"You don't have to tell me," Rachel gagged plugging her nose. Holly B jammed her pistol in her back pocket and jerked the flashlight up and down. With her stomach in knots, she entered the room without hesitation. She glanced at the ceiling. The lightbulb swung back and forth, flickering in and out, giving the place a spooky, creepy feeling.

She ventured further in and noticed the backside of a large human being slumped in a chair by a wood desk. She moved closer in, adjusting the flashlight to a higher beam. Then she noticed a satchel hanging off the arm of the chair. Her eyes wandered to the desk. The burnt butt of a marijuana joint was lying on a pile of bloodstained alcohol wipes, and two inches from there was a pair of bloodied scissors. Her eyes then dropped to the floor, and there was a dried patch of crusty black blood. She swallowed hard and spun around, shining the light directly on the human figure. She recoiled in horror when she laid eyes on him. His body rigid like a rod. His hazel eyes, smeared with black mascara, stared back at her. His knit dress was soiled with dried blood, and she screamed panting in short breaths. Rachel ran to her aid.

"What's the matter?!" She squealed. When she saw Robert Harris for the first time in three weeks, her knees buckled, and it felt like she was about to faint. She tried to speak, but no words came out. Gripped tight in his right hand was a pair of bloodied metal clippers and his knit black dress, reeked with the smell of old blood. He sat there with his legs propped open. His fishnet stockings twisted around his ankles and he still had on his red high heel shoes. On the floor, white maggots crawled on a bloodied heap of hard flesh, his genitals smeared on the concrete floor. The rancid odor was too much for them, and they both threw up. Holly B wiped her lips with her coat sleeve, and words of shock rushed from her lips at once.

"In all my years, I never have in my career witnessed anything like this!"

"Me either!" Rachel said as she wiped away tears.

CHAPTER TWENTY-FIVE

Robert Harris was gone. The story around the hospital was the man killed himself. Setting off a media firestorm throughout the town. When the news broke, Ethan just lost it. Staying in her coffin for a total of three days, and not answering her phone. As hard as it was for her to accept, Robert Harris died under her watch. A reality she had to embrace. A career disaster she never thought she would face. By the time Friday, July Fourth rolled around, she had hired Sugar Foot Kent. She knew her career was on the line and she needed to do everything possible to save it. As for Robert's wife, Ginger, she too had hired an attorney. Every day her angry, bloated face would appear on KIRO news television adding more drama to the already media frenzy.

Rachel, recovering from the shock of Robert's death, also took refuge in her bed. Curled up under the covers in a fetal position, plagued by nightmares and exhaustion. Every night, like clockwork, she would wake up from a brutal nightmare. The dream, always the same, like a replay in a horror flick. The dark gray sky beckoning rain, the thunder clapping in a distant, the rain pelting down on the dark tunnel, dead rodents and birds floating in puddles, the flashing light, Peepers, the smell of rotting flesh and then him. His six-foot, four-inch frame slumped in a chair. Caked in blood from the waist down. His rotting genitals on the floor immersed in a dried patch of black blood covered with slithering white maggots. The grisly image a permanent imprint in her fragile state of mind.

Holly B, Betty Jo, Sally, Beth, and Cathy have all called several times and left messages, but she didn't feel like talking. She could barely speak to Everett about it, preferring to focus on Peepers instead. However, her refusal to talk about it had created distance between them. A situation she had not counted on. Then there was Susan. Susan Cole. Her arch rival. Susan's horrible secret weighed on her. It gnawed on her conscience, making her feel guilty. Susan sent messages through Everett out of desperation, requesting she come see her, but she refused to do so. She already knew why Susan needed to see her. She knew she had a decision to make and it wouldn't bode well for Susan. Everett grew more and more suspicious as time went by. He questioned her many times, but she refused to disclose any details.

Several times, she thought about telling him the truth, but each time she would talk herself out of it. She wasn't ready to deal with his disappointment once he learned the horrible secret. George Benny was his friend, his colleague. A fellow graduate from the same medical school. Harvard University. She knew she must tell him, but when? She scooted further down on the bed feeling more and more guilty. Despite those feelings, she was determined to keep Susan's horrific crime to herself. Then she heard Everett and Jamie Lee stirring in the next room, and a few minutes later, there was silence. Suddenly the door opened and slammed against the wall. Quick, hard footsteps approached the bed and then halted. The blanket covering her half-naked body was snatched off, and she sat straight up.

"What the hell are you doing?" She screamed only wearing her red lacy panties.

"It's time to stop moping," Everett said looking serious. "Time to join the land of the living baby girl!"

"You are a psychiatrist! Don't you have any empathy for what I am going through?! What's wrong with you?!" She reached for the blanket and tried to snatch it from him. He whipped it out of her reach.

"Oh no you don't, baby doll! It's time to get up! The self-pity party is over! We need to talk!" She was peeved, but she knew he was right.

"Go to hell," she yelled as she scooted out of bed. She ran to the bathroom. "You make me sick!" He whistled and clapped.

"That's my girl," he hollered after her. "Take a shower while you are at it! You smell a little ripe this morning!"

"Go to hell!" She screamed again, her voice muffled behind the door. A minute later, a rush of water beats against the shower wall, and he sighed with relief.

July Fourth, at twelve noon, Betty Jo sat on her deck enjoying a can of coke with her mind on Mark. She wondered if he was drunk somewhere celebrating the holiday. She hadn't seen or heard from him since their blow up three days ago, and she was worried about him. Although divorce seemed imminent, she still had trouble believing her marriage was over. They were married for fifteen years. A long time for most unions. She thought about looking for him but dismissed the thought. Until he addresses his alcohol problem, their marriage was doomed. Four hundred miles away, in a town called Port Townsend, Mark Brewer laid on his bunk in a rehab center, taking a break between AA meetings.

He checked himself in three days ago after his fight with Betty Jo. Facing divorce, he now realized Betty Jo was serious about him seeking treatment. She had never changed the locks on him before and the fact she did bothered him. He had taken her for granted and deep down inside, he knew he had forced her hand. Doctor Beebe, after hearing his story, approved his request for time off. Promising to keep the reason for his absence and whereabouts a secret. So, here he was, in a six-month rehab program, trying to get his life on track. He knew the road would be tough, but he was up for the ride. He was determined to get sober for himself and his wife. So, while he sat there, he decided to write her a letter. When he finished, he felt a lot better.

Rachel, now dressed and out of the shower, was sitting at the kitchen table fuming again. Everett was preparing her a late breakfast, and Jamie Lee was taking a nap. Although she appreciated the gesture, she preferred to be curled up in bed and shut out from the world. However, her dear psychiatrist husband wasn't having it.

"Talk to me baby girl," he demanded, with his face serious. She flashed him a dirty look and then snapped him up.

"What's there to talk about?!" Knowing full well there was plenty to discuss.

"Come on! Get Real! How are you doing?"

"Compared to who?"

"Don't get smart!" He said getting irritated. "Let's talk about Susan," he said. "She's been asking about you."

"So, you keep telling me."

"What does she want with you?" He asked.

She sighed, still agonizing about telling him. She knew once she did all hell would break loose.

"I have no idea," she lied. "I guess I'll check with her when I return to work in the morning."

"You do that," he said looking peeved.

"Has she talked to you about George Benny?"

"Off and on," he quietly said. "I'm still not convinced she had anything to do with his murder."

"Mmmm, interesting," Rachel said avoiding eye contact with him. He finished breakfast, and he brought her plate to the table. Two pancakes, scrambled eggs, and turkey sausage. A small feast.

"Thanks honey," she said. "You are a gem!"

"You're welcome," he said grinning from ear-to-ear. He joined her at the table and watched her dive into her meal. Then he became solemn. His demeanor was honest and frank.

"I think you need counseling baby girl."

"Huh? Where the hell did that come from?!

"A lot has happened lately. You have been through a lot. You concern me when you keep talking about Peepers. The cat is gone. Dead. You need to consider counseling," he reiterated again. Her eyes went cold, and she threw her fork on her plate.

"Damn it, I don't need any counseling! I just need you to back off!" Inwardly pissed, he stuffed down his anger, falling silent. After a while, he got up and walked out. Frustrated, she lost her appetite. She folded her arms in a huff and thought about Peepers.

"He really thinks I'm crazy, but I'll show him!" She promised herself. "He will see."

Cathy Ray spent her holiday mixing up a batch of cupcakes for Tuesday's group. Separating the batter into four bowls and then adding the food coloring. She was not looking forward to working with Ethan Poppy again, still angry about her tattling on her. She was sure Robert Harris' death would send her over the edge and permanently out the door, but even that didn't work. The more she thought about working with Ethan, the more riled up she became.

"I poisoned your patients and your pet rats, and I still can't get rid of you! Why, Why, Why?!" She fussed slamming a bowl of batter on the counter. She thought hard about another plan. Then, an hour later, an idea came to her.

"I'll make her some chocolate cupcakes to take home with her after group tomorrow! Once she eats one.......!"

She fell out laughing like a wicked witch. Then her icy cold eyes wandered to the cabinet above the sink. She reached up and yanked the door opened and took out a bottle of rat poison. She twisted the cap off and shook the poison over the batter. She mixed it up, stirring vigorously. Then the corners of her mouth curled up into a twisted grin.

"This will do the trick!" She cackled. "I can't wait!"

CHAPTER TWENTY-SIX

"Doctor Poppy, it's me! I got a surprise for you!" Cathy yelled out as she banged on the doctor's office door. Ethan yanked the door open, and she stood there looking wide-eyed.

"A surprise for me?"

"Yes ma'am," Cathy said with a wicked gleam in her eye. It was Tuesday morning, the day after the holiday, July Fourth.

"Can I come in?"

"Oh, sure," Ethan said moving to the side. Cathy struts in and places the cupcakes on the doctor's desk. Ethan's face brightened.

"Chocolate cupcakes?"

"Yes ma'am!" Cathy cheerful responded. "I know you like them. I made extra so you can take some home with you after group today!" She said smiling.

"How thoughtful!" Ethan said smiling back. Cathy bounced to the door.

"Enjoy," she hollered. "They are really good! Good enough to die for!" She was gone in an instant before Ethan could say another word. She unwrapped the cupcakes and carefully inspected them. She lifted one up to her nose and sniffed it. The sweet aroma of chocolate swept her senses, and she sighed with pure joy.

"I'll have one of these little treats with a cup of Starbucks coffee later this afternoon," she decided. "How nice of Cathy to do this for me," she beamed.

Betty Jo was thrilled when she received Mark's letter in the mail and discovered he checked himself into a rehab center over the weekend. For the first time since their separation, she had hope. Maybe their marriage will work out after all. She unlocked the door to her office and went inside. Her face lit up when she saw the plate of chocolate cupcakes on her desk.

"Chocolate, my favorite!" She proclaimed. A note was taped on top of the wrapping, and she read it to herself.

"Oh, how sweet," she said. She reached for her phone and dialed Cathy's number. It rang twice and then she answered.

"Cathy Ray here."

"This is Betty Jo. Thanks for the cupcakes," she said. "Apology accepted!"

"I know I have been a bitch lately, that's the least I can do," Cathy humbly said with a smile in her voice.

"No worries," Betty Jo said. "So how was your fourth?"

"Quiet," Cathy said. "How was yours?"

"Well, I heard from Mark," Betty Jo disclosed.

"Really?! What's he up to?"

"He checked himself into rehab! Isn't that great?!" Betty Jo said looking pleased.

"Well, it's about time," Cathy said. "I know you're happy!"

"Yes, I am," Betty Jo said. "Well, I got to go… Talk to you later." Cathy slammed the phone down, and a twisted smile appeared on her face.

"Mark in rehab and you six feet under! Now, that's a way to go!"

Rachel came at last to Susan Cole's room to talk to her.

"Where have you been?" Susan questioned her, looking very despondent.

"I have been under the weather," Rachel yawned, still not getting enough sleep.

"Did Doctor James give you my messages?"

"Yes, he did," Rachel quipped getting annoyed.

"You need to calm down!" You are going to bring suspicion on yourself!" She warned. Susan looked visibly flustered, even angry.

"So, what are you going to do? Are you going to the police?! I need......" She stopped talking, realizing the answer before Rachel responded.

"You know I have to," Rachel said feeling pressured. "I'm just trying to figure out if you have a way out of this!"

"Girl, I'm screwed!" Susan told her. "There is no way out!"

"Don't give up just yet," Rachel said. She was silent for a moment. Thinking through options. Susan misread her silence and became even angrier.

"Well I'm sorry for bothering you with this problem! But you pressured me into telling you! I didn't want to!" Rachel was quick to reassure her.

"I'm not mad at you Susan! So, stop pestering me so I can think, please!" Susan concentrated on doing her deep breathing exercises and then after she was done, she rested her chin in her hands.

"Okay. So, what can I do?" Rachel puts her finger up.

"Hold on." She sat there thinking while Susan fidgeted in her seat. Outside Susan's door, listening with great interest, was Everett. He came by to see Susan. Her therapy session was due to start in fifteen minutes. He was shocked by what he heard, but he managed to stay quiet and out of sight.

"You need to get yourself a good lawyer before you go to the police!" Rachel finally suggested. Susan clenched her teeth.

"I don't have any money for a lawyer!"

"We will find one!" Rachel snapped back. "One who will work pro bono. Then you will call the police and tell them what happened." Susan wasn't having it.

"I can't," she said. "I can't go to jail!"

"Well, the problem isn't going to just go away......."

"I know that!" Fearing the worse, Rachel decided to give her an ultimatum.

"Either you take my suggestion, or I will call the police myself! I can't keep your secret forever! My conscience won't allow me to!"

"Fine," Susan said with a stricken face. They sat without conversation for a moment, then Susan whispered.

"Will you help me find a lawyer? I have no idea who to call."

"I'll ask Hiram," Rachel said. "He probably knows a good lawyer who can take a pro bono case. In the meantime, you need to stay calm."

"Okay," Susan said. She paused for a moment.

"What?" said Rachel bucking her eyes.

"Will you go with me to the police when the time comes?".

"I sure will," Rachel sighed with relief.

"Thank you," Susan said. Everett stepped away from the door and quietly returned to his office.

Betty Jo met Rachel in the cafeteria. She grabbed a salad and joined her in line.

"Guess what? Mark checked himself into rehab last Friday," she announced. Rachel's dark brown eyes widened like a couple of saucers.

"Girl, get out of here!"

"Yes, he did, yes, he did, yes, he did," Betty Jo sang.

"Girl, that's wonderful!" Rachel said looking pleased as she paid for her turkey burger.

"So how long is the program?"

"Six months," Betty Jo said.

"Well that should get him good and sober," Rachel chuckled. The two women found a table next to a window and sat down. Betty Jo took a stab at her salad and looked over at Rachel with concern.

"How are you doing since you know what?"

"As well as one can expect considering the circumstances," Rachel sadly interrupted. She bit into her burger, chewing slowly, and then she added.

"I have cried so much over these past few days, my eyeballs feel like they are on fire!" Betty Jo laughed at Rachel's expense. She couldn't help herself.

"I'm so sorry for everything," she said. "Finding him like that is certainly a nightmare!"

"Yeah, I know," Rachel agreed fighting back the tears.

"Have you heard from Holly B?" Rachel's response was swift.

"She's holding up. She has thrown herself full speed into the investigation. She's trying to find out who the drug dealer killer is." Betty Jo looked introspective.

"I wouldn't want her job."

"Me either," Rachel agreed, finishing off her burger. Betty Jo switched subjects.

"Guess who apologized to me for being so nasty and hateful?"

"Who?"

"Cathy, the little witch herself," she revealed. Rachel cracked up laughing.

"Really? I don't believe it," she said.

"Well, believe it! She even left me a plate of chocolate cupcakes on my desk this morning along with a note," she happily exclaimed.

"Now that's nice! I didn't know she had it in her," Rachel said looking surprised.

"Neither did I," Betty Jo said. "Would you like one?"

"No girl! I just got rid of my winter fat, and now I have spring rolls. I'm trying to get back to my prettiest," she said laughing.

"Girl you are a trip!" Betty Jo chuckled.

"I know," Rachel said. They finished their lunch and headed back to their offices.

"Let's hang out at Sully's after work this evening," Betty Jo suggested.

"Cool," Rachel said. "Should we invite Cathy?" She asked putting a good foot forward. Betty Jo smiled.

"Sure, why not," she said. "A truce is a truce!"

Nine o'clock, Tuesday Evening, Rachel received a telephone call from Betty Jo. She was ill. She had been throwing up for the past hour and was unable to make it to Sully's. Rachel became concerned and urged her to go to the emergency room, but Betty Jo decided to wait, thinking her condition would improve. Rachel wished her well and then ended the call.

She called her mother and told her she no longer needed her babysitting services. Then, the two women said goodbye and hung up the phone. Then she called Cathy. There was no answer at her residence, so she left a message on the answering machine. She glanced at the clock, and it was nine-thirty. Everett would be home soon, so she decided to wait up.

She showered and then slipped into her nightgown. She tiptoed across the hall and checked on Jamie Lee. The little girl was still awake, and she was slicked down from head to toe in greasy Vaseline. She laughed despite the messy cleanup she faced. When Rachel approached her crib, Jamie Lee giggled hysterically.

"You little bugger," she chuckled swooping her out of the crib. She dashed to the bathroom and filled the tub with warm water.

"You need a bath little girl," she chuckled to herself. She immersed Jamie Lee into the warm bath water. She giggled and splashed water everywhere while her mother washed the Vaseline off her skin. Rachel laughed.

"You are making mommy very messy little girl!" She said.

Everett speeded into the driveway and parked. It was eleven o'clock, and the lights were still on in the house. He was glad Rachel was up. He needed to talk to her about her little conversation with Susan Cole. He was disappointed, even angry she kept such a horrible secret from him. Susan Cole murdered George Benny, and he still couldn't wrap his head around it. He switched off his headlights, and he maneuvered out of the car. The warm breeze felt good against his skin, and the bluish-black sky was dotted with twinkling golden lights.

The crescent-shaped moon barely illuminated the deep black sky, and it traveled slowly, soon making its way behind the house. He dragged the garbage cans onto the curb for morning pick up, his general routine on Tuesday evenings. Nothing out of the ordinary, so it seemed. On his way to the house, he heard loud screeching by the garage, and he hesitated.

"Now what was that?" He said looking perplexed. Taking no chances, he rushed to his fiat and retrieved his pistol. He crept back to the garage with his heart beating wildly in his chest. With his weapon engaged, in one quick fluid swoop, he stepped around the garage. A big black cat with yellow-gold eyes pounced on a squirming rat, and the rodent's tail was wiggling underneath his massive paw. Everett, wide-eyed, disengaged his weapon and yelled.

"Peepers!" The cat froze in place and turned its head to one side. It seemed to recognize his voice, purring as it rested on its hind legs. Finally, freed, the rat scurried over the driveway and disappeared into the bushes. The cat, now captivated with Everett, swayed his bushy tail back and forth. Everett whistled, and the cat leaped up and landed in a bush next door in a neighbor's yard.

It wiggled free and then took off running down the street disappearing into the black night. Feeling out of sorts, he realized he must face Rachel. He regretted telling her the other day she needed counseling. She was right. Peepers was alive and well. Now he must tell her, he saw the big cat too. Rachel appeared in the doorway after hearing the commotion outside.

"Honey, what's going on out here?" With a quizzical look on her face.

"I saw Peepers," he answered with his voice very low.

"What?!" She said.

"I saw Peepers. The cat was by the garage attacking a rat," he said. She gave him a smug look.

"Peepers?!" She said. "You saw Peepers?!"

"Uh, huh," he said not giving her eye contact.

"So, do you still think I need counseling?" She taunted him. With a long face, he decided it was better not to respond. Not interested in a verbal fight about Peepers. Mainly since there was a more pressing issue to discuss. She looked him dead in his face, and his expression told it all.

"Apology accepted," she said smiling and feeling cocky. Then she turned around and went back in the house.

CHAPTER TWENTY-SEVEN

Everett put his gun away and came into the house.

"Rachel!" He called out. "Rachel!" She stormed out of the laundry room with her finger over her lips.

"Shush!" She scolded him. "You are going to wake Jamie Lee with all of that hollering you are doing! Now, what is it?!" Visibly crossed, he grabbed her hand and pulled her down the hall.

"What's wrong with you and where are we going?!" She fussed.

"To the living room. We need to talk!" He escorted her into the living room, and he sat on the edge of his lounging chair. He leaned forward with his elbows on his knees, and he cradled his chin between his fists. She stood in front of him, looking indignant with her hands on her hips.

"Tell me about Susan Cole," he said looking up at her, his face very tight. His statement, although demanding, caught her off guard. The last subject she wanted to discuss was Susan Cole. She threw her arms over her breast and answered him with a question.

"What about her?"

"Don't you have something to tell me?" He frowned with his eyebrows touching.

"What cocklenockled bull are you talking about?!"

"Why didn't you tell me Susan confessed?!" He said raising his voice and throwing her a curveball. "After all, I am her doctor! That's information I should know!" His question jolted her back, and her heart raced like an engine. She searched for the right words as she sat down on the sofa.

Bewildered, she spits out her words all at once.

"How long have you known this?"

"Just today. I stopped by Susan's room and heard the two of you talking," he said with his voice sharp.

"So, you were eavesdropping?!" He lunged out of his chair with his nostrils flaring. She jerked back, and her eyes got big.

"I shouldn't have to find out this way!" He shouted looking down at her, his face wolfish. "You were wrong not to tell me!"

"I'm sorry," she said with tears coming on. "I thought about it, but I promised her......" He cuts her off.

"Promised her what?!" He yelled with fire in his eyes. He pounded his fist on the coffee table, and she flinched.

"You are a professional! You don't promise her anything! You do your job!"

His angry words cut through her and tears streamed down her face. She tried to talk, but no words came out. Instead, she buried her head in her hands and sobbed. He glided to the bar and poured himself a half glass of Crown Whiskey. He downed the liquor and then poured himself another drink.

"You have a license to protect," he reminded her. "Keeping information to yourself such as that was unethical," he charged not mincing words. She raised her head, and her dark brown eyes met his.

"I didn't tell you because I wanted her to find a lawyer first," she explained with pain etched on her face. "She promised to go to the police once her legal was taken care of."

"How long have you known?" He asked, his voice wavering.

"Two weeks." He returned to his chair and sat down. He lowered his head, his mind in deep thought and then without hesitation, he belted out a firm directive.

"In the morning, you are going to see Thomas Marshall and tell him everything you know! No exceptions!"

She nodded her head in agreement; she had no other choice. All the time, feeling foolish and disappointed in herself. He glared at her for a long while, making her feel ten times worse. Then he finished off his last bit of whiskey, and without saying another word, he got up and left the room.

Downstairs on the ground floor, in the medical records office, Holly B, and Thomas Marshall were pouring over clinical records. Ground passes were spread out on the conference table, and they meticulously reviewed each one looking for clues. Checking the time and day when each patient left, who they left with, and how long they were gone.

"Nothing here," Thomas said after a long silence. Then he looked down the table at Holly B. "Anything?"

She arranged the lab results in alphabetical order and then she laid out the food intake records for each deceased patient. She studied the information for a moment and then took off her glasses. She rubbed her eyes.

"I think I may have something," she finally said with her voice very dry.

"Tell me what you got," Thomas said.

"Five patients died altogether. Only two had marijuana in their system at the time." Thomas looked confused.

"Doctor Beebe told me, they all had marijuana in their system. That couldn't be right!" Holly B puts her eyeglasses back on. She gave him a tongue lashing.

"The documentation is clear as a sunny day! I'm not making this up!"

"Okay, don't get excited," he said backing down. "Anything else?" She tapped her fingernails on the table and said.

"The clinical records show each patient had an episode of convulsions and vomiting right before they died......They all had symptoms associated with rat poison ingestion."

"Huh, huh," Thomas agreed, nodding his head.

"No one in their right mind, unless they are just plum crazy would eat rat poison for the heck of it. Whoever gave it to them camouflaged it with something else. Like a substance or food," she concluded.

"Marijuana! There you go!" Thomas readily reminded her. She shook her head in disagreement.

"Noooo, I don't think so," she said. "How about a cupcake?" She announced throwing him a curve ball.

"A cupcake?"

"Yes, a cupcake," she said. She gestured for him to come over to her side of the table.

"You need to look at these intake records," she said. He made his way over to review the records, studying each one.

"You are right. They all ate a cupcake the night they died," he said with his brow furrowing.

"Yep," Holly B said. She matched each nursing note with an intake record and then used a magic marker to highlight specific information.

"What are you doing?" Thomas wondered out loud. She looked at him. Her face was full of determination.

"The intake records show every deceased patient eating a cupcake shortly after attending Doctor Poppy's group."

"Go on," Thomas said listening carefully.

"An hour later, per the nursing notes, these patients begin experiencing convulsions and vomiting after eating a cupcake. I'll be willing to bet the cupcakes are laced with rat poison," she concluded. Thomas' face turned stark grave.

"Do you think Doctor Poppy is poisoning her patients?" He asked feeling sick to his stomach.

"It's a possibility," Holly B answered, looking somber. "I wouldn't put it past her! She is quite touched!"

"What do you mean?" Thomas inquired raising an eyebrow. Holly B chuckled to herself.

"The woman sleeps in a coffin! Very creepy, don't you think?"

"A coffin?! Are you kidding me?!" Thomas said shaking his head. "I don't believe it!"

"No, it's true," she insisted. "I saw it with my own eyes last week when I went to her apartment to interview her!"

"What did you do?" He asked getting the heebie-jeebies.

"I inquired about it, completed the interview and left as soon as I could," Holly B calmly said.

"Brave lady," Thomas said still feeling queasy. "So, what's your next move?" Holly B took a moment to sort out her thoughts. Then she weighed in.

"I need to find out who or where these cupcakes came from. Once the source is located, then we have our serial killer," she said. Thomas was transfixed.

"So, you don't think it's Doctor Poppy?" He said.

"I don't know," Holly B said. "But I'm going to find out!"

She searched the room for a telephone, and her eyes landed on the fax machine.

"I'm going to call Doctor Poppy right now," she said.

"It's late," Thomas said glancing at his watch. "It's after midnight!" Holly B was very determined.

"I have to get some answers. Rachel should be up." She dialed the social worker's number. Rachel answered on the third ring. She sounded groggy.

"Hello?"

"This is Holly B! Sorry to wake you! Do you have a minute?" She asked.

Rachel yawned. "You're up late. What's going on?"

"Need a question answered," Holly B said.

"Okay, I am listening," Rachel replied still yawning.

"Doctor Poppy's group...... What's the name of the bakery she orders the cupcakes from?"

"Bakery?!" Rachel laughed. "There's no bakery. Cathy Ray makes those cupcakes."

Holly B's jaw dropped. "Are you sure?!"

"Yep," Rachel said. Then she paused.

"Is something wrong?" Holly B got herself together in a hurry. Not wanting to alarm Rachel just yet.

"No, no, no. Nothing is wrong," she fibbed. "Thanks for the clarification."

"You're welcome," Rachel said. Holly B hung up the phone.

Her face was ghostly white. She looked down the table at Thomas Marshall and said,

"Guess who makes those cupcakes?"

"I'm afraid to ask," Thomas responded looking bug-eyed. She let out a long sigh, and Thomas became irritated.

"Don't keep me in suspense! Who makes them?!" He demanded.

"Cathy Ray," she said, with her voice wavering. "I'm afraid it's Cathy Ray!"

Sammie found Ethan on the floor in her office, with her eyes rolled back in her head, jerking with convulsions and with salvia foaming around her mouth.

"Doctor Poppy, what did you take?!" He hollered into her ear. She heard him but was unable to speak. She pointed to her desk, but he misread her gesture, shoving a half-eaten cupcake to the side and reaching for the phone. He dialed 911, and a woman's voice answered on the first ring.

"What's your emergency?"

"I need an ambulance pronto! One of our doctors is having a seizure!" He shouted into the phone.

"Is this Salter's Point Regional?" She asked with her voice sharp. Sammie examined Ethan's face, and he could tell she was running out of time. Her eyelids drooped, and her breathing was shallow.

"Yes, this is Salter's Point Regional you nitwit!" He yelled into the phone. "Hurry up! She's fading fast!"

Betty Jo's neck and shoulders rippled with pain. She tumbled into her Nissan Maxima and the urge to vomit suddenly overwhelmed her. She stuck her head out the door hovering over the driveway, but nothing came out. She slammed the door and switched on the ignition. With her neck tightening and her stomach in knots, she backed out of the driveway. The muscles in her legs knotted up as she speeded down the highway. Thinking she may have food poisoning, she tried to recall the foods she ate earlier in the day. After some thought, nothing she ate, not even one of Cathy's chocolate cupcakes could cause her this much pain, she reasoned. She made a sharp right onto Tacoma Avenue, and Lakewood General Hospital was there two blocks down.

She drove into the parking lot, and her shoulders ached with excruciating pain. She parked in front of the emergency room and struggled out of the car. Her legs felt like rubber, and she could hardly stand. She managed to lock her car door and hobbled down the walkway. When she finally reached the emergency room check-in counter, her knees buckled. She began to fall, and two nurses ran over and lowered her to the floor.

"Help me! Somebody, please help me!" She whispered.

"Code 99, Code 99!" One nurse yelled cradling her head in her lap. Betty Jo's eyes rolled back in her head, and her limbs sank to the floor. A curtain fell over her vision and then her world went black.

CHAPTER TWENTY-EIGHT

Wearied from reviewing notes, Holly B and Thomas Marshall decided to close shop for the evening. As they strolled to the hospital exit, they were surprised when two medics rushed by them carrying Ethan Poppy on a gurney. Fearing the worse, Holly B rushed to her side.

"What happened?" She asked staring down at her face. The terror in Ethan's eyes gave her pause then a queasy feeling came over her.

"Talk to me!" Holly B urged grabbing her hand and squeezing it tight.

Ethan slid her oxygen mask down over her chin, and she mouthed out words, but the detective had trouble understanding her. Holly B leaned in closer, this time within an earshot to the doctor's dry, cracked lips. Ethan whispered.

"You will find the answer to all of your questions on my desk." Holly B gently squeezed her hand again and nodded.

"I understand," she assured her. Relieved, Ethan gave her a weak smile and slid the oxygen mask back over her nose. She waved as the medics ushered her out the door. Wasting no time, Holly B raced across the lobby and then down the narrow hall to the admissions unit. Once there, she banged on the door with both fists, stopping once to peer through the glass window. Sammy heard the commotion and sprang to his feet. When he stepped into the hall, he saw Holly B peering through the glass window.

He rushed to the door and shoved it opened, gesturing for her to come inside.

"What's wrong with you?!" He asked.

"Where is Doctor Poppy's office?!" She asked with big eyes.

"It's the door on the right, before you get to the nursing station." She rushed past him and raced down the hall. He ran after her, and by the time she reached Ethan's office, he had caught up with her. She tugged at the doorknob looking flustered.

"It's locked," she said looking back at him. "Do you have a key?"

"I do," he replied. He hesitated and searched her face looking for answers.

"What is it you need in there?" He asked. She glared at him through her black-rimmed glasses, impatient with his slow response and prying question. Her mother used to tell her on many occasions she was short on patience, especially when she needed something done in a hurry. Realizing time was of the essence, she pulled rank.

"Sir, you are impeding my investigation, which is a federal offense! Now if you don't want to go to jail, open this door!" She demanded.

Her idle threat frightened him, and he backed off. He jammed the key in the lock and jiggled it. Then the door clicked open. He flicked on the light switch, and the ceiling light came on. Holly B stepped inside, and her eyes fell on Ethan's desk. Just like the doctor instructed her, the answer was right there, a plate of chocolate cupcakes sitting on the desk. Three whole ones and a half-eaten one with tangled saran wrapping on the side.

Holly B dug down into her coat pocket and pulled out a pair of green gloves. She put the gloves on and stepped to the desk. She took the saran wrap and untangled it, and then she wrapped the cupcakes.

"Did Doctor Poppy have a group this evening?" She asked out of the blue. Sammie gave her a funny look. Then he spoke with caution.

"No, she canceled it. She wasn't feeling well," he said.

"Why? What was going on with her?" Holly B probed, curious to know how much the nurse knew.

"I found her on the floor seizing, so I called 911," Sammie said. Holly B pushed her glasses up on her nose with one index finger.

"Are there any more cupcakes stashed on this unit?" She asked looking worried.

"There's some in the fridge in the med room," he disclosed. "Why do you ask?" Thinking the worse. She blurted out her next question without much thought.

"Did you or your staff give the patients any of these cupcakes?!"

"Not yet," he said. She sighed with relief and then her face turned serious again.

"Go to the med room and get rid of those cupcakes right now!" She demanded.

"Why?" He asked getting irritated. Growing tired of her demands.

"Just do it!" She said as she grabbed the plate of cupcakes and rushed to the door.

"Where are you going with those cupcakes?" Sammie asked following her out the door.

"I'm taking these babies with me," Holly B answered.

"Why?" He demanded, with his voice rough. She stopped in mid-stride and looked straight into his eyes.

"This is an on-going investigation," she told him. "I need you to keep this quiet." She started down the hall again, and he grabbed her elbow stopping her.

"I need to know why you want me to get rid of these cupcakes! The patients are looking forward to eating these cupcakes for snack tomorrow morning!" He said. She huffed, refusing to answer him, frustrated with his questions. She jerked away and brushed by him taking off down the hall. He stayed with her all the way to the exit, refusing to let up.

"I need an answer right now!" He insisted. When she came to the exit, she turned to face him. She saw annoyance and irritation on his face prompting her to tell him the truth.

"The cupcakes may be laced with rat poison. If you give these babies to your patients, you will kill them!" Sammie's eyes grew big like saucers, and he reared back.

"Oh, I.... I didn't...." She cuts him off.

"Get rid of the cupcakes right now!" She demanded again. "Now unlock this door!" He unlocked the door and shoved it open. She dashed out and hurried down the hall. He watched her until he couldn't see her anymore, then he let the door slam. It rattled like a pop of thunder. He hoofed down the hall making a beeline to the med room.

He went to the refrigerator and yanked the door open. A plate of chocolate cupcakes sat on the middle shelf, and he grabbed it and tossed it in the trashcan. He searched the room for a telephone and found one on the wall by the cabinet. He snatched it off the receiver and dialed a number. After he keyed in a return number, he hangs up. A second later, it rung, and he snatched it off the wall again.

"Sammie here," he barked.

"You called?" The med tech asked on the other end, his voice heavy.

"I need you to come to the med room and take a bag of trash to the dumpster," Sammie said.

"Why Now?" The med tech asked.

"Just do it!" Sammie said. He slammed the phone on the receiver and waited.

Thomas Marshall stood outside in the chilly air. He gazed into the grey, black sky, and admired the twinkling stars. Occasionally, a formation of bats would soar over the parking lot, dropping little piles of waste. He lights up a cigarette, breaking a promise to himself to quit smoking. The details of the investigation had worn on him, and he was feeling stressed out. He took another drag off his cigarette and then threw it on the sidewalk stamping it out with his shoe. It wasn't long before Holly B joined him. Surprised he was still around, her hazel-green eyes filled every space in her prescription glasses.

"You waited for me?" She said.

"Why wouldn't I?" He said with smiling eyes. "Have you forgotten I am the police chief?" She gave him a half smile.

"No need to get smart!" She chided him. He laughed and then noticed the plate of cupcakes in her hand.

"So, you found some?" He said.

"Right where she told me," Holly B replied. "We need to run labs on these little gems. I bet the results will turn up with rat poison." She handed him the plate, and he inspected it looking visibly cross.

"It's amazing something this good can cause so much pain and death," he sadly said. "Cathy Ray is worse than Satan," he brutally added. Holly B shoved her glasses up over her nose and pondered for a moment. Then she asked a question.

"How long will it take to get the results back?"

"Probably a good twenty-four hours, but not fast enough," he said. "If the results are positive, I will take great joy in arresting her and putting her away for good!"

"Did you call Doctor Beebe?" She asked staying on task.

"Yes, and he was devastated after hearing the news," Thomas said. "In the morning, he plans to meet with Beth and a few of his doctors to inform them of the latest developments."

"I need to be there," she said quickly. Thomas nodded his head in agreement.

"We both need to be there. They will have lots of questions for us," he warned her.

"I also want to be there when you arrest Cathy Ray," she informed him.

"Once we receive those results, I will notify you with a plan, and soon this debacle will come to an end!" He angrily said.

Mark Brewer hung up the phone, and he was inwardly shaken. With his mind on speed dial, he was not sure if he grasped the nitty-gritty details of his wife's condition. Betty Jo was in Lakewood General, fighting for her life. He just couldn't fathom it.

Although he was despondent and heartbroken, he managed to pack an overnight bag, shower, and dress in less than an hour. Before leaving, he gave his room a once over and then he jetted out the door. The night counselor saw him coming and hopped off her stool.

"Doctor Brewer, is there something wrong?"

"My wife………. I need to get to my wife! I'll be back soon!" He shouted as he rushed passed her. Before she could say another word, he was out the door.

Doctor Beebe changed into his pajamas and then transferred out of his wheelchair onto the bed. He scooted to the middle of the bed and laid down. He pulled the comforter up to his chin and thought about the news Thomas shared with him earlier. Shocked to learn a staff social worker could be responsible for such a terrifying act.

"Where did she come from?" The chief repeatedly asked him. "Does she have a criminal record? Is she really a social worker?" When asked these questions, Doctor Beebe couldn't supply any answers. As far as he knew, her background check and legal record came back clean as a whistle. An upstanding citizen.

Now, with a serial killer in their midst, he must act to ensure patient safety. He entertained calling Beth and telling her the news but thought better of it.

"I'll wait until tomorrow morning," he said. "That will be soon enough."

CHAPTER TWENTY-NINE

Five o' clock, Wednesday morning, A Mercedes Benz screeched into the parking lot and parked in front of Lakewood General Hospital Emergency Room. Mark hopped out of his car and ran inside. A bright-eyed candy striper volunteer was there at the visitor's desk, and he stopped there to ask for directions.

"What floor is intensive care on?" He asked with fear in his eyes.

"On the third floor," she said pointing to the elevators.

"Where are the stairs?" He asked, too impatient to wait for the elevator.

"On your right around the corner," she told him.

"Thanks," he said as he took off running. He found the stairs and hightailed it up to the third floor. He forced his way through the double doors, and intensive care was right there. With his breathing heavy and ragged, he quickened his pace, and within seconds he was there at Betty Jo's side. At first, he didn't know what to expect. However, when he saw her lying there not moving, with an oxygen mask taped to her ashy grey face, he fell apart. He took her hand and held it to his lips, rocking back and forth with tears rolling down his face.

"Betty Jo," he whispered. "My sweet, sweet Betty Jo!" Ethan, now feeling a little better, had just finished her third trek around the ICU with IV in tow. She heard Mark sobbing from Betty Jo's room, and she stopped and looked in. She lingered there in the doorway quite a while giving him space to grieve and then she tiptoed inside.

"Mark, it's Ethan," she said as she moved closer to him. At first, he wouldn't look up. He rocked back and forth, holding his wife's hand, mumbling to himself. Ethan, moved by his outward emotion, gently squeezed his shoulder.

"Mark, come with me. I have something to tell you," she said. He turned to face her with confusion in his red, blurry eyes.

"What?!" He said.

"Come," she urged. "I can explain everything." When he realized she too was in a hospital gown with an IV attached to her arm, he dropped Betty Jo's hand and said,

"What the hell happened to you?!"

"Food poisoning," she explained. "Your wife also was poisoned," she told him. Mark was beside himself.

"What?!" He said not believing his ears.

"Come walk with me. I'll tell you everything," Ethan said again in a calm, direct voice. She offered her hand, and he took it. He followed her into the hall. For a long while, they walked side by side holding hands without conversation and then Ethan broke the news to him.

"Remember in the meeting a couple of weeks ago, Doctor Beebe told us my patients had rat poison in their systems?" She said.

"Huh, huh," Mark said wiping tears from his face and giving her his full attention.

"I know how it got there and so do the police," she said. Mark stopped in his tracks.

"Tell me!" He insisted. She took a few deep breaths, hesitating to answer. Fearful he might lose it and go after Cathy Ray. He read her like a book. Her face told it all.

"Ethan, stop stalling and just tell me!" He demanded.

"You know those cupcakes Cathy Ray makes for my skills group?" She reminded him. He threw one hand up.

"Wait don't tell me!" He blurted out. He paced back and forth, his face etched in pain. Then he stopped and looked at her, visibly angry. He knew what she was going to say, and he was livid. Ethan walked over to him, and her violet eyes stared straight into his blue-green eyes.

"Cathy Ray poisoned my patients, Mark. She also tried to poison Betty Jo and me."

"Why?!" He whispered frowning up like a gremlin. "Why would she do such a thing?!" Ethan shook her head.

"I really don't know." Rage builds within him replacing his grief.

"I'm going to need prayer and a bottle of vodka!" He said, red-faced with his brow furrowing.

"Vodka?!" Ethan asked, looking perplexed. "Why vodka?!

"I need vodka to give me permission to rip her ass to pieces!" He said, gritting his teeth.

"Now Mark, let the police take care of Cathy Ray! She will get what's coming to her," Ethan reassured him.

"I hope so. Otherwise, I'll rip her apart myself! You can bet on that," he said. He turned away and stomped down the hall to Betty Jo's room.

Sally glanced at her watch. It was seven o'clock in the morning, and she was five minutes late for report. When she unlocked the door, and stepped onto the unit, Sammie was racing like the wind in her direction with his hands frantic in the air.

"Oh dear, what now?" She asked herself, blinking like a peacock.

"I got something to tell you," he said as he came to a screeching halt. With his breath short and heavy, he grabbed her arm and ushered her into the clean linen room. He shut the door and faced her. His eyes filled with anguish and fear.

"What is going on?" She said in exasperation. "You are scaring me!"

"I got something to tell you," he repeated very excitedly.

"Then tell me," she demanded.

"You know those cupcakes Cathy Ray makes for Doctor Poppy's skills group?" He said.

"Yeah, what about them?" Sally said batting her eyes.

"The cupcakes have rat poison in them," he said in a matter of fact tone. Sally's jaw dropped opened.

"Rat poison?" She said with a quizzical expression on her face. Not sure she heard right.

"Rat poison," he said again. "Cathy Ray has been poisoning the patients with rat poison," he said not holding back. Sally was speechless. After a moment, she posed a question using great caution.

"How do you know this?"

"The little detective………. What's her name?" He said
snapping his fingers as he tried to recall the detective's name.
Sally helps him out.

"You mean Holly B!"

"Yes, Holly B!" He said. "She told me to get rid of the
cupcakes because of the rat poison!" Sally slapped one hand over
her mouth and cursed under her breath.

"I'll be damned!" She grabbed Sammie's shoulders and looked
him dead in his face.

"Who else knows about this?!" She whispered.

"Just me. Holly B asked me not to tell anyone," he said.

"Well, she picked the wrong person to keep a secret," Sally
nervously chuckled. A frown came over Sammie's face, irritated
by her comment.

"I couldn't keep this to myself! I thought you should know!"

"I'm sorry," she said, her face apologetic. "I'm just trying to
come to terms with all of this!"

"Sally, what are you going to do?" Sally mulled over her
thoughts for a minute and then she said,

"I think we should act normal. First, let's do report and then I'll
pay Doctor Beebe a visit."

"Sounds like a plan," he said sighing heavily. When he opened
the door to go out, he bumped into Rachel.

"Oops," Sally said trying to duck behind him. Rachel laughed
out loud.

"I see you, Sally! What are you two doing in there?!" Sally
brushed by him and became indignant.

"It's not what you think," she insisted with her hand on one
hip.

"Then enlighten me," Rachel giggled. Sammie broke out in a lopsided grin and took up for Sally.

"We were having a meeting," he said. "A crucial meeting!"

"A meeting?!"

"Yes, a meeting," he insisted.

"Can I be in on this meeting?" She asked with beaming eyes.

"NO!" They both yelled at once. Rachel scrunched her face up.

"Well, excuse me!" She said. "You don't have to yell!" Sally hurried up and changed the subject.

"I see you are here early! Don't you come in at eight-thirty?!"

"Most days," Rachel acknowledged. "But, this morning, I have a meeting with Thomas Marshall. I came in to get my notes," she revealed. Sally arched an eyebrow.

"A meeting with the police chief?! What's this about?"

"None of your business!" Rachel said, fluttering her eyelashes to get back at her.

"Not funny," Sally said twisting up her face. Rachel smiled and started for the exit.

"Have to go folks! See you two later!" Sally and Sammie gave each other anxious looks.

"I wonder what's that all about," said Sally.

"Me too," Sammie said.

Everett and Rachel were in front of Thomas Marshall's office precisely at eight thirty. Still very angry, Everett stooped over and whispered in her ear.

"I want you to tell him everything! Don't leave anything out," he said looking crossed.

"I won't," she hissed. "Stop pestering me!" He glared at her, and she averted her eyes from his penetrating gaze. Too ashamed to look him in the face. Everett pounded on the door.

"Come in," said a gruff voice. He opened the door and strolled inside with Rachel right behind him.

Thomas sprang to his feet and extended his hand to greet Everett.

"Good Morning Doctor," he said shaking his hand.

"Good Morning," Everett said with a stone face. Thomas' eyes fell on Rachel, and he broke out into a wide grin.

"So, this is the little Mrs.! How are you this fine day?" Rachel cringed.

"It's Rachel James," she coolly said with her dark eyes smoldering. Thomas ignored her frosty attitude and gestured for the couple to take a seat. They both make themselves comfortable on the red velvet couch trimmed in black leather across from the chief's desk. Rachel gave the room a once-over. Every wall was decorated with an oil painting either of Mount Rainier, The Space Needle or Pike Place Market. On one end of the room, two leather chairs trimmed in gold sat against the wall. In the middle of the floor, a huge potted ivy plant sat on a coffee table.

"You have good taste," Rachel warmly said admiring his office.

"Why, thank you, little lady," he grinned. Rachel's blood boiled. She despised men who called her little lady. However, she forced a smile, shrugging it off.

"What brings you here this morning?" He asked. Rachel gave Everett a quick look. He nodded, giving her permission to speak.

"Go ahead and tell him," he urged with blazing eyes.

Thomas' eyebrows went up. "Tell me what?!" Rachel sighed in exasperation. Anxious about spilling her well-kept secret. Feeling bad about betraying Susan's confidence, but despite her feelings, she knew she couldn't lie. Besides, Everett wouldn't stand for it.

"Susan Cole killed Doctor Benny," she said in a hurry giving the chief direct eye contact. Thomas leaned forward and folded his arms on the desk.

"How do you know this?" He calmly asked.

"She told me," Rachel disclosed. She hesitated while she gathered her thoughts. He knew she had more to say so he waited and then he said,

"Go on, I'm listening." She took a deep breath and said,

"Two weeks ago, Susan and I had an impromptu conversation. Apparently, Doctor Benny cheated on her making her very jealous and angry. So, she shot him. I don't think she meant to kill him, but she did." Thomas' ferret-like eyes zeroed in on her.

"She told you this?" He said in a firm questioning voice.

"Yep," Rachel said. Thomas was silent for a moment, then he said,

"What took you so long to report this?!"

"I don't know," she said shrugging her shoulders. He gave her a disapproving look.

"Do you know it's a crime to interfere with a murder investigation?" He said chastising her.

"I realize that," she frowned, with the little vein protruding in her forehead.

"I guess I felt sorry for her," she off-handedly replied. He winced at the absurdity of her reasoning. He was about to snap her up, but he decided to let it go.

"I suppose you are willing to put this in an affidavit?"

"I am," she dryly said.

"Someone will call you later to take down your information," he informed her.

"Okay," Rachel said. Thomas zeroed in on Everett and posed a question.

"Is Susan stable enough to leave the hospital?" He inquired. Everett chose his words carefully.

"Give it a couple of days. She probably will be ready then."

"Very well then. Arrangements will be made to pick her up. Is there anything else?" He asked with a clenched jaw.

"No, nothing," Rachel said rubbing her forehead and ready for this meeting to be over.

"I need you to keep this quiet until we have her in custody," he instructed them.

"Will do," Everett said. Rachel didn't say a word. She nodded her head and gazed down into her lap. Thomas leaped to his feet, and Rachel and Everett departed for the door.

"We'll be in touch!" He said. Everett opened the door, and Rachel stepped out with Everett behind her. She fumed while they walked together in silence. By the time they reached the parking lot, she was good and angry.

"Are you satisfied now?!" She snapped. His dark brown eyes carried a mixture of shock and barely contained anger. He decided not to answer. Instead, he quickened his pace and left her alone in the parking lot.

CHAPTER THIRTY

Rachel called Betty Jo as soon as she returned to her office. The phone rang and rang, and no one answered. She knew she wasn't feeling well the last time she spoke to her, and she began to wonder if she was alright. Feeling uneasy, she picked up the phone to call Cathy Ray, but a knock on the door interrupted her. She hangs up.

"Come in!" She hollered. The door swung opened, and Sally rushed in slamming the door behind her. Red-faced and breathing hard, she collapsed in a nearby chair. She struggled to speak.

"I.... I...."

"What in the hell is wrong with you?!" Rachel asked looking flabbergasted.

"I... I... Just finished talking to Beth and Doctor Beebe," she finally stammered out. "You are not going to believe what they told me! Are you sitting down?!" Rachel, feeling comical, looked down at her chair.

"I guess I'm sitting down," she giggled in hysterics. Sally was so apprehensive the joke went over her head. Beads of sweat broke out on her forehead as she fidgeted in her seat. Then she hopped up and locked the door. Fear crossed Rachel's face.

"Girl, What's wrong with you?! You are scaring the hell out of me!"

"I'm sorry," Sally said as she hurried back to her seat. "I have to make sure no one busts in on us!"

"Girrrl, you better tell me what's going on before I physically jack you up," she said, half annoyed.

Sally squeezed her eyes shut. She took deep breaths, pursing her lips together and then she let out short, quick sighs. Rachel snapped her fingers and yelled.

"Sally, are you clinically insane or incredibly annoying?!"

"I don't know, probably both," Sally said opening her eyes and blinking them hard.

"What's got you spooked?!" Rachel asked looking infuriated.

"There's a serial killer here at Salter's Point Regional," Sally said. Rachel cracked up laughing. She couldn't help herself.

"Have you lost your blasted mind, girl?! A serial killer?! The hell there is!"

"I'm not making this up!" Sally exclaimed, bolting out of her chair, causing Rachel to jerk back. "Look at the number of patients who have died over the past three weeks?!" She said. Rachel fumbled her words.

"Maybe, four or five. Don't you need more than six to call it serial?!" She innocently asked with big eyes.

"Girl, wake up!" Sally hissed getting livid. "Ask yourself this...... Have you seen Betty Jo, Doctor Poppy or Cathy Ray this morning?!" Rachel was dumbfounded.

"Is this a trick question?"

"Noooo," Sally said dropping her head in her hands.

"Okay, I give up! You are going to have to tell me," Rachel said getting frustrated. When Sally looked up, her face was flushed and stern.

"Promise me you keep this quiet until the police make an arrest," she said.

"An arrest?! Sally, come on!"

"Promise me, you won't tell anyone, not even Everett," she urged. Rachel threw her hands up. Great, another secret she must keep from Everett. She was not happy about it and felt strong-armed. However, she reluctantly accepted Sally's request.

"Okay, I promise!" She said. Sally cleared her throat.

"Cathy Ray killed those patients!" She spilled out.

"Our Cathy Ray?" Rachel said in a high pitch soprano voice almost falling over in her chair.

"Shush!" Sally said looking at the door. "We must keep this quiet!"

"I'm sorry," Rachel said straightening her chair. "I didn't expect to hear that coming out of your mouth! Besides I don't believe it!" Sally became ornery, even angry. "Stop being difficult! This information came straight from Beth and Doctor Beebe!"

"Okay, okay," Rachel said backing off at first. Then she turned obstinate.

"I'm sorry, I need more information before I believe this nonsense!"

"Okay then!" Sally said getting indignant. "You know those cupcakes Cathy makes for Doctor Poppy's group?" She reminded her.

"Yep, what about them?" Rachel asked bucking her eyes.

"The cupcakes have rat poison in them. Holly B had Sammie get rid of a batch last evening," she informed her. "So there!" The impact of Sally's words hit her like a ton of bricks.

Terror consumed her, and she popped out of her seat like a weasel in a hole.

"Oh, my god! Cathy gave Betty Jo a plate of those cupcakes yesterday! Have you seen her this morning?!"

"Well, this is the other part I need to tell you....... Doctor Poppy and Betty Jo are at Lakewood General as we speak," she said looking grim. Rachel felt her legs getting weak, and she collapsed down in her chair. She folded her arms on her desk and laid her head down.

"Now do you believe me?" Sally said.

"Yes," Rachel said in a muffled voice. She lifted her head and with eyes swimming in tears, she stared uncompromising into Sally's eyes.

"I need to see Betty Jo!"

"Rachel, you can't!" Sally warned. "The police aren't finished collecting evidence!" A thought crossed her mind. She remembered she was going to call Cathy Ray earlier before Sally's disturbing visit.

"By the way, where is Cathy Ray?"

"She called out sick," Sally said. "She has no idea we all know."

"Good," Rachel sighed. She grabbed her Coach handbag and headed for the door.

"Where are you going?" Sally asked leaping to her feet.

"To Lakewood General! I have to make sure Betty Jo is alright!" She said yanking the door open. She hurried out with Sally hollering after her.

"Be careful, and remember not to tell a soul!"

Thirty minutes later, Rachel was in the elevator at Lakewood General Hospital. The elevator stopped on the third floor, and she stepped out into the hall in front of intensive care. She tapped on the buzzer, and the double doors swung open. When she rushed through the doors, Ethan Poppy was standing in the hall. She rushed over to her.

"Are you alright?" Rachel asked trying not to look too rattled.

"I'm fine," Ethan said. She sized Rachel up. She could tell the social worker was about to lose it. She grabbed her arm.

"I think you need to calm down and walk with me," she calmly said. Rachel jerked her arm away.

"I need to see Betty Jo right now! I need to know she's alright!"

"She is alright, but you need to calm down before I take you in there to see her. She does not need the stress," Ethan said taking control.

"Okay!" Rachel relented. She followed Ethan to Betty Jo's room. She could see Mark through the window. He was weeping like a baby, holding her hand, very distraught. Rachel felt tears coming on and opted not to go in.

"Are you sure she's going to be alright?!" She asked feeling helpless.

"I'm sure. She woke up this morning for a few minutes," Ethan said. "Her doctor told us, she is stable but needs rest." She turned and faced Ethan. The features on her face were very grave.

"Do you know why Cathy did this?!" Ethan was taken aback by her question. Very surprised Rachel knew anything at all.

"Who told you?" She asked.

"I'm not at liberty to say," Rachel said with a quickness. She realized she broke Sally's confidence and for that reason, she flipped the script.

"I want to hear your side of it," she said. Ethan eyed her with skepticism but decided to tell her side anyway. She became incensed when she thought about Cathy Ray almost taking her life, and she responded with malice in her voice.

"Cathy has been using her cupcakes to poison my patients! She even tried to poison Betty Jo and me!"

"Poison you and the patients with what?!" Rachel asked pretending not to know.

"She used rat poison," Ethan said. "The little wench used rat poison!"

"Damn!" Rachel cursed as she recalled the conversation she had with Cathy Ray weeks ago. "She really does hate you!" Ethan's radar went up.

"What are you saying?!"

"I remember Cathy telling Betty Jo and me, you remind her of her stepmother," Rachel disclosed.

"How so?"

"She told us you criticize her a lot like her stepmother," Rachel said. Ethan fell mute for a minute and then said with watery eyes,

"I admit I was a little hard on her at times, but did I deserve to be poisoned for it?!"

"No, you didn't, and Betty Jo and your patients didn't either!" Rachel said. "Cathy will pay for this!"

"Yes, she will," Ethan nodded in agreement. "Yes, she will!"

When Rachel returned to her office, she found Susan Cole waiting for her at the door. Her blue eyes locked on her like a couple of magnets, causing the social worker to feel uneasy.

"What's up?" She said.

"I need to talk to you," Susan said fidgeting in place.

"Okay," Rachel replied as she unlocked the door. The door clicked opened, and she gestured for Susan to go in before her. Susan went inside and flopped into a chair. Rachel shuts the door. She strolls to her desk and drops her handbag in the drawer. She remained standing with her arms folded across her chest.

"What's up?" She asked again.

"I want you to know I told Doctor James I killed George," she said with a straight face.

"When?" Rachel asked looking wide-eyed.

"This morning," she replied.

"How did he take it?"

"Calm and stoic as usual," Susan said. "He told me I must tell the police."

"Are you?" Rachel probed now feeling bad about betraying her. Tears shimmered in Susan's eyes.

"I have no choice," She sadly said. Rachel felt guilty and sad all at once. She decided to tell her the truth.

"I have something to tell you," she quietly said.

"What?" said Susan.

"I went to see Thomas Marshall this morning and told him everything." Susan tenses up.

"I knew you would," she said.

"I was torn," Rachel said with her bottom lip trembling. "I couldn't hold on to it much longer. It was the right thing to do."

"I know," Susan said looking miserable. A hush fell on the room, and they sat there together without conversation for a very long time. Then Susan stood up and said,

"I guess I'll go," she said heading to the door. She opened the door and stopped in the archway. She looked at Rachel, suddenly feeling bad for her.

Don't fret over it," she said. "You made the right call."

"I appreciate those kind words," Rachel said emotionally exhausted. Susan nodded and walked out, shutting the door behind her. Rachel closed her eyes and fell back in her chair. She sighed with relief.

CHAPTER THIRTY-ONE

Cathy Ray stood in the archway of her balcony, breathing in the crisp, cool air, as her calculating eyes admired the snow-peaked tips of Mount Rainier. It was sixty-five degrees, and the sky, absent of clouds was a deep crimson blue. She braided her long strawberry blonde hair into two thick ponytails and then tied little yellow ribbons on the ends. She thought about Ethan Poppy and Betty Jo. Wondering, if the two women were already dead or managed to stay alive by some small miracle. She cackled out loud, feeling full of herself. Basking in her own craftiness and her artful ability to rid herself of people she perceived were against her. Her stomach growled, reminding her she hadn't eaten for two days.

"A late breakfast will do the trick," she said heading to the kitchen. She fried two pieces of bacon and scrambled some eggs. She shuffled the food onto her plate and sat at the bar. While devouring her eggs, she jumped in her seat when the phone rang. She dropped her fork and snatched the phone off the receiver.

"Hello?!" No answer.

"Hello?" No answer. She hangs up the phone looking disgusted.

"What an idiot," she mumbled picking up her fork again. She finished off her breakfast and ran to the bathroom. Still obsessed with her weight, she had gained one pound, and she wasn't happy about it. She jabbed two fingers down her throat and made herself retch.

Five seconds later, her breakfast was in the commode, and she felt hungry again. She dragged herself back to the kitchen and then began scrimmaging through every cabinet until she found a bag of microwave popcorn. She threw it in the microwave oven and stood by the counter and waited.

Holly B hung up the phone when she heard Cathy Ray's voice on the other end.

"She's at home just like Beth said," she told Thomas.

"Good," he said. "As soon as we receive those results back, I'm going straight to the courthouse." Holly B sprung out of her seat and paced back and forth. She stopped one time to push her glasses up on the bridge of her nose, and she started again.

"What's taking so long anyway?! It's been over twenty-four hours!" She complained.

"Be patient. We will get her. Don't you worry," Thomas tried to reassure her.

"I hope so," she said. "I certainly hope so."

A day later, ten-thirty in the morning, a UPS truck parked in front of Salter's Point Police Station. The driver, a short, dowdy man dressed in brown shorts and a shirt with the UPS logo on it, hopped out of the truck with a large manila envelope in his hand. He hightailed it into the station and stopped at the security counter. A police officer, tall and rough looking, approached him.

"Whatcha got there?" He asked with a long straight face.

"Here," the driver said with his arms stretched out giving him the envelope.

"It's for the police chief! See to it that he gets it!"

Before the officer could say another word, the driver ran off, sprinting out the door.

"Jerk!" The officer grumbled. His eyes scanned the area and landed on Lisa. She was a tall woman with a bald head and bleary red eyes, a condition brought on by her night surveillance job. She spotted the officer checking her out, and with a poker face, she yelled,

"Who are you looking at you creep?!"

"It's not what you think," he yelled back. He held the envelope up for her to see.

"I can't leave my post, so I need you to take this to the chief." She sashayed over rolling her eyes and then she snatched the envelope out of his hand.

"Fine," she huffed. "Anything else?!"

"Nope," he grimaced. She turned away and hurried to the chief's office. Holly B and Thomas were going over their notes again.

"All we need are those lab results, and we are in business," he said, with his face brightening a little.

"It's been at least forty-eight hours, what's taking so long?" Holly B complained again as she took off her eyeglasses. With her eyes scratchy and bloodshot, she rubbed them hard. She was jittery from too much coffee and raw from lack of sleep.

"I know you are tired," Thomas said noticing the exhaustion on her face. "But we are so close now. You have to be patient."

"I know," Holly B yawned. Suddenly there was pounding on the door, and she jumped up.

"My, whoever that is... Do they have to knock so hard?!" Thomas flashed her a grin and yelled,

"Come in!" Lisa busted through the door and stood in the doorway.

"This is for you chief," she announced tossing him the envelope. "Google eyes told me to give it to you!" Thomas gave her a strange look.

"Who in the hell is google eyes?!"

"The dude who mans the front desk," she said. Thomas laughed.

"Thanks," he said.

"No problem," Lisa said. She turned around and slammed the door behind her.

"Boy, she's something," Holly B said in a silvery voice.

"That's not even the half of it," he chuckled. Holly B eyed the envelope like silver lightning.

"Is that what I think it is?"

"Well, let's see," Thomas replied. He tore the envelope open and pulled out a report. He scanned it, and the corners of his mouth turned up.

"We got her, Miss Presley!" As tired as she was, she managed to pop out her seat like a boomerang.

"Let's get this witch!" She shouted.

"I'm on it," Thomas said as he reached for the telephone. He dialed the courthouse and a representative answered the phone. "Salter's Point Magistrate Court," she announced. "This Is Thomas Marshall. I need an arrest warrant on Cathy Ray as soon as possible!"

Rachel and Sally were hunkered down in the nursing office, dictating notes from the previous day. After Sally finished her last note, she broke the silence between them.

"Cathy called out sick again today," she softly said.

"Yeah, Beth told me," Rachel said not looking up.

"Did she tell you anything else?" Sally asked blinking her eyes and feeling antsy.

"Nope, except, she did tell me Betty Jo and Doctor Poppy are in the hospital," she said.

"Did she give a reason why?" Sally asked.

"No, she didn't. But, I must tell you, Everett knows about it. Doctor Poppy called him last night and told him." Sally sighed.

"I guess the secret is out," she said.

"Yeah, I hope it doesn't get back to Cathy before the police have a chance to arrest her," Rachel said with a grim face.

"Me too," Sally murmured.

"It's hard to believe Cathy Ray did this," Rachel sadly said. "It's so troubling!"

"I know," Sally said.

"Once she's convicted, I wonder if she will get the death penalty," Rachel pondered shaking her head. Sally's face looked grave.

"Does this state have a death penalty law?"

"Yep," said Rachel. "It sure does."

"Well, she's in trouble," Sally said.

"Definitely," said Rachel.

Cathy started her morning getting attacked by a bouquet of birthday balloons while shopping at Safeway. A little girl in a red dress ran into her carrying the balloons, and the strings became tangled up around her head. With the little girl's help, she managed to escape, and her day was about to get worse from there.

Forty minutes away, across town, Holly B parked her Honda Civic a block from Salter's Point Duplex Apartments. It was misty outside, and the thick gray fog hampered visibility. Dressed in black from head to toe, her frizzy blonde locks were crammed underneath her Mariner's baseball cap. She scooted down in her seat. Her head was barely above the dashboard, and her hazel-green eyes looked like shiny green marbles in her prescription glasses. She scoped out the area looking for Cathy Ray. Determined to bring her to justice at any cost, she yawned; tired of being up all night. Then, she pulled her hat over her eyes and settled in for a very long wait.

Thomas glanced at his watch and the time was twelve noon. His left eyelid twitched as he paced the floor in front of the judge's chambers. Soon his constant pacing tired him out, and he found a seat near the vicinity and sat down. He squirmed in his seat, tapping his right foot, and then he became angry.

"Damn it, what's taking so long?! "He cursed under his breath. He jumped up and began pacing the floor again. Then the courtroom doors flew open.

"Got your warrant," said a sleepy-eyed court clerk waving the document in the air. Thomas rushed over.

"Thanks!" He said snatching the document out of her hand. He took off running down the hall while she looked on.

"Good Luck!" She hollered after him. He didn't respond or look back. He just kept going.

Meanwhile, Susan Cole was camped out in her room, sitting cross-legged on the bed contemplating her next move. She knew her time was short and soon she would be carted off to jail. Hiram gave her the name of a colorful attorney named Sugar Foot Kent. The name worried her. She wondered if he had the credentials to represent her.

"With a name like that, how would anyone take him seriously?!" She pondered to herself. Her calf muscles twitched with pain, and she uncrossed her legs. She slid off the bed and stretched for several minutes until the pain subsided. Then there was a knock on the door. She limped to the door and opened it. Doctor James' dark brown eyes stared back at her.

"Miss Cole, I am discharging you in the morning," he said with a deep, stern voice. "The police will be here to pick you up after breakfast."

"And my medication? Where will I get my medication?" She asked with wet eyes.

"I'll make sure a six-month supply is ready for you when you leave," he promised. "But, after that, the jail psychiatrist must fill your prescriptions."

Her head dropped, and a tear rolled down her cheek. He noticed her discomfort and felt empathy for her.

"Look, I am sorry you are in this fix, but you have to face the music," he said.

"I know," she murmured.

"Did Hiram give you a name of a lawyer?" He asked.

"Yes, Sugar Foot Kent," she said not looking up. He sighed and shook his head. Leery of Hiram's choice.

"Are you okay with using this lawyer?"

"I guess so," Susan said.

"Well I wish you luck, and I'll see you in the morning," he said. He leaves her, and she shuts the door.

CHAPTER THIRTY-TWO

On the way home, Cathy thought about Doctor Poppy and Betty Jo again. The thought of never seeing the doctor again gave her great joy. Disposing of people whom she didn't like or didn't like her had always been her method. Her favorite weapon, rat poison, a handy, undetectable solution. Her killing spree started with her stepmother a long time ago. Just barely twelve, she successfully killed her with the substance. Then as time went on, her best friend in high school also met the same demise after she discovered her in bed with her boyfriend. And then her college sweetheart suddenly dropped dead in his dorm room after she laced his orange juice with the poison following an argument. She was angry with him for jilting her for another woman. Despite intrusive investigations by the police, no one ever connected her to the murders. Now Salter's Point Regional has fallen into her murderous crosshairs and unbeknownst to her, her time of obscurity had just run out.

Doctor Beebe and Michael Louis were behind closed doors in Doctor Beebe's office. They were having a field day discussing the latest news on Cathy Ray. Michael, his face red and bloated, raised his fist and pounded on the desk.

"That woman needs to fry like a piece of chicken!" He said. "The court should not allow her to breathe another breath!" Doctor Beebe's eyebrows snapped together.

"Do you think she should get the death penalty?!" He squealed.

"Damn right I do!" Michael said in a matter of fact tone, scowling. He dawdled for a minute, and then he quietly said,

"Carl, you know this is our fault."

"How do you mean?" Doctor Beebe asked taking a dim view of his comment.

"Our hiring process sucks," he pointed out. "We don't take time to really check people out!"

"I am of the same mind," Doctor Beebe nodded. "We have to do better."

"Well it's nothing we can do about it now," Michael said. "What's done is done. I'm just glad we are able to stop her murderous campaign before she kills anyone else!" Doctor Beebe sighed looking somber.

"It's still a travesty against the hospital. It will take a while to live this down," he said.

"And this Susan Cole debacle," Michael said veering off to another subject. "When does James plan to discharge her so she can go to jail?" He asked.

"Tomorrow morning, he told me," said Doctor Beebe.

"I hope she hires herself a good lawyer," Michael said. "Her ass is about to fry too!" Doctor Beebe chuckled to himself.

"I heard she hired Sugar Foot Kent."

"Damn, what a hasty and ill-informed decision!" Michael mused.

"She didn't know anybody, so she asked Hiram for a name," Doctor Beebe said. Michael busted out laughing.

"She seeks counsel from a knucklehead who has his hair done at a strip joint?! I sure hope it works out," he joked.

"It's not a strip joint Michael, it's a hair salon," said Doctor Beebe correcting him.

"Whatever," said Michael rolling his eyes. "What about Ethan? What's her game plan since she's off the hook?" He growled looking halfway disappointed. Doctor Beebe's bushy eyebrows snapped together again in a perfectly straight line.

"You need to back off that poor lady! She's been through enough!" He said pushing back.

"If you say so," Michael smirked, shaking his head and popping out of his seat. He heads to the door.

"I got work to do! So, I will see you later!"

"See you in a few," said Doctor Beebe. Michael left his office without saying another word.

Cathy speeded into her driveway and parked. She turned off the ignition and glanced out the rearview window. Bright blue flashing lights were behind her car, blinding her.

"Oh shit," she grumbled. She turned on her ignition and tried to back out of the driveway. A man with a bullhorn hollered at her from behind.

"DO NOT MOVE!" Men in black surrounded her mustang and drew their guns. She shrank back when Holly B tapped on the window with her forty-four Magnum pointing it at her.

"GET OUT!" She yelled. Cathy rolled down the window and gave her a broad twisted grin.

"Holly B, why are you slithering around in my neighborhood? Did I do something wrong?" She sweetly asked.

"We are arresting you for the murders of Celeste Brown, Donald Curtis…..."

Cathy appeared childlike as she wrapped a braid around her fingers and said.

"Sweet Holly B, murder wasn't on my agenda today so why are you here?"

"It's wasn't on anyone's agenda!" Holly B snapped back still pointing her weapon at her.

"No, but it's still on mine, just not until next Tuesday!" She wickedly cackled.

"You scare me!" said Holly B, suddenly getting the heebie-jeebies. Cathy winked at her and cunningly said.

"Well, don't you know I'm naturally terrifying?"

"Get out of the car before I unload on you!" Holly B hollered, now getting very angry.

Cathy opened the door and got out with her hands up. She stood there, face-to-face with Holly B. Her cold, piercing eyes bored into the detective. Holly B stared back holding her ground until Thomas rushed over and flipped Cathy around. He slammed her up against the car and handcuffed her.

"Hey, I didn't kill anybody today! Why all the fuss?!" She snickered. He turned her back around, and his fiery eyes met hers.

"What do you want? A Gold Star?" He quipped.

"Something like that!" She grinned puckering her lips.

"Stop that!" He said.

"Stop what?!"

"Trying to kiss me!" He confronted her. She cracked up laughing.

"I'd rather have a thousand fleas invade my armpits than kiss you!" She said. Red-faced, he rattled off her rights and shoved her into the arms of another officer. She batted her eyes as the officer patted her down.

"You, horny devil, are you trying to molest me?!"

"You wish!" Said the officer. Cathy cackled, and Holly B jammed her forty-four Magnum in her holster and shoved Cathy in the direction of the police van.

"There's not enough salt in this world to protect you from the hell that's about to be unleashed on you!" She said. Cathy Ray threw her head back and laughed like a hyena.

"Don't be so sure, honey bunch! The demon in me will protect me!"

"Ugggh," Holly B moaned. "Get her out of my sight! She disgusts me!" Two police officers escort her to the van with the others following close behind. Holly B shook her head in disdain. Thomas, usually a man of many words, was quiet and sullen. Grim-faced, he finally spoke.

"She's frightening!"

"Seriously?" Holly B said taking off her eyeglasses and rubbing her eyes. "I had worse nightmares...... Like failing chemistry in college!" Thomas gave her a quizzical look.

"Huh?" He said.

"Never mind," Holly B said. "It's a joke." She took off trotting back to her black Civic Honda, and thunder clapped in the distance. It began to sprinkle.

After a while, the sky grew dark, and a large raindrop splattered on Thomas' bald head. He broke out in a slow jog with a lot on his mind.

"One arrest down and another one to go," he panted. "Tomorrow will be another crazy day!"

CHAPTER THIRTY-THREE

The Next Day, Thomas wasted no time obtaining an arrest warrant on Susan Cole. By twelve noon, he had arranged a van to pick her up. Susan Cole with her unruly blonde curls tied up in a ponytail joined three female inmates in a police van. The pupils in her eyes grew larger when she realized one of the inmates was Cathy Ray. She grinned like a Cheshire cat as she slid onto the metal bench next to her. She poked her on the shoulder.

"Aren't you the social worker I saw the other day?" She asked.

"Yes, I am," Cathy Ray said looking a hot mess with her strawberry blonde hair tangled and matted. Susan's smile quickly faded when Cathy glared at her with such disdain and hatred. Spooked, Susan slid to the other end of the bench so fast, she nearly fell off. Cathy howled with laughter. Her laughter drew the attention of the officer who shot her a dirty look. Cathy made a face and fidgeted in her seat pulling on her handcuffs and ignoring her. The officer, extremely bow-legged with a heavy-set body frame, chewed on a toothpick as she checked out Cathy Ray from a distance. Then she reverted her attention to her checklist and began roll call.

"Susan Cole!" She shouted.

"Here!" Susan said.

"Tanya Davis!"

"Here!" Tanya said.

"Cathy Ray!"

"Here, here, honey bunch!" Hollered Cathy.

The officer halted her roll call. She glared at Cathy with an evil eye.

"The name is not Honey Bunch!" She sneered gritting her teeth. "The word "here" is all you need to say smarty pants!" Cathy snickered and tugged on her handcuffs, flashing the officer a fake smile. The officer gave her a fake one back, and she continued with her roll call.

"Gretchen Peters!"

"Here!" Gretchen said.

"Very good," the officer said looking very pleased. "Everyone is here with bells on. I need to check your handcuffs." The officer climbed up in the van and checked every woman's handcuffs making sure each cuff was locked and fastened.

"It looks like you girls are ready to roll," she smirked. She secured the van and took a seat by the door. She looked down at her holster and her gun was still there. With a poker face, she caressed her weapon while belting out a warning.

"Don't any of you try any monkey business up in here! If you do, I promise you I will unload some serious lead into you!" No one makes a sound except for Cathy Ray who was snickering out loud. The officer shot her a blazing look and Cathy ignored her. The officer grunted rolling her eyes, and then her attention focused on the front of the van. She craned her neck to see through the cubby hole window. David was in the driver's seat with both hands tight on the steering wheel. Itching to take off with his left foot tapping the accelerator. The engine raced like a rocket beckoning to take off.

"David, we are secured back here! Let's go!" She yelled.

"Roger," he said.

He stepped on the accelerator and zoomed off. Within minutes he had cleared the hospital parking lot and was speeding down Salter's Point Boulevard. Blaine County Jail agreed to house the women after Salter's Point Jail didn't have any room. Their expected time of arrival was precisely three hours, and heavy rain was in the forecast. Susan Cole squeezed her eyes shut trying to block out the reality waiting ahead. She daydreamed about being on the beach with her toes buried deep in the warm, gritty sand. She imagined the feel of the ocean's cooling waves rushing over her slender body, a welcomed diversion from the hard reality ahead. Then her mind floated back to Sugar Foot Kent, her colorful, outlandish attorney. She wondered if he had the right muster to fight on her behalf and keep her out of prison. She jumped when ice pellets bounced off the roof of the van.

"Is that hail?" She asked.

"Yep," Cathy Ray replied.

"It sounds horrible out there," said Gretchen looking worried. The howling and the whistling wind was so loud, it frightened Tanya.

"I'm scared," she said biting her lower lip.

"Stop being a baby!" Cathy chastised her. "It's just wind, you idiot!" Tanya scrunched up her face and lunged at her. Cathy reared back, and the officer wedged her heavy frame between them.

"Alright girls, I'm not having this!" She shouted. She pointed at Tanya. "Go back to your seat... Now!" Tanya obeyed her order and reluctantly returned to her seat. The officer then focused on Cathy with hot, burning eyes.

"I don't want to hear another peep out of you young lady!" She said clenching her teeth. Cathy made a face and then stared at Tanya with evil, icy eyes. Tanya ignored her choosing instead to gaze out the window. A gust of wind roared over them like a freight train, swaying the van back and forth over the steep road. The women screamed when the van violently jerked forward and threw everyone on the floor.

"The officer is driving too fast! He needs to slow down!" Tanya said getting angry. The women, still handcuffed, struggled back onto the bench and then the van jerked again. Susan and Cathy hit the wall bumping their heads.

"Ouch!" They both hollered. Small cuts appeared on their foreheads, and blood dripped off the end of their nose. Cathy tried to wipe her nose with her shirt sleeve, but with no success. Her head throbbed, and she lashed out in anger.

"Will you tell that asshole to slow down?!"

"David slow down!" The female officer shouted, but there was no answer. Instead, the van picked up more speed, and terror crossed the officer's face.

"David, you are scaring everybody back here! Slow down!" She yelled again.

The van swerved back and forth all over the road. Jerking everyone off the bench again and onto the floor. The women screamed, and the officer climbed over them to see about David. She looked through the cubby hole window, and David was slumped over passed out.

"Oh, my god! David, wake up!" She yelled pounding on the glass. "David, can you hear me?!"

White foam drooled from David's mouth, and his left foot was pressed hard on the accelerator. The speedometer was registered at ninety, and the officer freaked out.

"Oh, my god!" She snatched her keys from her belt and in a hurry, she unlocked everyone's handcuffs. Then she kicked the back door open and yelled.

"Jump! We are going to crash!" The officer hopped out, and the van flipped over the highway banister. It rolled down the rocky embankment sending David through the front window and glass shattered everywhere. One woman, unable to hold onto the bench, flew out the back door. The other women rolled back and forth on the floor of the van; bashing their heads against the wall, knocking them out cold. Then suddenly the van came to an immediate halt, landing in the Muddy river. Two minutes later, the weight of the water blew the windows out. Water rushed in, and the van went under. Then the sky broke up, and rain assaulted the earth. The precipitation turned into a fierce hailstorm. Large ice pellets danced on the Muddy River like ping pong balls while lightening sizzled across the dark sky.

Soon the storm fizzled out, and a human head emerged from the muddy waters. She gulped down water, gasping for breath as she wiped mud from her eyes. She began to swim. Every muscle in her body burned with each stroke, and she ached all over. When she finally reached the bottom of the embankment, she rested for a moment. She breathed in deep, trying to catch her breath and with a sudden burst of energy, she managed to hoist herself up. The heavy rain beat her down, but she trudged on clawing her way up the rocky embankment.

Grabbing at every branch, nook, cranny and sharp rock. Her hands bloodied in the process. She kept pushing forward despite her body aching with stabbing pain. An hour had passed by the time she reached the top of the embankment. She fell over the banister onto the slippery wet highway. Weak and exhausted, she lay there bruised and muddied while the rain beat down on her. With no one to help her, it soon dawned on her she may die at any minute. Six minutes. That's all the time she had, she thought to herself. Six minutes until the pain was over...... Six minutes her world turned black.

A half hour later, the rain ceased to a drizzle. A logging truck rattled down the highway at a slow pace due to the wet conditions. His headlights caught the motionless body in the road, and he brought his logging rig to a screeching, grinding halt. He backed the rig up about ten feet from the prone body. Then he parked and turned off the ignition. He stretched his neck, looking over the dashboard.

"My word! That's a woman down there!" He muttered to himself. As he eased himself down from the cab, he felt himself trembling inside. It was dusk. He was all alone. There could be more to this situation than he was willing to handle. He warily approached the motionless body expecting the worse. He squatted down and flipped her over. Drenched with mud, he shook her, hoping she was still alive.

"Lady, wake up," he yelled. "Can you hear me?!" Her bright blue eyes blinked wide open, and he jumped back as she startled him.

"Help me," she whispered. "Please help me!"

"Stay here, I'm going to call for help," he reassured her getting himself together. He jetted back to his truck and reached for his CB radio. He called the ambulance and then tossed the radio in the seat. He began searching his cab for a blanket. He found one in the back seat. As he hopped down from the cab, his face turned ashy gray. His eyes frantically scanned the vacant area, his mind unable to comprehend what he saw. The woman he left lying in the road while he called for help was nowhere to be found.

Seventy-two hours later, the news of Cathy Ray's arrest sent shock waves throughout the hospital, and her terrifying story took on a life of its own. The arrest of Susan Cole paled in comparison. Staff, more willing to give her a pass, after learning why she killed George Benny in the first place. However, Cathy Ray was another story. Her serial killer alter ego took everyone by surprise. It spooked Doctor Beebe so bad, he immediately implemented a hiring freeze on new staff until he came up with a safer method to weed out bad actors or suspected criminals. Betty Jo's condition improved and she was discharged from the hospital. Mark, who never once left her side, waited on her hand and foot, often slipping away to sip on a shot of vodka.

Rachel and Everett's marriage survived their disagreement and Beth put Rachel on a three-day suspension from work as punishment for keeping Susan Cole's secret. Rachel gladly accepted it, relieved she still had her job. As for Doctor Ethan Poppy, she recovered physically, but the emotional scars of almost being murdered by a social worker haunted her every day.

Despite her emotional state, she was back at the hospital in rare form creating welcome comedic relief for the hospital staff there. Instead of rats, she bought herself a red pet ferret and now no one visits her office. Not even her patients. With Beth's backing, Rachel agreed to work with Doctor Poppy, at least until another social worker was hired on staff. One morning, Ethan and Rachel sat in the conference room reviewing the day's discharges. Still rattled and upset, Rachel felt a need to let off steam.

"Doctor Poppy, how could anyone be evil enough to kill innocent patients or their co-workers?" She innocently asked.

"Cathy had a dark forest living inside her. Her personality was anti-social, and those types sometimes commit murder," Doctor Poppy explained.

"I never heard it explained quite that way," Rachel said with sadness clouding her features. "Social workers are supposed to help people not kill them." Ethan got up and patted her on the back.

"It's going to be okay. The police have captured her. It's over now," she said.

"I have a feeling it's not," she said sounding worried. Then the door swung open, and Hiram stepped in. He looked pale as if he had seen a ghost with his wiry blonde locks tangled all over his head.

"What's the matter with you?!" Ethan asked getting concerned.

"There was an accident," he said wrinkling his nose.

"An accident? Where?" Rachel asked looking wide-eyed.

"On the freeway, up in the woods in Blaine County," he said. Fear crossed Rachel's face, and she rose to her feet in a hurry.

"Who died?! Is it someone we know?"

"They don't have a lot of information, but five bodies were recovered, and one survived," he told them. Rachel's face turned from fear to red-hot angry.

"Damn it Hiram! Quit beating around the bush and tell us who died," she shouted.

"The van carrying both Cathy Ray and Susan Cole sank in the Muddy River," he said. "There were seven people on board. Two officers and five women. One officer survived, four inmates died, and one inmate is missing," he quietly said. Ethan's jaw tightened, and she bit her lower lip.

"Of the four who died, is one of them Cathy Ray?" She asked, inwardly hoping it was. Hiram looked at her funny.

"They don't know. The body was bloated. It was difficult to tell who it was," he said. "But I can tell you this, her hair was blonde," he added.

"Cathy had blonde hair," Rachel quickly recalled.

"And so did Susan Cole," Hiram reminded her. "Like I said, they don't know yet." Rachel sank in her seat.

"I suppose Holly B told you all of this," she said softly.

"Yep, she sure did," he murmured.

"What happens next?"

"The medical examiner is working on identifying the bloated body in the morgue, and the police will continue to look for the one who's missing," he said. Rachel eyeballed Ethan.

"I told you it wasn't over. It hasn't even begun."

Down in Blaine County, at a hole-in-the-wall eatery called Oakwood Table; a woman stood outside in the cold air, shivering and rubbing her shoulders. The Canadian Border was only two hours away, and she was desperate for a ride. Although she loved her life in Salter's Point, it was no longer her home. She was a fugitive now, on the run, a cold-blooded killer. When the trucker stopped to help her two days ago, she panicked when he ran off to call for help. As bad as her body ached with excruciating pain, she managed to pick herself up and hightailed it out of there. It was either escape or go to prison, and she wasn't ready to give up her freedom just yet. She showed up at a little bungalow house in the woods, soaking wet, bruised and covered in mud. The owner, an elderly man in his seventies, took one look at her and invited her in. He knew she was in trouble, but he elected not to ask any questions. He allowed her to shower and change into a pair of his old pajamas. She inquired if he had any hair dye and he said no, but he promised to buy her a bottle the next day.

Exhausted and drained, she climbed into bed and fell fast asleep. When she finally woke up two days later, he had bought her a set of clothes, hair dye, and some personal items. She dyed her hair a dark brown, deciding black was too harsh for her skin color. The old man, feeling sorry for her, treated the throbbing cut on her forehead using peroxide, and by the second day, the pain subsided. By the third day, she had regained her strength, and she told the old man she had to go. He didn't ask why. He just gave her money and wished her well.

Dressed in blue jeans, a heavy sweatshirt and wearing a large baseball cap on her dark brown curly hair, she waited with her backpack on her shoulder. She stood there scrutinizing every trucker who entered the restaurant. Trying to find the one she could trust. Soon, a Buick Eight-Wheeler Truck rumbled into the parking lot and parked. A short, bearded, burly looking man with kind twinkling eyes jumped out of the cab. As he approached her, she decided he was the one. She sized him up, confident if he tried anything amiss, she could take him if she had to. So, she stepped out in front of him, and he stopped in his tracks.

"Whoa, little lady! What's up?!" He growled.

"I need a ride," she quickly said.

"Oh! Where to?" He asked looking surprised.

"To Canada," she said. He checked her out, suddenly getting suspicious.

"Why Canada?"

"My stepmother is ill," she fibbed talking very fast. "I have no way to get there, and she needs me," she said with forced crocodile tears. He felt sorry for her, and his suspicion quickly faded.

"Look, I have to drop a load off in Canada," he said. "You are welcome to ride with me." Her face brightened, and she rejoiced inwardly.

"Thank you," she said. "I appreciate your kindness."

"I'm going in here to buy breakfast to go. Do you want anything?" He asked.

"No thank you," she said. He went to the restaurant, and she waited outside. After a while, he re-emerged with a box of piping, hot food.

"Ready to go?" he said smiling.

"Yes," she said with a nod. She followed him to his truck, and he helped her up into the cab. He turned on the ignition and reared up the engine. She settled in and fastened her seat belt. As he drove out of the parking lot, he faced her with a broad smile.

"So, Miss Lady, let me introduce myself. My name is Doug Foghorn. What's yours?" He asked.

"Susan," she said. "My name is Susan Cole."

Made in the USA
Lexington, KY
27 March 2018